THE
HERETIC
CYPHER

Murray Bailey

.

This story was originally published as part of the treasure hunt book entitled Map of the Dead. It has been rewritten as the first book of the Egyptian Stones trilogy. Within the original book, the ancient Egyptian story has been published separately as the first of Yanhamu's Letters: Scorpion and the Tomb.

ISBN 978-1-916382848

Three Daggers
An imprint of
Heritage Books, Cornwall

By Murray Bailey

The Heretic Cypher
The Mark of Eternity
Codex of the Gods

The Lost Pharaoh
Scorpion and the Tomb
The Second Truth

Singapore 52, Singapore Girl
Singapore Boxer, Singapore Ghost
Singapore Killer, Singapore Fire
Singapore Rain, Singapore Worlds

Singapore and Other Stories Vol. 1
Singapore and Other Stories Vol. 2

Cyprus Kiss, The Troodos Secret
The Killing Crew, The Prisoner of Acre
Dead Man's Line

Wolfe's Gambit, Wolfe's Shadows, Wolfe's Traitor

No Safe Place to Hide

Black Creek White Lies

Chapter 1

Dr Ellen Champion pedalled harder, her breath clouding in the November air. The narrow country road ahead twisted through the Hampshire countryside, shrouded in blackness. Alex's warnings echoed in her mind.

"You are eleven times more likely to be killed cycling than in a car—mile for mile." That was Alex. Her best friend. Always thinking about numbers. If only he'd listened last weekend. She'd been anxious and needed to talk but the time hadn't been right.

A sudden flash of headlights blinded her. A car surged around the bend, engine growling. Ellen instinctively veered toward the verge, gravel spraying under her tires. The bike wobbled dangerously, but she managed to stop just short of the ditch. Her pulse hammered. One more mile. Just one more.

Old Bramsclere appeared in the distance, a smattering of orange streetlights casting long, skeletal shadows across the oak trees. Relief flooded through her. Almost home. Her mind drifted back to the Egyptian exhibition, to the research she and Marek had been piecing together like an ancient puzzle. His last email lingered in her mind:

Hide it.

Ellen had typed back, If anyone finds out, I'll be in trouble.

Marek's reply had been swift.

You'll be in more trouble if we lose it. Let's not take any risks.

Paranoia? Or something more? Last week, Marek had sworn someone was following him. But that was Marek— intense and dramatic. Yet something about his fear had unnerved her. And she hadn't heard from him since.

She reached her bungalow, the rear door looming in the darkness. She stepped off the bike, reached for her key—

The door wasn't locked.

A trick of memory? She must have forgotten in her rush earlier. Still, a prickle crept up her spine. Ellen pushed inside, locked it behind her, and exhaled. She set her bag on the dining table, pulling out her notebook and laptop. The room, her makeshift office, felt colder than usual. The kitchen clock read 2:00am.

Two sleeping pills and a quick descent into darkness.

Something woke her.

Ellen blinked at her phone, the edges of sleep still clinging to her mind. 5:45am.

She rolled over, about to drift off again—

A sound.

Downstairs.

Pete? He usually came by on weekends, sometimes crashing in his aunt's old bedroom. Maybe he had let himself in. She heard the rustling of papers, the subtle creak of wood shifting under weight.

Ellen swung her legs out of bed, tightened the belt on her robe, and made her way down the narrow staircase.

She turned the corner.

A figure stood in her dining room, silhouetted against the window.

"Pete?" she said hesitantly.

The man straightened.

Not Pete.

Ellen's stomach lurched. Her eyes flicked to the table—her laptop open, her notes scattered.

"What the hell are you doing? Get out!"

The man raised his hands, stepping forward. "Sorry. I didn't think anyone was in. I was just—"

"Get out!"

His expression shifted. Calculating. Cold.

Ellen backed toward the stairs, pulse slamming against her ribs. He took another step.

She turned and bolted. The stairs blurred beneath her feet. Three strides to the top. She felt his presence right behind her.

Phone. Get the phone. Call the police.

Instead, she lunged for something else—a solid, familiar weight beneath her bed.

Her father's gift. A cricket bat.

Fingers closed around the handle. She spun, heart hammering.

The intruder lunged.

Ellen swung with everything she had. The bat connected. A grunt. A thud. But he wasn't down.

He was on her again, gripping her arms, shoving her back.

She kicked, twisted, clawed—anything to break free.

A sudden explosion of pain. A blow to her head.

The world tilted. A sickening sense of weightlessness.

Her final thoughts were fast and fragmented. Relief. She'd hidden the item. Copied the research. *Expose the truth.* And then—

Darkness.

The man stood at the top of the staircase, breathing hard. Crazy bitch had fought like a wild animal. He peered down at her crumpled form. The awkward angle of her neck told him everything.

Shit.

He stepped over her, dialled a number. The call connected.

"She's dead."

"What?"

"Freaked out, attacked me. Fell down the stairs. Broke her damn neck."

Silence. Then: "Did you get it?"

He glanced at the scattered papers. The laptop. The notebook.

"I've got everything."

"What about her? Did she talk?"

The man exhaled sharply. "Didn't get the chance. She went full Tasmanian Devil."

A pause. "What's the risk?"

He looked around.

Fought me. Scratched me. DNA everywhere. Shit.

"High."

"The boss isn't going to like this."

"Yeah, well, he can get in line."

Another pause. Then, flatly: "Bring the evidence. Destroy everything else."

The call ended.

The man looked down at Ellen Champion's motionless body.

He had one more job to do.

Chapter 2

Alex MacLure descended the steps of the British Museum, absently adjusting his glasses with the back of his hand. His mind was still lodged in the distant past, not in the grandeur of pharaohs but in the murkier, less-documented world that came before them—the enigmatic rulers of pre-dynastic Egypt, whose names had been eroded by time. He sifted through centuries like a man flipping through an old, familiar book, searching for the missing pages.

The museum's towering columns caught his gaze—Doric, austere, a construct of a civilization thousands of years younger than the ones that occupied his thoughts. It was strange, the way history chose its champions. The Greeks and Romans, preserved in marble and literature, while the earliest kings of the Nile remained whispers in the sand.

The late afternoon sun gilded the museum's façade, lengthening the shadows at his feet. He blinked, momentarily disoriented by the sudden shift from dimly lit archives to open sky. Eddie, the security guard, sat in his usual glass box by the gate, tapping a cigarette from a crumpled pack.

"See you tomorrow?" Eddie called.

Alex pushed his glasses up again, momentarily thrown by the question. "Unless I make a historical breakthrough overnight."

Eddie smirked. "Yeah? Let me know if you need a shovel."

Alex gave a distracted chuckle but was already elsewhere—his mind locked on the translation he had been poring over all afternoon. A fragment of text, dismissed as an epitaph, but something about the structure nagged at him. Patterns. There were always patterns, and this one was whispering to him, just out of reach.

As he moved through Bloomsbury, his gaze flickered across the architecture—Regency façade blending into Victorian refurbishments, each building a palimpsest of time. He loved that about cities. They were layered, always hiding something beneath the surface. He wondered if the museum's archives were the same. What had been misfiled, mislabelled, forgotten? He itched to go back and check.

Then something pricked at his awareness—a vague unease, like a note played out of key. A presence. He slowed his pace, casually adjusting the strap of his satchel as he took in his surroundings with newfound intent.

Across the street, a man in a well-fitted blue suit browsed a bookseller's stall. His fingers moved over pages as though considering the words. And yet his attention seemed elsewhere. Alex frowned. He had seen this man before—outside the museum three days ago. Coincidence? Statistically possible. But probable?

Alex changed course, turning down a narrower street. His steps remained measured, but his mind raced. He wasn't just heading home now; he was running a small experiment. The noises of the city softened as the buildings pressed in, and he caught a glimpse of himself in a café window—reflected behind him, the man in the blue suit had shifted his trajectory to match.

Adrenaline spiked, uncomfortably at odds with the academic part of his brain. He had spent years with books, not in back alleys, but even he knew this wasn't nothing. Someone was following him.

Why?

He mentally indexed everything he had worked on recently—early dynastic inscriptions, lost burial sites, an incomplete translation of a stela that suggested an undocumented ruler. Hardly spy-thriller material. Unless...

A memory surfaced. Three weeks ago, a private collector in Istanbul had sent him an email with an image of an artifact fragment. The hieroglyphs had been too precise, their meanings too deliberate. It felt wrong, like a forgery—except if it was, it was the best forgery he had ever seen. He had dismissed it as a hoax. Had someone assumed he knew more than he did?

By the time he reached Marylebone Village, the knot in his stomach had tightened. He spotted an outdoor café and slipped into a seat, setting his satchel down with more care than usual. The waiter—Jamaican accent, name tag reading Sammie—gave him an easy smile.

"What yuh 'avin'?"

"Sumac grilled chicken. And a Sanpellegrino limonata."

Sammie nodded and disappeared into the café. Alex exhaled and opened his notebook, flipping to the page where he had copied the Istanbul inscription. He stared at the symbols, trying to see what he had missed.

A shadow crossed his table. The man in the blue suit had stopped across the street. Watching. Not pretending to read, not pretending to be lost. Just watching.

Alex's grip on his pen tightened. The back of his mind began assembling a dozen theories at once, each branching into a hundred more. What was he supposed to do now? Confront him? Run? What if this was some misunderstanding—an academic rival trying to be intimidating for no reason? He had once been scolded for mispronouncing Middle Kingdom grammar at a conference. Academia could be cutthroat. But this felt... different.

Sammie reappeared, setting the plate in front of him. The warm scent of sumac and charred pitta curled into the evening air. "Penny fer 'em?" he asked, nodding at the open notebook.

Alex hesitated. Then, with a careful smile, he said, "Just an old puzzle."

Sammie leaned in slightly, lowering his voice. "Then yuh betta be careful who else wants to solve it."

A shiver crept up Alex's spine. He glanced back across the street.

The man in the blue suit was gone.

Forty minutes later, Alex stood outside his Maida Vale flat, shifting the weight of his leather satchel. The red-brick Georgian building was unassuming, tucked within a neighbourhood poised on the brink of gentrification. Five years ago, he had invested in the property, calculating the inevitable creep of London's housing market with the same meticulous precision he applied to deciphering lost languages.

As he climbed the six stone steps to the communal entrance, his mind drifted to his latest research. The pre-dynastic Egyptian symbols he had encountered at the British Museum were unlike any he had seen before—fragments of an unknown script, potentially older than Sumerian cuneiform. If his theory was correct, history itself would have to be rewritten.

His thoughts were interrupted by the persistent ring of his phone inside the flat. It stopped just as he turned the key in the lock.

"Topsy?" he called.

Silence. Odd. His cocker spaniel cross usually bounded to the door like a sentry eager to report. He scanned the dimly lit hallway, then moved toward the back of the apartment, where he heard an urgent scrabbling.

"Topsy?"

The sound was coming from the garden door. He flicked on the light. The dog stood outside, tail wagging, eyes bright with excitement. The dog flap—normally ajar—was inexplicably locked from the inside.

"How did you manage that?" he muttered, flipping the latch open. Topsy dashed in, circling his legs before leaping onto the sofa as if nothing was amiss.

He lingered at the door, inspecting the lock. The mechanism was stiff, but intact. Could the wind have rattled it shut? Unlikely. He frowned, making a mental note to examine it more closely in the morning.

The television hummed in the background, filling the space with idle chatter. He left it on for Topsy's company, a habit born of long hours spent buried in research.

Settling onto the sofa, he absently ruffled the dog's ears. "Daft dog, locking yourself out... So, tell me about your day," he murmured, half-smiling. Topsy gazed up at him with liquid brown eyes, her silent response somehow deeply reassuring.

The phone rang again. This time, he reached it just in time.

"Hello?"

His mother's voice cut through the receiver, thick with urgency. "Alex, have you heard the news?"

He straightened. Changed the channel. "I've got it on now. What's happened?"

His mother exhaled sharply. "I don't mean on the TV."

"What news, Mum?"

"About Ellen? About the accident?"

"What accident?" His throat tightened. Topsy looked at him, concerned.

"Ellen's house. There's been an explosion."

He couldn't speak. His mother continued.

"Ellen's dead, Alex. Your friend is dead."

Chapter 3

Alex nursed his second cup of coffee, but the hangover clung to him like a stubborn shadow. He blamed it on the bottle of red wine he'd polished off last night. But maybe it wasn't just the alcohol. Maybe it was the grief, raw and unyielding, that made him feel rotten.

The café, perched by the canal, was a stone's throw from Paddington Station. London's sixty miles of canals wove through the city like hidden veins, with the Grand Union meeting Regent's Canal at Little Venice, a picturesque spot just a hundred yards away. But today, the view held no beauty for Alex.

Ellen was dead.

It hadn't fully sunk in. His best friend since university was gone, just like that. He sighed at his reflection in the window, as if the image could offer some solace. On the towpath, a man untied a barge while a woman on board laughed—a sound that stabbed at Alex's heart. Ellen used to laugh like that, bright and carefree. But she could also be intensely serious, especially about her Egyptology research. Her passion had been infectious, pulling Alex into a new career path. She was a neutron star, brilliant and chaotic, yet prone to dark, depressive phases.

Alex tracked a young man entering the café. Wiry with haunted eyes and tousled dark hair. Pete Tonkin.

Alex raised a hand, and Pete nodded, pointing at the counter before mouthing something about getting a drink. Alex showed him his cup, signalling he was good. A few minutes later, Pete pulled up a bar stool beside him, staring out the window. The barge Alex had watched was gone, replaced by another manoeuvring into the space, dark, oily water churning around its stern.

Pete took a slug of his coffee and broke the long silence. "I just got back from the house," he said, his voice thick with pain.

The house—the bungalow where Ellen had lived. Alex turned to Pete, a relative stranger despite Ellen's introduction. Pete had been her landlord while she stayed near Highclere Castle, where Lord Carnarvon had lived. Pete's hand shook as he held it out in front of him. "I can't believe it," he said.

"I know."

"Sorry. You must be... devastated."

"Numb. Numb is the best way I can describe it."

Ellen hadn't just been Alex's friend. They'd had a brief fling after university, and though it had ended, their closeness never faded. She'd never shown interest in anyone else, at least as far as Alex knew. He'd kept a room for her at his place, filled with some of her things. What was he going to do with them now?

Alex asked, "So, what was the house like?"

Pete stared outside. "Like matchsticks. Hardly anything left. It was flattened; wood strewn everywhere. Hard to believe it was a house." He paused and seemed on the verge of tears.

"You can't blame yourself," Alex said.

Pete sighed, fingers over his mouth. The bungalow had been destroyed by a gas explosion. It hadn't made the national news, but Alex had seen the photo on a local newspaper's website.

Pete said, "I was responsible for the house, responsible for the gas."

"Did you know there was a leak?"

"No."

"Did you have the boiler serviced?"

"My aunt had it checked before she went away. The certificate's gone, but I'm trying to trace the plumber who did it. We'll need proof for the insurance."

"How's your aunt taking it?"

"More upset about Ellen getting killed than worrying about the house. She might stay in the Canaries now. Nothing to come back for, really."

Alex pushed away from his stool. "Good to see you, Pete. I guess I'll see you at the funeral?"

Pete nodded, then added, "Did she tell you about her research, Alex?"

"A little. She'd been working on a new interpretation of the Amarna Letters... translating and linking to other geo-political events and communiques. But not why she'd started investigating something at Highclere. What did she tell you?"

"She was really excited about it last week. Seemed to be making progress or had a breakthrough."

Alex smiled at the memory. "That was Ellen. She could get so thrilled over the smallest things. I helped her once with a numerical problem—she was looking at a cuneiform number, not a hieroglyph. It represented eight. She was over the moon. I also realised a symbol might be a surveyor's measuring rope. You'd think she'd solved The Times crossword puzzle she was so happy."

"She described you the same way."

Alex blinked, pushed back his glasses. Did she? Well, he supposed... Pete interrupted his thoughts.

"She mentioned treasure or gold. I think she was following clues to something hidden." Pete looked intense. "You don't think...?"

"What?"

"Maybe Carter and Carnarvon hid something. I read they were in trouble with the Egyptian authorities after finding King Tut's tomb."

Alex winced. Ellen hated Tutankhamun's nickname. "Do you think Ellen found something?"

"I don't know."

"She didn't tell you?"

"No." Alex thought about the last time he'd seen her, two days before the explosion. She'd seemed agitated, stayed the night, and was gone by morning.

Pete gripped Alex's arm. "Maybe you should finish her research."

"Do what?"

"Finish it. She must have been close—with the breakthrough and all."

It seemed reasonable. Alex's own research wasn't progressing. Completing hers could ensure she got the recognition she deserved. But he didn't know much about it. Let's see. She'd been translating documents from the New Kingdom period. There had been the breakthrough with the recognition of numbers...

Pete broke his thoughts. "Let me get you another coffee." He guided Alex back to the stool. "White? Sugar?"

"Small Americano. White, one sugar."

Pete returned with two cups. Alex said, "It's hopeless. Her notes were probably destroyed."

Pete rubbed his head, thinking. "But what if she didn't have all her notes with her?"

"Maybe, but unlikely. She wouldn't have left her laptop overnight at Highclere. Do you know if it was found?"

"Nothing left except large items. Even the fridge was in pieces."

"Maybe the police picked up something valuable? I don't know how these things work."

"I'll check with the cops," Pete said. "Meanwhile, maybe you could check her stuff at your place?"

Alex was sure Ellen hadn't left any research at his house. A few books and clothes, yes, but he agreed to look. They drank in silence for a while, Alex watching the canal activity again.

"I really cared about her, you know," Pete said quietly.

"Me too."

Pete's gaze lingered. Alex thought, *He really hasn't slept.*

"What?" Alex prompted.

"We might have become an item. Early days, but there was something there."

Alex didn't comment. Would Ellen have fallen for this guy? She would have told him, wouldn't she? Best friends shared things like that. Pete didn't seem like her type. But who knew? People surprised you.

He tried not to sound dismissive. "We'll never know."

"Sorry, it was insensitive to mention." Pete touched Alex's arm. "Almost forgot—she prepaid her rent. Two thousand pounds. I can't keep it. Can I transfer it to you to pass to her folks?"

"Why not send it to them yourself?"

"I met her parents. They didn't like me. Silly, but I'd rather not contact them. Please?"

Alex considered. What did it matter? "Fine," he said and gave Pete his bank details.

Pete finished his drink. "I've got an idea."

Alex leaned forward. "What?"

"Highclere Castle."

"What about it?"

"We should go there. See if it triggers anything. You have a pass, right?"

Alex hesitated, then nodded. "Yeah."

They made a plan. On the walk home, Alex felt a glimmer of purpose. Taking action was better than moping. Maybe he could finish her research after all.

Chapter 4

Pete's plan was to arrive after closing so that they wouldn't be disturbed. The gatehouse was in darkness and the gates locked. They parked on the grass and climbed over fencing that bounded a field.

Highclere Castle was not really a castle. It was a manor house that had once been classically Georgian in appearance. Less than 150 years ago it had been transformed to look castle-like with a central tower and ramparts.

"I remember it from *Downton Abbey*," Pete said, and quickly added, "Though I never watched it. It looks smaller."

At night, the main entrance doors were locked, and Alex led the way around the side, through tall wooden gates into a courtyard.

"The servant's entrance," Pete said, and put on a baseball cap. He pulled it low over his brow. He handed one to Alex, who shook his head.

"Come on, man," Pete said with a laugh. "We're a team, aren't we? Put it on and play along."

Alex acquiesced and stuck it on his head. "The Egyptian exhibition was mothballed during the years of the TV series here," he said. "Now it's back and covers most of below-stairs. It's bigger now too. Now that the British Museum has supported it." He took out his museum ID card. "There's extra security but my ID can get us in."

"What sort of security?"

"Oh, most of the exhibits from the museum are in locked and alarmed cabinets. And there's a security guard..."

Pete shook his head. "You didn't say anything about a guard!"

Alex knew the guy would be upstairs in the comfortable office. He'd most likely be watching TV or asleep. And, anyway, what if he did see them on the monitors? Maybe it would seem odd being there so late, but Alex could argue he was doing research.

"He won't be a problem," Alex said as he swiped the card. The door lock clicked open.

"Pete?" The other guy had taken a few steps away. "Really, there won't be a problem. I've a right to be here."

"But I haven't."

"We'll blag it. Not a problem."

Pete took another step away. "You go in. I'll just do a quick recce outside."

Alex was about to respond, but Pete had gone. He stepped into the hallway and hit the light switch. There was nothing in here, just a long corridor. Alex went to the end and through a door. A few minutes later, Pete came in behind him, a little out of breath.

Pete said, "Are the lights a good idea? I thought we would use torches."

"Why? We're not being secretive." Alex studied Pete's face for a moment, suddenly concerned. "You better not be up to anything. This is about Ellen's research."

"Sure, I just thought... I just don't want us to be disturbed."

"We won't be. The guard can't see the basement lights from his room, plus the house is pretty hidden. Lights down here aren't going to attract anyone. And, on the off chance we get discovered, how bad would it look if we were snooping around with torches?"

"Fair point." Pete stepped past. They were at the bottom of some stairs. "Where are we?"

Alex walked on into a small room. "This is the start of the exhibition," he explained. "These are all genuine artifacts from Carnarvon's collection. They are all from tombs, so we have lots of these doll-like things called shabti, as well as personal items like combs and jewellery."

"Good. When you explain things, keep it simple for me. None of the fancy historical names. Okay?"

"Not a problem."

Pete walked around slowly and asked a few questions about items that were displayed inside secure glass cabinets. Finally, he said, "Anything leap out at you?"

"No."

They descended a ramp and saw a large cabinet with a more modern display. It was about Lord Carnarvon. There were photographs and toys from his childhood but also diaries and photographs relating to his work with Howard Carter.

"Carter was really the Egyptologist," Alex said. "Carnarvon financed his digs, most of which weren't very successful."

"Have you read these diaries?"

"No, but I know Ellen did. She was interested in the man as well as the history."

Pete tried the cabinet. "Can you unlock it?"

"To get the diaries, you mean?"

"Sure."

"I don't have a key. I'd need to be here on official research. We'd have to come back… Hey!"

Pete had a penknife out and was trying to jimmy the lock. Alex grabbed his arm and pulled it away.

"Don't…" Pete's eyes flared with anger, but it was only brief. "Sorry, you're right. Maybe we'll come back… officially."

Alex led them onwards into semi-darkness. The next display was a glimpse at what Carnarvon and Carter allegedly saw before they broke into Tutankhamun's tomb. Pete peered through a slit in blackened glass. "Wow! It must have been incredible."

"Yes, but it's of no interest to us. It's all fake."

They proceeded through a blackout screen and Alex hit the lights. A wall of gold dazzled them. "Wow!" Pete said again.

"The main exhibition," Alex said. "This used to be mostly replicas, but most of the artifacts in glass cabinets are real.

"What about this?" Pete touched the huge, ornately carved box-like object that had blinded them with reflected light.

"It's an outer casket. The sarcophagus was surrounded by a series of caskets like this. And no, it's not real gold."

"So, Ellen wouldn't have been interested in it?"

"Unlikely."

"And this is the famous death mask?" Pete was standing in front of a glass cabinet.

"Again, a replica."

"Shame. So apart from Carnarvon the man, what else was she interested in?"

"At the moment her focus is… was on New Kingdom communication."

"Sounds exciting," Pete said with sarcasm.

"You see the hieroglyphs on everything?" He ran a hand over the carved symbols on the casket. "Well, it was really an ancient language mostly used by priests and the higher echelons of society. They believed it was the language of the gods. A more cursive form developed, but everyday writing was cuneiform. Cuneiform was widely used internationally in the region. It was literally a wedge-based alphabet that could be easily written in clay."

"Uh-huh." Pete studied a royal-blue and golden vase.

"Ellen was particularly interested in hidden and double meanings. I couldn't help very much because I'm a numbers guy rather than language. She showed me some symbols and it was part of a puzzle she was solving."

Now Pete looked interested. "See them anywhere— these symbols? What are they? What are we looking for?"

Alex was already checking out the hieroglyphs. "Lots, but in particular you could look for spirals, pillars and geese. Maybe anything that looks like cuneiform."

"The wedges."

"Right. Like an arrow with the head the wrong way round."

They both completed a circuit of the main exhibition. Alex shrugged. "I don't see any of them."

"Go round again. Maybe you missed them, or maybe you'll spot something else she might have been interested in."

They spent almost an hour in the room, with Pete going back over items and showing frustration each time Alex drew a blank on Ellen's research.

There was one more exhibition room. The old kitchen had been converted, with glass display cabinets all around. Pete led the way.

Alex said, "This room used to just contain the Carnarvon family memorabilia. The items you now see are all mostly from the British Museum, minor Egyptian artifacts that weren't displayed in London. These are genuine, but any link to Carnarvon is tenuous at best."

Pete did a quick circuit. "So, nothing else?"

"The research room."

"What? Where Ellen did her research?" Pete could barely contain his excitement.

Alex took him across the first corridor and into a small side room, probably once a boot room. "Well, more of a coffee room. I don't think…"

Pete was already opening cupboards and searching for clues. Alex looked in the bin. Empty.

He moved it aside to get at a cupboard door.

"What's that?" Pete said over Alex's shoulder. There was a ball of paper in the gap between the last cupboard and wall. Someone probably missed the bin and it just got wedged there.

Alex fished it out and smoothed open the small piece of paper. It looked like it had been torn from a notebook. Ellen's writing. She'd thrown it away because of doodles and word games. That's what he first thought. He read: Watcher Road. Charter Roars. Toward Reach.

It made him smile when he realised.

"What is it?" Pete asked, looking over his shoulder.

"Anagrams of Howard Carter."

"Meaning?"

"Just something she did."

She'd also written Tutankhamun, but Pete didn't mention it.

"What about those… 'Stone' and 'Block'?" he asked. "And that… Looks like 'Carnarvon table'?"

"Carnarvon tablet. It's about a stela—"

"Simple, remember," Pete interrupted. "What's a stela?"

"A stone marker known as a stela. Sometimes to mark a boundary. Sometimes like a plaque. The Carnarvon Tablet was taken from one of the temples. There had originally been two."

"What happened to the other one?"

"No one knows. Carnarvon's notes said there were two, but these were later changed to one tablet. Anyway, looks like she's crossed it out. I don't think—"

Pete wasn't listening. "So, Ellen was trying to find out what was on the other tablet? That's the research. And maybe the other tablet was gold?"

Alex shrugged. He remembered Pete mentioning treasure when they were in the coffee bar. It didn't seem likely. "Could have been, but..." For some reason Alex held back. He could see imprints in the paper—numbers written on a previous page, he guessed. Forty and twelve and eight were repeated over and over. Twelve had been one of the symbols he'd interpreted for Ellen. To him it looked like a surveyor's measuring device. It was a line with twelve knots, two of which were bigger: the third and seventh. He'd told her it was much more than just a measure. Twelve knots could make up a triangle with sides of three, four and five. The ancient Egyptians thought of it as having magical powers. They called it the golden triangle.

Rather than mention this, he said, "Tutankhamun is obvious. Most of this exhibition is about Carter and Carnarvon's discovery."

Pete said, "What else then? Maybe it was a message about some treasure. I keep thinking maybe Ellen was onto where more of King Tut's wealth was buried."

"Tutankhamun. Ellen hated the name King Tut."

"Okay, *Toot-an-car-mun* then. What do you think? Could she have been onto something?"

Alex shrugged again. "Look, Pete, you've got to understand what it's like to be an archaeologist. It's not Indiana Jones. It's hardly ever about finding buried treasure. It's about piecing together the past. It's like solving part of a puzzle. Archaeologists get a kick out of discovering the tiniest thing."

Pete asked more questions, but Alex's energy drained away. What had started out as a diversion, a distraction from Ellen's death, now seemed pointless. There was nothing here of interest. What he really needed was her laptop. That's where her research would have been. And that had been destroyed in the explosion. However, as they drove back to London in silence, Alex couldn't help but think he had missed something.

Chapter 5

Alex took Topsy for a long walk through Regent's Park, but the fresh air did nothing to clear his mind. The next day drifted past in a haze. He wandered from room to room, unable to focus on work, flipping through books and old photographs of Ellen. A familiar paperback caught his eye—*The Oxford History of Ancient Egypt*, wedged among novels instead of textbooks. He pulled it out and traced the worn spine with his thumb. Ellen had given it to him two years ago, scrawling a note inside the cover.

Think you can memorise the King List? she had written, teasing him on his birthday. The King List—the accepted chronology of pharaohs. He had once managed to recall fifty-eight names from the Eighteenth to the Twenty-first Dynasty. Now, he could barely remember half. He tried again, flipping pages, mouthing names under his breath, but lost interest. The walls of the flat felt too close. He needed to get out.

Sitting on a park bench, watching kids kick a football across the grass, his phone rang. Nadja.

"You don't want me walk Topsy today, Mr MacLure?"

Alex blinked, glancing at his watch. "Damn. Sorry, Nadja, I lost track of time."

"I walk her later, if you like?"

He looked down at Topsy, who perked up at the mention of her name. "I think she'd like that. What time suits you?"

"Five all right?"

"That's great." He was about to hang up when Nadja hesitated.

"Mr MacLure?"

"Yes?"

"I've been cleaning..." Another pause. "I found mobile phone. In your house, I mean."

Alex sat up straighter. "What? Where?" He tried to remember if he had any old phones lying around. Maybe an old Nokia?

"Behind the bedside table," she said, sounding uncertain. "I know you don't ask me clean in there much, but it has been a while, and... well, I had time in the spare room."

His mind reeled. Nadja didn't know Ellen was dead. If she had found a phone, it had to be Ellen's.

"I'll be home soon," he said. "Just leave it on the coffee table."

The phone was an older iPhone, scuffed and lifeless. He pressed the power button. It turned on. Passcode locked. He tried a few numbers—birthdays, anniversaries—but stopped after five attempts. A quick search online warned him that ten failed tries would lock it permanently.

Ten thousand possible combinations. He put the phone down.

In his rush, he had ignored his own phone. The answering machine flashed three messages. His mother checking in, and two from Aysha Milwanee of *The Sunday Times*, requesting an interview about Ellen. Curious, he looked her up. An investigative journalist. Not a tabloid hack.

He called back.

"Aysha Milwanee," she answered, her voice brisk yet warm.

"Alex MacLure, returning your call. You wanted to talk about Ellen?"

"Yes. I understand she was remarkable. I'd like to write a piece about her life."

"And the accident?" His tone sharpened.

"I can't promise publication," she said quickly, "but I've spoken to her family and colleagues. Just a bit of depth from your perspective. Wouldn't you like to celebrate her life?"

He hesitated. What harm could it do?

"Fine. When?"

"I'm nearby. Twenty minutes?"

He hung up and glanced at Ellen's phone. Should he tell Pete? He had promised to report anything he found. Instead, he sent a text.

Hi, Pete. Did the police find anything?

Five minutes passed. Nothing. He made coffee, trying to ignore the itch of unease creeping up his spine. Half an hour later, the doorbell rang.

Aysha was professional, setting up a digital recorder and flipping open a notebook. "Let's start with your career change. You left finance?"

"I was the financial controller at Shelley's Recruitment Agency. Quit to study archaeology."

"At?"

"Macquarie University. Ancient Egyptian studies."

"Not many people can afford to just quit."

"I won the lottery."

She raised an eyebrow.

He smirked. "Really. Paid off my mortgage and did what I wanted. I was always good with numbers, but accountancy? Thought it would be more interesting than it was. Just a job in the end."

"Everyone's dream." She smiled. "You weren't drawn to Egypt because of Tutankhamun?"

He shook his head. "That was Ellen's passion. The New Kingdom period anyway."

She watched him carefully. "You were close?"

His throat tightened. "Yes."

"Was it Ellen who got you interested?"

"In a way. She had an eidetic memory, was brilliant, but struggled with bipolar disorder."

They spoke about Ellen's research, her sharp mind, her theories. He realised he'd been speaking too quickly, getting excited. He looked up and noticed the reporter wasn't writing it down.

She nodded politely then surprised him with a question. "Were you two involved?"

He hesitated. "We dated, briefly... Ah... It didn't work."

His phone vibrated. A text from Pete.

>Don't speak to anyone!

Alex frowned. **Why?**

>Police. Reporters. Stay low

Immediately followed by another message.

>Ellen's death suspicious

Alex's skin prickled.

He looked up at Aysha, suddenly wary. "What's this really about?"

She didn't blink. "Ellen Champion."

"I hope that helps your article."

"Is the interview over?"

"Yes. Something's come up."

She smiled sweetly. "One last question?"

"What?"

"Were you involved in Ellen's murder?"

Chapter 6

Alex's fingers trembled as he swiped through the BBC news app. The headline made his stomach churn:

Gas explosion: Police treat woman's death as suspicious

The news article outlined the tragic details. Dr Ellen Champion, found dead in a house near Newbury, was now the focus of a police investigation. Detective Superintendent Charles Wardby of Thames Valley Police had noted significant discrepancies that ruled out a simple gas explosion. Post-mortem tests were pending, but the police were already urging anyone who had seen Ellen recently to come forward.

Alex called Pete, his anxiety bubbling over.

The phone rang forever before Pete's groggy voice answered, "Hello?"

"I can't believe it," Alex blurted. "The police think she was murdered!"

Pete's tone shifted from sleepy to irritated. "They're just suspicious. It doesn't mean—"

"Have the police contacted you?"

"Yeah, a short interview," Pete admitted with a sigh. "I'm sorry, mate. I'm tired. Working nights. Didn't get to bed until six-thirty this morning."

"No, I didn't know."

"Listen," Pete's voice softened, "we shouldn't mention we've been in touch. Cops can be funny about connections. They latch onto them, and next thing you know, you're a suspect."

"Jesus. Have you—"

"Yeah, been there before. They wreck your life, find you innocent, and leave. No apologies, no compensation, and your reputation's in shambles. You haven't talked to the press, have you?"

Alex's heart skipped a beat. "No, why would I?" he lied.

"Good. The cops catch wind of it, the reporters twist your words, and the police take it as gospel."

Alex kept silent. He hoped the interview with Milwanee wouldn't be published. Pete warned him again, "Be careful what you say and to whom. They found my number somehow. Stay under the radar."

Alex spent the afternoon combing through news updates, finding little beyond the police's vague suspicions. Milwanee had hinted at murder, but the official reports were more cautious. He scanned other articles, noting a pattern: police often confirmed suspicions of foul play within days. Ellen's fears suddenly seemed all too justified. Maybe Pete's treasure theory wasn't so far-fetched after all.

The doorbell's buzz jolted him. It was Nadja.

"I didn't want to just let myself in," she explained, seeing his distressed face. "Mr MacLure, you look like you've seen a ghost."

"I thought…" He forced a smile, waving away his thoughts. "What were you...?"

She pointed to Topsy, who was wagging her tail. "I said I'd walk her."

The doorbell buzzed again, followed by firm knocking. Nadja picked up the intercom phone, then handed it to Alex.

"Thames Valley Police. Can we come in?"

Moments later, a tall, swarthy man stood in the doorway, his ID badge reading Detective Constable Dixit. A shorter woman with untidy dark hair, Detective Sergeant Belmarsh, stood behind him.

"Interesting name," Alex commented. "Belmarsh, like the prison."

She nodded slightly, then looked at Nadja. "Who are you?"

"A neighbour," Alex interjected, "just about to walk my dog."

Belmarsh's eyes narrowed. "I'm sure she can speak for herself. Your name, Miss?"

"Nadja."

She took out a notebook. "Miss Nadja...?"

"Dabrowska." Nadja spelled it out, and Belmarsh wrote it down.

"Can we sit?" Belmarsh asked. Nadja, looking relieved, said, "Can I go then, if that's all right?"

Belmarsh looked at Alex. "You have Miss Dabrowska's contact details?"

"Yes."

"Then you are free to walk Mr MacLure's dog, Miss Dabrowska." The detective's tone suggested she didn't fully trust them.

With Nadja gone, Alex resumed his seat on the sofa. "How can I help you, Detectives?"

Dixit introduced himself formally, stating they were making enquiries following Ellen's death.

"I've seen the news. You think she was murdered."

"There is an enquiry due to suspicions," Dixit replied, his eyes squinting, perhaps for effect. Belmarsh sat silently, her gaze disconcertingly above his eyeline.

"We have some questions," Dixit continued.

Alex, recalling Pete's advice, asked, "How did you know where I live?"

Dixit's mouth twitched a smile. "We interviewed Dr Champion's family. So…"

"Of course, they know my address. And phone number. You could have called."

"We prefer face-to-face," Belmarsh said, her tone suggesting they aimed to catch him off guard.

"Tell me about your relationship with Dr Champion," Dixit began.

Alex explained their fifteen-year friendship, how they met at school and had remained close.

"She moved there. Started in year 11," he added unnecessarily.

"She was your girlfriend?"

"Once. Briefly. Not recently. Just friends now. Her parents could confirm that."

Belmarsh raised an eyebrow. "Friends-with-benefits, then?"

"Just friends," Alex snapped, his chest tightening with anger. The detectives moved on.

Dixit asked, "Did she often stay here?"

"Yes, in the spare room," Alex said, pointing down the hall. "Not my bedroom."

"We'll take a look in a moment." Dixit checked his notes, maybe biding time. "And you worked together?"

"Not exactly. She worked for the British Museum. I'm a research fellow there."

Belmarsh interjected, "Splitting hairs, Mr MacLure?"

Alex's frustration boiled over. "You suspect me, don't you? That's what this is about. I didn't hurt her. She was my best friend. If you're looking for a killer, then you are looking in the wrong direction. For God's sake, I didn't do it. You need to be out there looking for the person who did!"

"Person?" Belmarsh continued the stare.

"Just a figure of speech. If you mean, do I know if it was one person rather than two or more, I don't." Alex breathed in and out. He was riled and could see that Belmarsh was more interested now he was angry.

Dixit appeared distracted by his bookshelf.

Belmarsh said, "Talk us through your employment history, please."

Alex recounted his transition from accountant to Egyptologist, noting the odd intersection of mathematics and history.

"When did you leave Shelley's Recruitment?" Belmarsh snapped.

"Six months ago."

"When was the last time you saw Dr Champion?"

"Last weekend, just before the explosion."

"Before she died…" Belmarsh clarified unnecessarily.

"Yes, that's right."

Dixit noted it down. "The weekend of the 7th and 8th? All weekend?"

"From Saturday night until Sunday morning. She left early to see her mum for dinner."

"Did she?" Dixit's tone implied disbelief.

"That's what she said." Alex's confidence wavered. "I'm pretty sure."

"How was she?"

"Anxious, maybe depressed. She denied it, but that's why she stayed here. Her parents knew she was on medication—Venlafaxine."

Dixit noted it. "What did you do?"

"Watched a film, had an Indian takeaway." Alex named the restaurant and the film. Dixit asked for a receipt, and Alex promised to check his card statement.

"And Monday night?"

"I was home. Walked my dog, Topsy, for forty minutes. Then ate, watched TV, and went to bed."

"Alone?"

"Yes. Alone." Alex realised this meant no alibi.

"And what were you doing during the early hours of Tuesday morning?"

"I slept until six, maybe a bit after, but definitely got up before six thirty."

Dixit pursed his lips as he jotted it down. After a moment of silence, he looked up sharply. "Who would want to kill Ellen?"

Alex blinked. "I don't know."

"No enemies? No one upset with her?"

"No."

"Can you think of any reason, any reason at all, that someone would do this?"

"No."

Dixit flipped through his notes, then closed his book. "Can you show us around?"

The tour was brief. Belmarsh inspected the spare room, photographing Ellen's belongings, while Dixit studied the bookcase. The meticulousness of the police was unnerving.

Returning to the lounge, Belmarsh remarked, "The bathroom's spotless. You have a cleaner?"

"Yes, Nadja. She walks the dog too."

"Not another friend-with-benefits, then?"

Alex seethed but stayed silent.

As they returned to the lounge, Dixit was standing in front of the bookcase. He turned and exchanged a nod with Belmarsh.

Dixit said, "You certainly have an eclectic mix of books, Mr MacLure."

Alex shrugged. "I'm a mathematician. But I've been drawn to Egyptology because of the mysteries."

Belmarsh smiled thinly. "Thank you for your help. We'll be in touch if we need anything further."

As they left, Alex said, "One more thing—did you find a laptop at the house?"

Dixit paused. "Why?"

"What about her briefcase? It's burgundy. Old."

"Again, Mr MacLure: Why?"

"Her research. I can't find it. If she was murdered, then maybe it's related to that."

The man who had been in the blue suit, knocked on the rear door of a white transit van. His codename was Fox. Without waiting, he climbed in. Another man, sat before a bank of equipment, looked up.

"Any news?" Fox asked.

"Thames Valley detectives. The woman got the rabbit riled, but it was routine."

Rabbit. Alex MacLure.

"Think he knows anything?"

"If he does, he's good at hiding it. But listen." The seated man played the recording.

Alex's voice crackled through, "Her research. I can't find it. If she was murdered, maybe it's related to that."

Fox pulled out his phone and dialled. After a brief conversation, he said, "Nothing so far. My opinion? If it wasn't an accident, someone did us a favour."

Chapter 7

Detective Inspector Jackson leaned back in his creaky chair, staring at the autopsy report. His instincts had been right: murder. The younger detectives might see him as the washed-up old-timer, bypassed for promotion, a relic the Super didn't like. Maybe they worried their careers would stagnate under his command. But he didn't give a damn. They should respect his instincts. He smiled grimly. He'd known the Champion case was fishy from the start.

His eyes drifted over the three junior detectives in front of him. There was Limb, always impeccably dressed, a goatee framing his smug face. Beside him, Belmarsh, looking weary, her hair pulled back in a no-nonsense ponytail. And then there was Dixit, sharp and ambitious, reminding Jackson of himself twenty-five years ago.

"Time of death was about three hours before the explosion," Jackson grunted.

Limb, the dandy in grey suit trousers, matching waistcoat, and burgundy loafers, chimed in, "Three hours before the explosion, sir."

Jackson resisted the urge to roll his eyes at Limb's footwear—tassels, for God's sake! Turning to Belmarsh, he continued, "The trauma to the back of the head... an occipital fracture, probably from a blunt instrument.

Most of the contusions are post-mortem, likely from the explosion. But perimortem marks suggest a struggle."

Jackson flipped through the CSI report. "The forensic report confirms it was a gas explosion. No surprise there. A gas explosion happens when the gas-air mixture hits a critical point. Any spark can set it off. We get an explosion rather than a fire because of the pressure build-up."

Limb interjected, "And the explosion can stop the fire from spreading."

"Exactly. The blast blows itself out. The report pinpointed the leak and ignition source—the boiler. Likely ignited when it fired up to heat the water."

Limb nodded. "Between three and three and a half hours after Dr Champion's death."

"Right." Jackson's tone was curt. "But there was an inconsistency, wasn't there?"

Dixit jumped in, "There was evidence of a fire in the lounge."

"A fire in the lounge, not near the boiler, and not the cause of the explosion." Jackson tapped the report. "So what the hell was it?"

Belmarsh leaned forward, showing rare engagement. "The explosion was deliberate. The person who caused the gas leak wanted to ensure it happened."

"Like an accelerant or primer," Dixit suggested.

"But it went out," Jackson nodded. "I don't think the perp intended an explosion. It was supposed to be a fire caused by a gas leak. We wouldn't have the discrepancy in the time of death if he'd just set a fire."

He spun the manila folder around. "We have our confirmed murder investigation. Each of you read the file later. Now, how have your investigations gone so far?"

Limb reported first. "Interviewed Ellen Champion's parents. They confirmed Alex MacLure was a friend from school. They haven't seen him in years. She has a brother in Singapore, working at a financial institution. Do you want me to speak to him?"

"Not yet," Jackson replied.

Limb continued: "Nothing from the neighbours. They were both home all night and Tuesday morning. No one saw or heard anything unusual until the explosion."

"What about her landlady?" Jackson asked.

"She's in Lanzarote. She hasn't returned in four months. Never met Dr Champion, was shocked by the news, suffers from angina, and the insurance claim is stressing her out."

"Give her a few days and try again. See if her story holds. There might be a connection."

Belmarsh said, "You think Champion was collateral damage?"

"Until we get a firm lead, rule nothing out," Jackson said. He shifted his gaze to Belmarsh, who looked more exhausted than usual. "What did you find at Highclere?"

"Staff confirmed she worked long hours and didn't interact much. Her boss at the British Museum, Professor Beatrice Lloyd, said she'd been an employee and research fellow for six years. No trouble. Recently turned down a dig in Egypt to help at Highclere instead.

"Lloyd said the dig was a big opportunity."

"Why was she so keen to stay behind?" Jackson mused. "Most archaeologists jump at a dig opportunity. Why Highclere?"

Belmarsh nodded at the rhetorical question.

Jackson switched to Dixit. "Alex MacLure?"

"MacLure confirmed he was the ex-boyfriend. No signs they were more than friends, but he found it odd she left Sunday morning for her parents' place."

Limb interjected, "Parents didn't see her on Sunday. They hadn't seen her for three weeks."

"Either he's lying or didn't know," Dixit said, looking at Belmarsh. "She got under his skin. He got agitated when we suggested there was more to their relationship. There was also an attractive Polish woman, Nadja Dabrowska, who walks his dog and cleans. Maybe she was more. Maybe Miss Champion found out. The house was spotless. Could be innocent but could also be hiding something."

"MacLure picked up on Belmarsh's name," Dixit added with a grin. "I didn't know it was so infamous. Jo has an interesting ancestor."

Belmarsh said, "Each time I mentioned there was something more between them, MacLure flushed. Friends-with-benefits, I kept saying. He didn't like that."

"Alibi?" Jackson asked.

"Claims he was alone Monday evening, in bed all night."

Jackson waited.

"But he seemed very keen to know if we'd found her briefcase. Her research."

Jackson looked at Limb, who pulled out a sheaf of papers. "One leather briefcase. Burgundy."

"Anything else?" Jackson prompted.

"Nothing unusual in the apartment except the books," Dixit said.

"Eclectic!" Belmarsh coughed through her fist.

"Quite a mix. Mostly non-fiction. One caught my eye: a karate handbook."

"Karate?" Jackson pondered. The victim had died in a struggle. The cause of death was a broken neck, not blunt trauma. Could it be MacLure? "Okay," he said, dismissing them. "Let's get a look at the briefcase. And Belmarsh—"

"Sir?"

"Talk to MacLure's neighbours. I want to know if they had an argument when she stayed over."

Chapter 8

Alex lay in bed, staring at the ceiling, wrestling with the thoughts that tormented him since the detective's visit. Ellen's murder plagued his mind. Who had the motive? Every time he drifted into an uneasy sleep, the same dream returned.

In the dream, he was walking on the path from the gym, heading towards the lone low-rise block. The echo of his footfalls on the flagstones was dull and heavy. The air was biting cold, and the sky, a mix of pewter and tangerine, hinted at impending snow. It was as if he had returned to that day, back in school, at fifteen, and aware he was dreaming. But knowing it didn't change the outcome.

Behind him, an odd pitter-patter grew louder until— thwack! He was nearly knocked off his feet. Arms wrapped around his neck, choking him. He swung around, forcing his attacker to release him. It was Tommy East, the small scrum half, fresh from the playing fields in his rugby kit. More boys formed a circle around them. Tommy threw a roundhouse punch to Alex's jaw, sending him stumbling.

Tommy kicked Alex's legs, sweeping him to the ground. A stamp on his chest was followed by a barrage of kicks. Pain shot through his head as one connected above his right eye. Laughter echoed as the boys walked away, leaving Alex in a fog on the verge of unconsciousness.

In the assembly hall, the scene shifted. The varnished block wood floor and Prussian blue velvet curtains were unchanged. The form master appeared, accusing the rugby team due to the stud marks on Alex's shirt. The team lined up, cold and menacing. As Alex walked the line, their eyes met Tommy's, but, just like then, he couldn't point him out. The form master's face morphed into Detective Dixit's.

"Who did it?" Dixit snarled. "Point out the murderer!"

Panic surged in Alex. "I don't know! I don't know!"

He jerked awake, drenched in sweat. It was 4am, Sunday morning. Fully awake, he got up, made tea, and settled on the sofa with Topsy. The news blared on the TV—Highclere Castle had been burgled.

At 8:30am, his phone rang. DS Dixit.

"Have you seen the news?" Dixit asked.

"Yes."

"Stay home. Colleagues from the Met are on their way. We'd like you to help with our enquiries." The words were laced with hidden meanings.

Nineteen minutes later, Alex's doorbell and phone rang at the same time. He ignored both and continued reading the news. Heavy footsteps in the hall followed a neighbour opening the outside door. A sharp knock on his apartment door.

"Police, Mr MacLure," a voice called.

Alex rubbed Topsy's head. "I won't be long," he said. "Don't worry."

In the hallway, three uniformed policemen waited impassively. Alex stepped out, shutting the door behind him. He walked down the hall, flanked by officers. Outside, the lead officers cleared a path through a huddle of reporters and photographers, leading to a silver Omega with twin orange Metropolitan Police lines. An officer looped his arm through Alex's, guiding him briskly through the mob.

Reporters surged like a rugby maul. A boom microphone swung close, and the officer beside Alex swatted it away. Alex ducked into the car, cameras flashing, a reporter shouting, "What have you got to say about the allegations?" The door slammed shut, silencing the chaos.

Inside the police car, Alex settled into the black leather seat, staring ahead, oblivious to the paparazzi chasing the car. His mind wrestled with the unfolding events.

At the Chiswick police station, Alex waited for nearly an hour before being ushered into a room with DC Dixit and an older man with grey hair and weary eyes.

DI Jackson introduced himself.

Alex scanned the spotless cream walls. No pins, no Blu-Tack marks, no two-way mirror, no camera. A digital recorder sat on the table, switched off. Alex sat upright, hands relaxed on the table. Between the detectives, but closer to Dixit, was a manila file. Dixit twirled a cheap blue pen, while Jackson, directly opposite, kept his hands under the table like a card player.

"So, I've not been arrested?" Alex asked.

"We'd just like you to help with our enquiries."

"Can I have a solicitor?"

"If you want one," Jackson said. "Do you need a solicitor?"

Alex shrugged. "I'm not guilty of anything, so no, I don't need a solicitor."

"Good." Jackson smiled.

Alex asked, "Is this about the burglary at Highclere last night?"

Dixit replied, "We'll come to that. Firstly, just to be open and clear, were you involved in any way in Ellen Champion's death?"

"No."

"You suggested we look at Dr Champion's briefcase, correct?" Dixit waited for Alex to nod. "Why was that?"

"I wondered... if Ellen was murdered, maybe it had something to do with her research. Maybe it was in her briefcase. Did you find it?"

"Was her research about something at Highclere?"

"I think so, but I don't know the details. And you know what it's like to be a detective. She was following threads, trying to answer questions about the past. That's what she found so fascinating."

"And you?"

"Yes, I find it interesting."

"But not always so. For many years, you were an accountant."

"Yes."

"Latterly at Shelley's Recruitment."

"Yes. But accountancy wasn't the—"

Dixit leaned forward. "You like to think of yourself as a mathematician, right?"

"I like numbers. I like looking for patterns. Same thing again—like detective work, I mean."

"What are the odds of winning the national lottery?"

"Do you mean getting all six numbers correct?"

"That'll do. What are the odds?"

"The probability of pulling six balls out of forty-nine is one in forty-nine times one in forty-eight times—"

"What's the answer?"

"One chance in thirteen million, nine hundred and eighty-three thousand, eight hundred and sixteen."

"So, about fourteen million to one." Dixit raised an eyebrow.

"Yes, if you want to be less accurate."

"You know that and yet you claim to have played and won."

"It was a whim, and I like certain numbers."

Jackson said, "You don't strike me as someone who acts on whims." He emphasised whims, almost mocking.

"Well, each number has an equal chance of being drawn, irrespective of past draws—the so-called law of averages is nonsense. And sequential numbers are just as likely as any random combination. However, I play the lottery every now and then when the whim takes me, and the numbers I chose were 2, 5, 10, 17, 28, and 41." Alex smiled but could see they didn't get it. "They are the ascending sum of the first six prime numbers, so 2 plus 3 is 5. Then add 5, the next prime, gives you 10. Then add 7, then add 11."

Jackson again: "And you won?"

"Five of the numbers…"

Dixit leaned forward and smiled. "So, you won millions?"

Alex shrugged ruefully. "The problem was that there was a bunch of people playing the same sequence. Probably all number freaks like me. I got a few pounds shy of seven hundred thousand. Did you know there's a one in fifteen chance that a London telephone number is prime?"

Dixit ignored the question. "What was the date of your win?"

Alex gave him a date, almost six months ago.

Dixit said, "We'll check, of course."

Jackson said, "Because otherwise you can see why we might be suspicious of you coming into a large amount of money."

Alex looked from Jackson to Dixit and back. "Is this what you wanted to speak to me so urgently about?"

Dixit said, "We spoke to your ex-colleagues. They said you just resigned. They knew nothing about you winning the lottery."

"I did win. I didn't tell them for obvious reasons. If you have money, other people get jealous and want it. The only people I told were Ellen, my brother and my mother."

After a beat, Jackson nodded as though to himself and said, "Let's talk about the matter exciting the press this morning, shall we?"

"The burglary at Highclere." Alex had read the reports, which were thin on information. The theft had been executed with surgical precision, it appeared. There was one witness to the arrival, but no one saw them leave. The guard had been "rendered unconscious" according to most, although one referred to chloroform or something similar. He was in his room and saw a dark-coloured van come through the gates. The CCTV was black and white so he couldn't report the colour, though he guessed blue and thought it looked like a Ford Transit. The guard hadn't been alarmed. It drove to the rear yard, and he thought it was maybe a delivery. He'd left the room and headed for the rear door. Before he got there, someone was already inside. He briefly thought he saw a movement, possibly someone big, but that was all. He was reported as not requiring medical attention.

Jackson asked, "Where were you last night between the hours of 2 and 4am?"

"At home in bed. Alone. No alibis."

"Did you go to Highclere?"

"No. I was at home in bed."

"With no alibi," Dixit repeated.

Alex said nothing and waited.

Dixit said, "How did they gain access?"

Alex looked from one to the other.

"I have no idea. Break the lock?"

Silence.

"They used a pass card—a British Museum pass card," Jackson said, and paused. "Your pass card, Mr MacLure."

Alex breathed in. He breathed out. "I think I'll call my solicitor now."

Chapter 9

They left Alex in the room, the quiet seeping in like a fog. He dialled his mother's number, his hands trembling slightly. She recommended Tanya Wilson, a family friend.

"Not a criminal lawyer, but good and reliable," she added before hanging up. "Be grateful, Alex. It's Sunday, and she's doing us a big favour."

Alex acknowledged with a nod, more to himself than to his mother.

Next, he called Pete, who answered groggily.

"Sorry, Pete. Were you working late?"

"As usual. What's going on?"

Alex hesitated. "Have you heard about the Highclere break-in?"

"No... wait." The line went silent, then Pete's voice returned, tight. "Shit."

"Yeah."

"Frickin' hell, Alex. We were there only a few nights before."

Alex exhaled, pinching the bridge of his nose. "The police brought me in for questioning."

More silence. Then a measured breath. "Alex... you weren't involved, were you?"

"Of course not! But they say my pass card was used."

Pete swore under his breath. "Do you have your pass on you?"

Alex checked his pockets again, as if this time it would magically appear. "No."

"That's not good, but maybe it was cloned."

"Maybe. But how do I prove that?"

Pete sighed. "Did they show you any evidence?"

"No, just talked about it."

"They might be bluffing. If they haven't cautioned you…"

"They haven't."

"Then you might be fine."

Alex hesitated. "But we were there, Pete."

More silence. Alex could hear Pete's breathing.

"Alex," Pete said slowly, "don't mention me."

"What?"

"Shit," Pete muttered. "Remember I sent Ellen's rent to you?"

"Yeah."

"Have you passed it on to her folks yet?"

Alex's stomach sank. "Not yet."

Pete swore again. "That looks bad, Alex. Really bad. The timing, the money—just don't mention me, okay?"

Alex rubbed his forehead, a deep sense of unease settling in. "I don't like this, Pete."

"Neither do I. But we didn't do anything wrong, right?"

Alex didn't answer right away. He didn't like the feeling of hiding things. It made him look guilty.

"Fine," he said, ending the call. The sick feeling in his gut didn't fade.

Tanya Wilson arrived late, murmuring an apology about the traffic. She was a petite woman in her sixties, her sharp eyes magnified by thick glasses. A severe haircut framed her face, and though her expression remained neutral, her hands, marked by time, gave away her age. She took in the details of Ellen's death and the break-in at Highclere with swift efficiency.

"You haven't confessed to anything, have you?" she asked.

"I haven't done anything to confess to," Alex said, his voice tight with desperation.

"They haven't cautioned or charged you?"

"No. They just said I was helping with inquiries."

Wilson knocked briskly on the door, signalling they were ready. Jackson and Dixit re-entered, settling into their chairs. Jackson gestured toward the recorder on the table.

"Mind if we record this?" he asked.

Wilson nodded. "My client is here voluntarily to assist with your inquiries. He has not been cautioned and maintains he had nothing to do with Dr Ellen Champion's death or the burglary."

Dixit slid a grainy black-and-white photograph across the table. "Do you recognise this person?"

Alex squinted. The image showed a man in a baseball cap. Wilson leaned in and whispered, "Could that be you?" Alex hesitated, then mouthed, "Yes."

"That could be anyone," Wilson said smoothly.

"This was taken from a security camera inside Highclere Castle," Dixit said. "I believe it's you, Mr MacLure."

Alex remained silent.

"The picture was taken just before the cameras failed. Not last night—Wednesday night, early hours of Thursday the 12th. 12:13am, to be exact. Do you deny it's you?"

Alex had shown Pete around that night, using his pass card. Dixit already knew this.

"I think it's me," Alex admitted. "I was there."

"You used your pass card to enter through the rear of the building."

"I did. I was looking for clues about Ellen's research."

"Why so clandestine? Why disable the cameras?"

"I went late because"—he almost said 'we' but remembered Pete's warning—"I wanted to be alone, to focus."

"To case the joint," Dixit countered.

Wilson gave Alex a sharp look, warning him. He shook his head. "No. I know the exhibit inside out. I didn't need to case anything."

"You disabled the cameras."

"No," Alex said firmly. "You have a photo of me entering. Why would I care about security after that?"

Jackson leaned forward. "Three days before the burglary. That looks bad."

"It's a coincidence. I'm innocent. Ellen was my friend. I was interested in her research, not the artifacts."

Dixit slid the photo back into the folder. "Let's talk about that, shall we?"

"Talk about what?"

"Hurting Miss Champion."

The phrasing made Alex bristle. 'Miss' rather than 'Dr'—a subtle but deliberate choice.

Before he could protest, Dixit continued. "Let's go back to the evening of Saturday the 7th. You got a takeaway and watched a movie?"

"Yes."

"And you had an argument."

"No."

"Your neighbours say otherwise."

Alex shook his head. "If you mean the woman in number four, she complains about everything."

Dixit persisted. "You had an argument."

Alex thought back. Ellen had been on edge, convinced someone was following her. She'd shouted during the film, said she saw someone outside. It was dark, and when Alex checked, he found nothing. She'd been irritable afterward. Had she raised her voice again? Maybe. He'd gone out to check again—still, no one. That was the end of it.

He relayed the story.

Dixit looked unconvinced. "So, no argument?"

Wilson interjected. "My client answered. Dr Champion believed she was being followed. That's the relevant fact here."

Dixit studied Alex. "And you didn't think to mention this before?"

"She was often paranoid. She was on medication. Her mind worked better without it, but then she got more paranoid."

Jackson tapped the table. "Do you think she was murdered?"

"Is that confirmed?"

"Assume it was. And assume the burglary was connected. Too much of a coincidence?"

Alex nodded. "Seems that way."

"You're smart. You must have a theory."

"Her research. That's why I asked about her briefcase."

"It was found, but no research notes."

"So, her work *was* taken."

Dixit shrugged. "Maybe."

"Any other theories?" Jackson asked.

"No."

Dixit changed direction. "You know martial arts—an expert."

"No."

"You have a book on karate."

"I studied it. Made it to second kyu. I wasn't very good, so I stopped."

The detectives waited. Alex said nothing.

Wilson stood. "If that's all—"

Jackson held up a hand. "One moment." Dixit left. A moment later, a new detective entered. "DS Belmarsh."

She sat and opened a file. "Tell us about your relationship with the deceased."

"We were friends."

Belmarsh produced a photograph of Nadja wearing very little.

"Who's this?"

"Nadja Dabrowska. She cleans for me and walks my dog."

"She worked at a lap dancing club."

"I didn't know. It's irrelevant. She cleans and walks my dog."

Belmarsh pressed. "She's attractive."

"So?"

"You are in a relationship with her."

"No."

"Tell us about the money in your bank account."

Alex hesitated, thinking of Pete's payment. "I won the lottery."

"You looked unsure. What's the truth?"

Wilson leaned in. "He won the lottery."

Alex added, "If you've checked, you know it's true."

"So, no one gave you money to gain access to Highclere Castle?"

"Of course not."

Belmarsh slid a letter across the table confirming Alex's appointment at the museum. He nodded at his own signature. She produced another letter.

"Your signature?"

"Yes."

"Your application states you have an MA in Egyptology and are enrolled for a PhD. Is that true?"

Alex said nothing.

"You aren't enrolled. Your application was fraudulent."

Before Alex could clarify, Wilson interjected. "Embellishing a CV isn't a crime. It's not fraud unless there's financial gain or unfair advantage. My client is not a fraudster."

Alex said, "I *am* enrolled. A remote PhD student at Macquarie University, using the British Museum as a base."

Jackson pressed. "Maybe you needed to take something from the exhibition. Maybe Ellen found out. Maybe you argued. Maybe she died because of it."

Alex shook his head. "None of that happened. I am innocent."

Belmarsh leaned in. "Or was it about the Polish tart? Was Ellen jealous?"

Wilson stood. "That's enough. This interview is over."

As Alex stood to leave, he met Jackson's gaze with quiet intensity. "You're wrong. I want to help find out who killed Ellen. She was my friend. I owe her that."

Jackson studied him for a moment, his expression unreadable. Then, with a slow nod, he said, "Don't leave the country."

Chapter 10

As Dixit and Belmarsh strode down the corridor, Dixit muttered, "You didn't get under his skin this time."

Belmarsh smirked. "Maybe he fell for my charms after all. Oh, and by the way," she added, lowering her voice, "Mike's here."

Dixit's brow furrowed. "Was he listening?"

"No, just arrived. The boss is with him now." She led the way through Chiswick Police Station, out into the car park. Jackson was there, engaged in a heated exchange with DS Mike Limb. Another man loomed beside them, thrusting a tape recorder toward Jackson's face.

The man had the unmistakable look of a reporter, his rapid-fire questions met with Jackson's terse replies. Dixit watched Jackson's lips form the words, "No comment."

As they approached, Jackson's patience snapped. "You're on police property. DS Limb, escort this gentleman out of the car park."

Limb stepped forward. The reporter held his ground until Limb reached for him, then he sidestepped deftly.

"One more question. Is there a connection between the death of the Champion girl and the burglary at Highclere?"

Jackson's face twisted with irritation. "Go away!"

Limb advanced again, but the reporter was already retreating, scuttling across the yard and through the gates. "Bloody hacks!" Limb muttered.

Jackson shook his head, turning to his team. "Right, what did you find out?"

"Nothing confirmed," Dixit said.

Belmarsh joined the circle. "Have I missed something?"

Limb shrugged. "There's a suspicion someone else was looking after the bungalow. The old lady in the Canaries hasn't been back for four months, so how could she be managing the property?"

Jackson frowned. "But no idea who yet?"

"No, and the old biddy isn't talking."

Jackson moved towards his silver Vauxhall Insignia. "Sir," Belmarsh interjected, a note of urgency in her voice.

Jackson raised an eyebrow. "I still think we should have arrested him—MacLure, I mean."

Dixit shook his head. "We don't have anything solid. All we have is speculation. MacLure didn't need to be in there just now. His solicitor kept reminding him, but I'd say he's honestly keen to help."

Jackson rubbed his chin. "We need to find a genuine motive."

"The Polish girl," Belmarsh suggested. "If there's something between them, she could be using him. Maybe she's connected to the Polish mafia. Follow that and maybe we find the link to the stolen goods."

Jackson sighed. "That's a lot of maybes."

"We should watch him at least," Limb said.

Jackson placed a hand on the car's roof, deep in thought. "Okay, we'll keep an eye on him. Limb..."

"Yes, Boss?"

"He hasn't seen you before, so you keep tabs on our guy. I want to know what he does, where he goes, who he sees. And Belmarsh..."

"Sir?"

"You chase down the Polish connection. See if you can find a link to a gang. And if any of you see that damn reporter again, give him a kick in the arse from me."

Fox, posing as the reporter, lingered under the overhang of the building by a pillar, just out of sight but close enough to pick up a signal. As he'd evaded Limb's grasp, he'd deftly planted a bug on the detective's jacket. The guy hadn't even noticed.

Fox listened in, every word clear in his earpiece. Eventually, the detectives called Limb, Jackson, and Belmarsh finished their discussion, and three car doors slammed. Moments later, the unmarked silver Vauxhall pulled out of the car park and headed west on Chiswick High Road. Jackson was driving, Belmarsh rode shotgun, and Dixit was in the back.

Fox pulled out his phone and dialled. "They haven't arrested the rabbit," he reported. "They've got nothing. They think he's involved but have no evidence. They're guessing it's the Polish mafia, but that seems unlikely to me."

"Because of the dog walker?" The voice on the other end was deep and gravelly, hardened by years of smoking.

"Yeah. They suspect there's more to it, though I don't think so."

A silence followed, punctuated only by the raspy breathing on the other end. "What do you want me to do?"

"Stay on him."

"There's a complication. The police have him under surveillance too."

"Anyone seen you?"

"Yes."

"All right, stay on it until you can make a switch with Dog. After that, check out this Polish thing, just in case."

As Fox ended the call, he saw MacLure and a bookish-looking woman exit the station. Fox also noticed the detective called Limb on the street, pretending to read a noticeboard.

MacLure shook the woman's hand and walked away from the station, crossing the road and turning right. Limb waited a moment and then followed. A few seconds later, Fox picked up the trail. The hunt was on.

Chapter 11

Alex scaled the fence into his backyard, moving with a mix of urgency and careful calculation, muttering to himself about the structural integrity of wooden fences as he went. The moment his feet hit the ground, he took a steadying breath and peered toward the street. A milling crowd and several parked vans—one bearing a TV company logo—made his stomach twist. "Ah. That's... unfortunate."

Instinctively, he ducked back, adjusting his glasses as if that might somehow help his predicament. With a quick mental recalibration, he took a wide detour, approaching from a different direction. A climb over a wall, a careful hop over another fence, and he was in his rear yard.

Slipping inside through the back door, he barely had time to exhale before Topsy bounded up, licking his face with unrelenting enthusiasm. "Topsy, please, I am attempting a tactical retreat here," he whispered, scratching behind her ears before crawling toward the lounge. He leaned against the sofa, calculating angles of visibility from the street. As long as nobody climbed on top of a van with a periscope, he was safe.

The temptation to peek outside was overwhelming, but he knew better. If they spotted him, he'd be the lead story on every channel. He needed an exit strategy. Immediately.

Two calls.

First, he dialled Nadja.

"Can you take Topsy?"

"For walk? Sure."

"No, I mean... indefinitely. At least for a few days."

A pause. Alex winced at his own lack of finesse.

"Nadja, I need your help. The press—lots of press. I need to vanish until this dies down."

Another pause, then a sigh. "It's okay, Mr MacLure. Of course, I do it."

Relief flooded him. "You are, quite possibly, my favourite person right now."

He hung up, feeling a fraction of tension ease. That had gone well. Now for the difficult call.

Pete answered immediately. "How was it?"

"Well, let's see. I wasn't arrested. So, by that measure—a flawless victory."

"You didn't mention me, did you?"

Alex adjusted his glasses and let the silence stretch just long enough to make Pete sweat.

"Alex."

"Oh, I'm sorry, I was just savouring the exquisite paranoia in your voice. No, I didn't mention you. However—"

"Fuck, what did you say?"

Alex exhaled dramatically. "I said, and I quote, 'I went late because I wanted to be alone, to focus.' You note that I said I was 'alone'. No mention of you. It was, frankly, exhausting work. The detective was sceptical, and I have serious concerns that my baseball cap may have inadvertently exuded an air of criminality."

"You owe me for that."

Alex scoffed. "Oh, no, no, my friend. If anyone is in debt, it's you. I would much rather explain some random cash in my account than, say, spend the foreseeable future in a cell."

A long silence stretched between them before Pete muttered, "What do you want?"

"I need a place to stay. Preferably somewhere free of news vans and existential dread."

Pete groaned. "Alex—"

"I'm coming over."

Alex packed quickly, pausing only to pat Topsy's head and whisper a heartfelt apology for the sudden change in circumstances.

Pete's apartment sat between Hammersmith and Fulham, an area Alex mentally categorised as 'urban purgatory'. He walked south along Fulham Palace Road, the air thick with exhaust fumes. Despite the pollution, the streets teemed with people.

As he approached Charing Cross Hospital, his mind wandered, as it often did, down a rabbit hole. He had once dated a nurse who worked here—Karen, the e-cigarette enthusiast. Their brief relationship had lasted precisely three weeks, ending when she prioritised her vape collection over meaningful conversation.

Alex leaned against the railing, watching orderlies on a break, when something odd caught his eye—a man in a sports jacket and a baseball cap marked 'Rule 62'. He had a beard, a gym-built physique, and an uncanny ability to repeatedly appear in Alex's general vicinity.

His brain kicked into high gear. He'd first spotted the guy on the Central Line. Then again at Hammersmith station. Now, here.

Alex turned slowly, nonchalantly adjusting his collar. The man glanced his way, then quickly looked down at what appeared to be a London A-Z guide.

"I am being followed," Alex muttered under his breath.

He hesitated a fraction of a second, then bolted in the opposite direction. His gym bag banged against his leg, then the railing. Annoyed, he slung it over his shoulder, narrowly avoiding colliding with a suited businessman. "Apologies! Urgent cardio!"

Ducking down an alley, he cut through Margravine Cemetery, zigzagging between tombstones. A perfect escape route—provided his pursuer wasn't a fan of gothic architecture and 19th-century funerary art.

At the south gate, he hesitated, then walked briskly away, resisting the urge to check over his shoulder.

Eight flights of stairs later, Alex found Pete waiting, his arms crossed.

"I hope you weren't followed," Pete grumbled.

"There was one, but I lost him in the cemetery."

"You're toxic right now, you know that?" Pete led him into his flat. The lounge was spartan. There was a large-screen TV, free-standing with a DVD player and an Xbox games console. Discs were piled high and scattered beside it. Two old, worn chairs with curved wooden arms were the only seating. The only other furniture was a side table by the door, with a tray for coins, a bunch of keys, and a yellow lanyard with a fob on the end.

"Cosy," Alex said.

"Beggars can't be choosers. And I'm doing you a huge favour."

Alex clasped his hands together. "Oh, believe me, I am choosing to be extremely grateful."

Pete nodded. "Okay, a quick tour of the place then I'm grabbing a few hours' kip before I have to go to work." He showed Alex the first room. It was next to the front door, with one wall that must have been at the top of the stairs, and the other side looked out at the rear.

There were no curtains, just grubby nets. The view was of the rear of an identical tenement block. They had gardens between them, although most had been paved and all had sheds, some so large they took up half the space. There was no furniture in the room, just a small, fitted wardrobe and a mattress.

Pete shrugged.

Alex said, "I know, beggars and choosers again."

"I'll get you a sheet, but I'm afraid I don't have a spare duvet."

Alex followed him into the kitchen and was shown what was in which cupboard: the usual stuff in the usual places. Pete said he would clear half of one so Alex could use it.

After the kitchen was a door to the right. "The bathroom," Pete said, pointing. "And that's my room at the end. Help yourself to tea or coffee, although when I'm asleep during the day you need to be a church mouse."

"Of course."

Pete walked back to the lounge and looked out the window. Alex joined him and checked up and down for anyone suspicious. Four storeys down, it was quiet except for a car trying to parallel park in a space that looked too small.

"That's rule one." Pete held up a hand and counted off with his fingers as he spoke. "Two: you do not tell anyone where you are staying."

The car trying to park bumped into a BMW and then took off without checking for damage. Alex turned back to Pete. "That's fine by me."

"Three," Pete continued, "you can only stay for three nights to help you out. And four, if the press or cops show up, you vanish."

"Understood." Alex stuck out his hand.

Pete hesitated before shaking it reluctantly. "You are way too happy about this."

"I just appreciate the hospitality. And the lack of immediate incarceration."

Pete rolled his eyes. "Just don't get me arrested."

Alex gave him an earnest smile. "That is absolutely the plan."

Fox sat in a parked BMW and pressed speed dial on his phone.

The smoker answered: "Where's the rabbit now?"

"He's still got one of the trackers on him." The trackers had been placed on and inside items when they'd broken into MacLure's flat—they'd dealt with the dog by locking it outside while they worked. "He's in a residential building on a road between Hammersmith and Fulham. I'm close by."

Fox had been lucky to find a slot, although another driver seemed to think he could get his car in the gap behind the BMW.

"And the detective?" the smoker asked.

"Dog was following him. Turned out there was another tail as well. Amateurs, both of them. Even the rabbit made them. There was a chase and the rabbit gave them the slip. The copper lost them both."

"And this other guy?"

"The other guy following the rabbit… Dog's on it. We don't know who he is or his connection, but if he's not with the rabbit…"

He didn't need to finish. They both knew this was their first big lead.

There was a crunching sound.

"What was that?" the man on the line asked.

Fox said, "I've just been pranged. Idiot thought he could get in a space." Fox watched the other driver take off as though nothing had happened. "I can't stay here."

"Not a problem," the smoker said. "Let's track him for a while. Find out about the other man following."

DS Limb called Jackson. "I lost him in Hammersmith."

"What was MacLure doing in Hammersmith?"

"I don't know, but here's the thing: someone else was tailing him too."

"Start at the beginning," Jackson said.

"After leaving Chiswick, MacLure took the tube to Maida Vale. From there he walked home via a roundabout route. He was avoiding the reporters at the front of his house, and it looked like he jumped a few walls to get in the rear. There's a sixth form college opposite and I managed to get high enough so I could see into his flat. He was squatting in the lounge for a while and then disappeared, I think, to his bedroom. Anyway, shortly after, he crawled to the back door and let himself out. I was just quick enough to see him heading down the road again. This time he walked to Paddington and caught the tube."

"To Hammersmith?"

"You'd think he'd have taken the Hammersmith and City line straight there, but he didn't. He headed east and kept changing tubes at different stations. All the time, he was looking around, checking for a tail. But he never made me. Finally, we got the District Line west and got off at Hammersmith. He stopped outside the hospital on Fulham Palace Road."

"For what reason?"

"Not sure, sir. I slowed down, hoping I wouldn't overtake him. After a moment, MacLure gave a guy a good, long stare. The guy walked past but then stopped and looked back, dodgy as hell. MacLure took flight—bumping into me as he spun round."

Limb hesitated, thinking Jackson would comment. When the boss didn't, Limb continued. "The guy started chasing MacLure. He ran past me, so I got a good look."

"Okay."

"They ran around the back and by the time I got there, I was just in time to see the other guy go into the cemetery. MacLure got away. I've no idea where he went, but the other guy lost him too."

"And you questioned this other guy?"

"I lost him." Limb heard Jackson take a deep breath, imagined his face reddening.

"Bloody marvellous, Limb."

"Yes, sir."

"Get your arse back here and... No, wait. I want a full written description of this other guy, and I want you to spend the rest of the day walking those bloody streets until you find either one of them. Now get off the phone and start searching."

Chapter 12

Alex was up and crunching through a bowl of Rice Krispies when Pete trudged in from work., the predawn light casting eerie shadows in the small kitchen.

Pete grunted and set a mug down next to the kettle. "Make us a tea, would you?" He flicked it on and rubbed his face. "You sleep okay?"

Alex, still stirring his already perfectly mixed tea, glanced up. "It was cold. I was thinking, statistically, a sleeping bag might be a wise investment."

Pete made a vague noise of agreement before disappearing into his bedroom. Moments later, he reappeared and headed for the lounge. Alex followed, two steaming mugs in hand, the tension between them settling into the silence like an uninvited guest.

Pete collapsed into a chair with a groan. "Knackered. I need a job that isn't nights. Though being up most of yesterday didn't help." He grabbed the controller and resumed his game, the flickering glow of the TV throwing erratic light across his face.

Alex hovered by the wall, sipping his tea. "I've been thinking."

Pete snorted without looking up. "Dangerous habit."

"I'm serious." Alex adjusted his glasses, his tone taking on a careful, measured cadence. "You don't want the press to know where you live. Which, frankly, I support."

Pete paused the game, his brows knitting together. "That's why you're here."

"Yes, but it also extends to the police."

Pete didn't respond. Alex took that as his cue to continue.

"The other day, you said you didn't want them knowing where you are. But that doesn't add up."

Pete's posture stiffened. "Not sure what you're getting at."

"You told me you spoke to the police. That they interviewed you."

"Yeah."

"But you also didn't want me to mention that you were at Highclere with me last Wednesday night."

"For your sake as much as mine. The money—"

"I don't think the police interviewed you at all." Alex set his tea down and folded his arms. "I don't think they know where you live. Do they even know you were Ellen's landlord?"

Pete's grip tightened around the controller, his fingers twitching against the buttons.

Alex took a step forward, blocking his view of the screen. "I think you're avoiding them. What's going on, Pete?"

Pete let out a short, humourless laugh. "What? Nothing. You're reading too much into things."

"Am I?" Alex tilted his head. "Because from where I'm standing, it looks an awful lot like you're hiding something."

Pete exhaled sharply and rubbed his face. "All right, fine. Sit down. I'll explain."

They settled into the armchairs, knees nearly touching. Pete leaned forward, his voice low, urgent. "I work security at an investment firm in Canary Wharf. They take background checks seriously. CRB stuff—criminal record checks."

Alex frowned. "And?"

Pete hesitated, then sighed. "I have a record. It was a long time ago. A stupid decision. I broke into a place—revenge thing. Juvie, nothing major, but enough to ruin my chances at jobs that care about that stuff."

Alex's tea had gone cold. "So, what did you do?"

"I changed my name." Pete ran a hand through his hair. "The checks don't cross-reference deed poll records or credit histories. It's all built on trust and the fear of getting caught lying. So, yeah. That's why I can't deal with the police. If they start looking into me, I'm screwed."

Silence hung between them.

Finally, Alex leaned back, exhaling. "Okay. New rules."

Pete groaned. "Oh, Christ."

"One: I don't mention you to the police, and in exchange, I stay here as long as I need."

Pete narrowed his eyes but nodded. "Fine. And the second?"

"You buy a spare duvet."

A beat. Then Pete huffed a laugh, shaking his head. "You're a pain in the arse, you know that?"

Alex sipped his tea, deadpan. "It has been mentioned."

By midday, Alex decided he needed air and lunch. He donned a beanie and found a gabardine coat in Pete's wardrobe. He thought about wearing a pair of wraparound sunglasses he found, but decided his vision was more important. Perhaps he should reconsider the contact lens option. Too late now though.

From his holdall, he pulled out a book: *The Oxford History of Ancient Egypt*. He stuck it in a pocket, turned up the collar of the coat, and headed out.

Walking south toward Putney Bridge, he stopped at a corner shop for a chicken salad sandwich. By the time he reached the bridge over the Thames, the coat felt too warm for the unusually balmy November day.

The bridge and road were clogged with traffic and pedestrians. On the far side, he descended a lane to the water, where only a few people strolled or jogged. He ambled along the embankment, past the rowing clubs, and found a quiet spot by the river's edge. The water lapped lazily against the shore; its surface dappled by weak afternoon light. A rower in a bright orange scull sliced through the tide, steady and determined.

He settled against a post, using the coat as a cushion, and flipped open his book. The rhythmic sounds of the river lulled him into a rare moment of stillness.

Then, a sharp honk broke the peace. He looked up to see a swan, wings half-raised, advancing on a woman scattering breadcrumbs. She backed away, hands raised in surrender.

Alex sighed, snapping his book shut. "Right. Time to play   the   hero."

Chapter 13

Alex tossed a piece of his sandwich bread, diverting the swan's attention.

"Thanks," the woman called. For a moment, he thought she was going to approach him, but she didn't.

He returned to his book and flicked to the contents page. After the list of contributors and before the introduction was a handwritten series of numbers.

2592523561 24071912

What the heck? Someone had written in his book!

Studying the pen strokes he calmed down, thinking it was probably Ellen's handwriting. Twenty numbers with no immediately obvious pattern or relevance. Why would she write in his book, and what did they mean?

A movement behind him made him jump.

"Hey!" Instinctively, Alex began to stand and turn, but a hand pressed on his shoulder, keeping him down.

"Don't move a muscle," growled a thick East London accent.

Alex froze.

"Time to talk, sonny," the man said.

Alex strained to see his assailant, expecting the man with the 62 cap. Instead, it was a clean-shaven, heavier-set man in a leather jacket and blue-mirrored Aviator glasses.

"You're from the papers, right? A reporter?" Alex said, trying to sound calmer than he felt. "I've got nothing to say."

Aviator-glasses man snorted. "I'll gut you like a fish. Now cut the crap and start talking!"

A knife's point pricked Alex's side. "Er... you're not with the press? Who are you?"

"Don't mess around with me, MacLure. I think you know all about the research. All about what your little friend found. Perhaps you need a little reminder."

"What do you know about Ellen's research?"

The knife pressed deeper, and Alex flinched as the blade pricked flesh.

"Okay! Okay," Alex stammered. "I'll tell you what you want to know."

"Where is it?"

Alex took a long breath. "You think I know where her research is? Well..."

"Shut up! The goods stolen from Highclere. Where's the item?"

"What item?" Alex's mind spun. The guy wasn't interested in all the stolen stuff, just a single item.

The thug's hand moved to Alex's head, squeezing his temples. His glasses came off and Alex screamed as pain burst through his skull.

"I don't know anything."

"Bullshit!" Aviator-glasses squeezed harder, darkness closing in on Alex's vision.

Blinking through tears, Alex was thrust against a wall between two boathouses, hidden from view. A punch to his ribs doubled him over.

"I really don't..."

"Bullshit!" Another blow to the head left Alex crumpled on the floor, his blurred vision homing in on a broken bottle—could he slash the guy and get away? It seemed the only option.

"Hey, what's going on here?" A woman's voice snapped Alex's attention away from the bottle. The duck-feeding woman stood at the entrance to the gap between the boathouses.

"Shove off, bitch, and mind yer own business!" Aviator-glasses snarled.

"I'm calling the police," she threatened, phone in hand.

Aviator-glasses turned, brandishing the knife. "Drop the phone and fuck off outta here, lady, before it's too late."

Alex seized the moment, grabbing the bottle. Too late. The thug had charged and was about to bulldoze into her.

But then he lurched sideways, staggering as he gripped his shoulder. Alex saw a dark patch spreading beneath the man's fingers, soon turning crimson.

A gunshot echoed in Alex's ears. "Run!" he shouted, adrenaline surging through his veins.

The woman stood frozen, her eyes wide with shock, hand still raised. Alex grabbed her wrist and pulled her down the alley, away from the river and the unseen gunman. As they reached the end, a thirty-foot wall loomed before them. Glancing back, Alex saw Aviator-glasses on his feet, closing in.

He yanked the woman into the narrow space behind a shed. She glanced back, understanding their need to escape. The area was cluttered with debris—bits of rope, a buoy, planks, a broken oar. They emerged on the other side just as Aviator entered the space behind them.

"Keep going," Alex urged as the woman slowed. "He's right behind us."

They squeezed between two more sheds and found themselves in the open. Alex's eyes darted around. The thug was nowhere to be seen.

A ping against the wood beside him made him duck instinctively. Someone was shooting at them! The earlier bullet must've hit Aviator-glasses by mistake. As Alex ducked back into the shadows, the thug reappeared, grinning despite the blood seeping through his fingers.

Alex hesitated. Confront the injured man or dodge the bullets? The decision was made for him when the woman bolted towards the ramp, head ducked. Alex sprinted after her, mirroring her movement to minimise their target area.

They reached the road together, gasping for breath. "We've got to get out of here," she panted, crossing the street.

Chapter 14

They reached the road together, and Alex finally breathed. The young woman's face was pale, her shoulders tense, her hands trembling slightly as she pushed back her hair. "We've got to get out of here," she said breathlessly, barely waiting for his response before crossing the road.

Alex hesitated for half a second, his mind working through possibilities. A man in aviator glasses was halfway up the ramp. Not good. Alex decided not to wait.

"This way," The woman called from the opposite side. She led him into an alley that funnelled them into a yard. She was fast—impressive, really. He chased after her as she slipped through a gap between buildings, only stopping when they hit a dead end.

She bent over, hands on her knees, trying to catch her breath. Alex glanced back. Any second now, their pursuer could round the corner. "We're trapped," he said, taking gulps of air. "We have to go back."

"No, this way." Without missing a beat, she pushed an industrial refuse cart to the wall, scrambled up, and disappeared over the top before Alex could process the manoeuvre.

"Oh, of course," he muttered. "Obviously, we're doing this." He climbed after her, landing in what looked like a backyard. The young woman was already moving, walking with the deliberate calm of someone who knew exactly where she was going. Alex quickened his pace to keep up.

She opened a green door and slipped inside. It was a fire exit. Once he was through, she jammed a metal bar into the handle. Smart.

Alex stared at her, half out of breath, half in admiration. "How did you—"

"Not yet," she interrupted. "Let's make sure we're safe first."

They climbed a narrow staircase, and on the first landing, she stopped beside a window. The backyard and alley were in full view. Even without his distance glasses, Alex could see no movement. No man in aviator glasses. No gunmen.

She exhaled slowly, tension leaving her shoulders. "I'm Rebecca." Then, with an edge to her voice, "What the hell was that about? Who was that guy? And why did he attack you?"

Alex wiped sweat from his forehead, his mind still sorting through possibilities. "Good questions. Equally good question: who was shooting at us?"

Her expression froze. "What?"

"Someone was firing. At him. At us. Hard to say." He frowned, mentally replaying the moment. "Either way, he got hit."

Rebecca's mouth opened in shock. Alex reached out, touching her arm gently. "You okay?"

"I— I thought I heard something but dismissed it as a starter's pistol. You get them all the time for the rowers. So that's why he fell over?" She took a steadying breath. "I thought he just slipped." She shook her head, as if trying to reset reality. "Oh my God!"

She was still trembling slightly, so Alex didn't let go of her arm just yet. "It's a lot. But you handled that brilliantly, by the way."

She gave a small, dry laugh. "I think I've just been too busy running to freak out." Then she forced a weak smile. "Come on, let's go downstairs. I'll introduce you to Simon."

Simon turned out to be the owner of the café they'd entered. Through the back door, Rebecca quickly glanced around before leading Alex to a table. The place was alive with chatter, a queue forming at the sandwich bar. It smelled of coffee, toasted bread, and something faintly citrusy.

"One minute," a voice called with a light accent. A man in a blue pinafore appeared. Rebecca stood and hugged him.

"Simon. My cousin," she said by way of introduction.

Simon extended a hand to Alex, eyeing him with curiosity. "And you are?"

"Alex." He shook the man's hand.

Simon turned to Rebecca with raised eyebrows. She swatted his arm. "Away with you. You have customers. And when you have a moment, we'll have… two teas with two sugars. That okay?" she asked, glancing at Alex.

Alex nodded, still studying her. He hadn't really looked at her properly before. Mid-twenties, dark eyes, sharp but not unkind features. A Mediterranean or Middle Eastern look. He found himself mentally categorising her—quick thinker, controlled under pressure, good spatial awareness. Useful skills.

She caught him staring. "What?"

He smiled, offering a hand. "I'm Alex."

She shook it. "We've established that already." Then her expression grew serious. "What we haven't established is what the hell is actually going on. And shouldn't we be calling the police?"

Alex sighed. "I don't know what's going on. Honestly. It's complicated." He could tell she wasn't buying that. "But you're right about the police."

Simon returned with two mugs of tea, and Alex took the opportunity to dial DI Jackson's number. When the inspector was unavailable, he was put through to DC Dixit.

After recounting everything that happened on the Putney embankment, Dixit asked for details—what the assailant looked like, where exactly the attack took place, and the location of the bullet hole in the shed. Alex answered mechanically, his mind half on the conversation, half on his surroundings. The café felt safe, but he still checked the door every time it opened.

When he hung up, Rebecca pushed his tea toward him. "Drink. It'll help."

He sipped. It was good. The warmth calming. His heart rate slowed.

She was watching him, an amused tilt to her lips. "Better?" she asked. "Maybe you should eat something, too."

Something clicked in his brain. "Damn, my book!"

"Your book?"

"My coat is on the embankment... and my glasses, but more importantly, I dropped a book when I was grabbed. It's got sentimental value." He hesitated. "I can't face going back. They might still be around. My prescription isn't strong but I... we'd probably recognise the guy with the aviators, but the shooter—we don't know what he looks like. And maybe there are more."

Rebecca tilted her head, intrigued. "What book?"

Alex hesitated, then told her.

She stood abruptly. "Just a minute." She disappeared behind the sandwich bar. When she returned, she smiled.

"Simon will send one of his staff to look for it. Hopefully, they'll find it for you."

Alex exhaled, staring at her. "I'm really glad I ran into you."

Rebecca smirked. "You didn't run into me. You ran *after* me."

"Semantics." He sipped his tea. "Still. Thanks."

Chapter 15

After a second cup of tea Alex began to tell Rebecca about the past week. She laughed softly at one point, and he stopped. "What's so funny?"

"I had a sense we'd met before," she said. "But we haven't, have we? I've seen your picture online. You were the Have-a-go Hero suspected of fraud. Is it true?"

"A hero? I don't think so. Anyway, you're a hero for stepping in earlier. My attacker had a weapon, whereas all I did was stop someone who snatched a woman's handbag. The press love to exaggerate."

"And the fraud bit?"

"It's rubbish. Pure conjecture. The reporter connected a problem with my previous employer to me leaving—and coming into money." She raised her eyebrows at that, so he explained: "I won a chunk on the lottery. Meant I could stop being an accountant and do something more interesting."

"Which is?"

"Archaeology—or more specifically, the study of ancient Egypt. And that's really what the story is about. That's why the police are interested in me. That and the recent burglary at Highclere you must have heard about."

She nodded thoughtfully. "So that guy... do you think he was one of the burglars?"

"Maybe. He seemed to think I knew something about an item."

"And do you?"

"I've no idea what he was talking about. If he was one of the Highclere burglars, why didn't he know…?" And then Alex realised something. The news reports hadn't mentioned what was taken, so if it was something specific, this guy *must* have been involved. "You know," Alex said, "I think the blue sunglasses guy was definitely one of the burglars and they were after a specific item. It was something they didn't find."

"But you don't know what?"

Just then a young man came to their table. He held out a folded gabardine coat with a book perched on top. The man also handed him a broken pair of spectacles. "If these are yours, I'm afraid you won't be wearing them again."

Alex took them with thanks, stuck the glasses in a pocket of the coat and placed the book on the table.

"You're smiling," she said.

He opened the book at the contents page. "I don't really know what's going on," he said. "I don't know what the man with blue sunglasses was looking for at the Highclere Castle exhibition. But I do know one thing." He pointed to the twenty numbers that Ellen had written in the book.

"I think my friend left me a clue."

DI Jackson's phone buzzed with a call from DS Limb.

"Boss, I'm at the scene," Limb reported, his voice crackling through the line. "Standing on the slipway by Putney Bridge."

"Any sign… of anything?" Jackson's voice was steady, seasoned by years of dealing with the unexpected.

"No sign of MacLure or the guy he described—the same one I saw chasing him outside the hospital. But that's not all."

Jackson's pulse quickened, but he maintained his calm. "Go on."

"There are sheds here, like MacLure said—rowing clubs. I've checked all around, no blood. Nothing visible, anyway."

"Could the tide have washed it away?"

"No chance. The water doesn't reach that high. MacLure said they were between two sheds. As for the bullet hole... these sheds are full of holes, being old wood. But no casings, no nothing."

"Any witnesses?"

"None, and no reports to the Met. If there were gunshots, surely—"

"So, you think he's lying?"

Limb hesitated. "He's definitely not lying about being chased, but something's off. I think we should bring him back in."

"Not yet," Jackson decided. Twenty-five years on the force had honed his instincts. DS Belmarsh hadn't turned up anything incriminating about the dog walker/cleaner, despite her dodgy connections. The Slimowiczs were involved in organised crime, but that's where the trail ended. He glanced at the wallboard cluttered with photos, lines, and questions. They were no closer to answers. He sighed, frustrated. "Time to come back to base, Sergeant."

Chapter 16

Rebecca's cousin arrived with sandwiches, replacing the squashed packet Alex had bought. As they ate, Rebecca listened with casual interest as Alex recounted his run-ins with the police and his breathless escape through the cemetery. She raised an eyebrow when he mentioned he was staying at Pete's despite disliking the guy. In turn, she shared snippets about her love for travel, her studies—psychology, mostly, though she had switched courses a few times—and her current place in Putney.

"Wait!" she suddenly exclaimed, pausing mid-bite. "The girl who died in that gas explosion—she was at Highclere too, wasn't she? Was she the friend you mentioned?"

Alex hesitated, shifting uncomfortably. "Yeah," he admitted, voice tinged with embarrassment. "So, you see, I'm a bit on edge. I don't think I'll be up for leaving the café anytime soon. Think I can stay here until dark?"

Rebecca considered for a moment. "I might have a better idea," she said, standing up. After a quick conversation with Simon at the counter, she made a phone call. At first she looked disappointed but after some hard persuasion, Alex thought, she returned satisfied.

"There's a room upstairs—a studio flat my uncle rents out. It's empty now and needs redecorating. You should come see it."

She led Alex through the rear door, up the stairs, past the scent of old cooking fat and into a bright but somewhat bare room. The space was clean enough, though the paint was chipped, and the window could use a serious scrubbing.

"What do you think?" Rebecca asked.

"It's nice," Alex said cautiously. "But why are you showing me this?"

"You can stay here for a few days," she explained. "I had to talk my uncle into it—he wasn't sure about letting someone stay yet, but I convinced him it won't be for long."

"How much?"

She waved a hand. "No charge. Unless you want to rent it after it's refurbished, then you can work something out with my uncle. But for now, you might as well make use of it."

Alex glanced around again, feeling an odd sense of gratitude he wasn't sure how to express. "That's... really generous of you."

She shrugged lightly, as if it wasn't a big deal. "I'll grab you some bedding. I have a spare set at home."

Rebecca returned twenty minutes later, carrying two black bin liners. One held a duvet and sheets, the other contained clothes.

"These were my ex-boyfriend's," she said, handing over the bag. "He was taller than you, but not by much."

Alex pulled out a blue football shirt. "Chelsea supporter, huh?"

Rebecca laughed. "Yeah, sorry. Didn't think to check your loyalties first." She smirked, watching as he examined the oversized shirt. "There's also some hair dye in there. In case you want to change things up. You'd look very different with black hair."

Alex hesitated, then nodded. "Might not be the worst idea."

After she left for her lecture, Alex got to work dyeing his hair. The dark colour looked startling at first, but after a few washes, it settled into something that felt almost natural. Satisfied, he flopped onto the sofa with his book, his thoughts drifting between Ellen's cryptic notes and the unexpected kindness Rebecca had shown.

That evening, she returned with a white paper bag. "Chinese for two," she announced, placing it in the small galley kitchen. "Hope you like Chinese—I got chicken with yellow bean and cashews, mixed vegetables, and sweet and sour prawns."

"Sounds great, but after everything you've done, I should be buying you dinner."

"Another time, perhaps," she said, giving him a crooked smile.

As they ate, he studied her, not entirely sure what to make of her. She was confident, sure of herself, yet hard to read. He found himself drawn to her, though whether it was gratitude, intrigue, or something else entirely, he couldn't yet tell. He liked her crooked smile.

"You mentioned studying psychology," he said, between bites.

She tilted her head. "It's just a module. My actual degree is in politics. Psychology is more of a side interest."

"Oh," Alex said, feeling strangely relieved. "So what do you want to do with it?"

She shrugged. "Lobbying, maybe? Environmental issues, sustainability—the way we treat nature is... careless, to say the least. People only seem to care when it directly affects them, and by then, it's usually too late."

He nodded, impressed. "That's admirable."

They ate in companionable silence until Rebecca spoke again. "Any luck with the code?"

"The one in my book? From Ellen?"

She nodded.

"No," Alex admitted. "It's strange because she wasn't really into numbers. Some people are more crossword than sudoku."

"And what are you?"

"Definitely sudoku."

She grinned. "Maybe that's why she used numbers. She knew you'd figure it out."

He leaned back, stretching. "If only."

Rebecca glanced at her phone. "I should go—I have a class in the morning."

Alex felt an unexpected pang of disappointment but pushed it aside. "Right. Thanks again, really."

She smiled. "I'll check in tomorrow. And by the way, if you're going to keep the black hair, you need to do your eyebrows too. I'll bring mascara."

Alex groaned. "Great."

"And I'll grab your stuff from Pete's. Don't argue, it's safer if I do it."

He hesitated but eventually relented. "All right. Thanks. There's a spare pair of specs in the bedside table."

They exchanged numbers, and he followed her downstairs, watching the way her ponytail swung as she walked. She reached the door and glanced outside before turning back.

"Tomorrow, tell me about your research," she said. "I googled your name and Egyptology came up. You've written about the gods of ancient Egypt?"

Alex raised an eyebrow. "A little. But the pre-dynastic period—"

She laughed and raised a hand, stopping him. "I have no idea what you're talking about. Tell me about it over dinner."

She stepped outside, leaving Alex standing there, mildly dazed. He shut the door, exhaling. Maybe this wasn't the worst place to be after all.

Chapter 17

The thing Rebecca had said about crosswords and sudoku played on his mind during the night. If they were a message for him, then Ellen was using numbers to express words. By morning he had it. In a film they'd recently watched together, spies had sent coded messages to one another using a book.

Alex leapt out of bed and snatched up his book and checked the numbers.

259252356124071912

Only now, he saw there were slightly larger gaps between some numbers. Deliberate? He hoped so. The first number was 259, the second 25. Let's see. He turned to page 259 and counted 25 lines. The next number was 2. He circled the second word on the line.

Isis

"Bloody hell!" Alex said out loud. Ellen had a fascination with the goddess Isis, and it couldn't be a coincidence. The code was a triumvirate of page, line and word numbers. He marked it up.

259-25-2/356-1-2/407-19-12

Alex turned to page 356 and read the second word: is On page 407 the word was key.

"My God, she's telling me Isis is the key!"

He paced the room. What did that mean? And then a thought struck him: sudoku not crossword. He texted Rebecca:

When you manage to get my stuff from Pete's, please check there's a phone as well as my laptop.

A moment later she replied:

>Already been and dropped off with Simon. See you later.

Alex dressed quickly and rushed down to the café. It was almost seven in the morning and already busy. The smell of sizzling sausages and bacon was intoxicating.

"Morning," Simon called. He scooted out from behind the counter and dropped Alex's bag on the floor. "Cooked breakfast for you?"

"And coffee, please," Alex said as he opened his bag. Everything was inside: clothes, laptop and Ellen's phone.

Isis was the key and keys unlock. But it wasn't ISIS.

Four numbers, not letters.

He keyed in 1515.

The phone unlocked.

Chapter 18

Alex's morning was a maze of Ellen's emails, each one a potential thread to unravel, a clue that could finally lead to something meaningful. His mind, always inclined to find patterns, sifted through message after message, hoping for some hidden meaning or overlooked detail.

After two hours of combing through it all, his optimism began to wane. The emails were filled with mundane academic discussions about Egyptology and some personal exchanges, none of which led to any breakthrough.

Frustration started to cloud his focus just as there was a knock on the door. Rebecca entered, arms full of a cafetiere and two mugs. She was wearing a sympathetic smile that only made him feel more deflated.

"Thanks for the bag," he said, trying to sound unaffected. "I hope it wasn't too much trouble."

Rebecca set the coffee down and looked at him, her eyes softening with concern. "You're welcome. No trouble at all. I didn't see anyone suspicious, though I can't say I liked your friend."

"Not really a friend," Alex muttered more to himself than to her.

Rebecca took a moment to study him. "You look very different with your glasses on. Very intelligent."

He laughed but it wasn't convincing.

"All right... You seem a bit down this morning, Alex. What's going on?"

He sighed, running a hand through his messy hair. "It's just... I cracked the code, the one you mentioned. You were right—the numbers connected to words." He pulled out Ellen's phone. "The clue was Isis."

Rebecca's eyes widened with alarm. "Isis?"

"Not the terrorist group." Alex spoke quickly. "The goddess Isis. I translated it to 1515, which unlocked Ellen's phone, but I'm starting to think it's not the big breakthrough I hoped for."

Rebecca sat down, making herself comfortable as she poured coffee. "So yesterday you said something about a dynasty..."

"The pharaohs ruled Egypt through dynasties," Alex began to explain, chopping his hand in the air to illustrate a series. "But the work I'm doing now for my PhD... it's on the pre-dynastic period... before the known dynasties. It's fascinating because we know so little."

"Because?"

"There's nothing but snippets... hints and implications. The list of pharaohs—the King List—has Narmer or Menes as the first, but even then, it's unclear because of the absence of written records."

"Hieroglyphs?"

"Yes. Before that there are archaeological limitations although discoveries occur all the time. But most information comes from myths and legends blending fact and fiction."

"You sound intrigued but... frustrated at the same time. Is that fair?"

He nodded. Very fair. Discoveries were challenging and it was the breakthroughs in understanding that gave Egyptology it's edge of excitement. He enjoyed the puzzle of it and yet he was a numbers guy. Which got him thinking about Ellen.

Rebecca was looking at him with curiosity as though reading his mind. "Was that your friend's area of expertise...?" she said then stopped herself. "I'm sorry for bringing her up."

"It's okay," Alex assured her after removing his glasses and giving his eyes a rub. "It's okay. I was just thinking about her and since we're talking about research..." He smiled reassuringly. "Ellen would have liked that."

"What about your paper on religion?"

"It was for my diploma. Ellen encouraged me, because she was interested in the 18th Dynasty."

"Okay..." she said seeming genuinely interested.

"There was pharaoh—Akhenaten—who believed in one god, Aten."

Rebecca raised an eyebrow. "Akhenaten? Can't say I've heard of him."

"He was pretty radical in his time, and it's been said that his followers were the *Ibiru*, a group of outcasts. Some say that the word Hebrew derives from *Ibiru*. One theory suggests he was Moses—"

"Moses?" she said slowly.

"Moses, yeah. Akhenaten isn't as famous as Tutankhamun, but he was his father. He's referred to as the 'heretic pharaoh' because of his monotheistic beliefs. No way he was Moses because he died and—"

Alex stopped, only now picking up on the expression on Rebecca's face.

"What is it?"

"I'm Jewish."

"What? Really? I hadn't guessed." Alex immediately felt foolish. What did he expect? A big sign above her head? There had been no clues, but then... why would there be?

Rebecca laughed, making him feel less uncomfortable. "I'm Jewish, though not Orthodox. There's a lot of anti-Semitism wrapped up in discussions about ancient Egypt and religion. And Moses always comes up in these kinds of discussions."

Alex held his hands up in mock surrender. "I assure you I'm not anti-Semitic and... well, Sigmund Freud also put forward the suggestion about Moses and he was Jewish, so there's no malice in it."

Rebecca raised her mug. "I'll allow it, but only because Freud said so."

They spent the next couple of hours lost in conversation, bouncing ideas about ancient Egyptian religion and the comparisons between Akhenaten's monotheism and the Ten Commandments. The coffee grew cold as Alex animatedly explained how gods like Ra and Aten had evolved over time.

"So, Aten was Ra?" she asked, clearly fascinated.

"Yeah, that's the theory. Aten was probably just Ra in a new form," Alex explained. "But when Akhenaten came into power, he rejected all the gods and only believed in Aten."

Rebecca seemed to follow his explanation, nodding thoughtfully. "And where does Isis fit into all of this?"

Alex grinned. "Ah, Isis. She was this all-encompassing goddess. Love, fertility, you name it. She was also associated with protection, especially of young life. Her image was often represented as a throne or a vulture, both symbols of nurturing."

Rebecca was thoughtful. "It's interesting how different goddesses seem to share similar roles. You mentioned Hathor too, right?"

"Yeah, Hathor was another goddess of motherhood and childbirth. They were all linked in some way, these goddesses of life, with Isis as the central figure."

Their lunch break came around, and they moved to a nearby café, sandwiches in hand. Rebecca's curiosity seemed boundless as she continued asking about Egypt's mythology, the gods, and their cultural significance.

"So, Osiris—he was Isis's husband, right?" she asked, her interest genuine.

"Yes, and he became the god of the afterlife after his death. It's one of the most famous myths: he was murdered, dismembered, and then reassembled by Isis. Some versions even say she became pregnant by him after he was mummified."

Rebecca looked horrified, then burst into laughter. "Only a god could pull that off!"

Alex laughed too. "It sounds ridiculous, but the ancient Egyptians really leaned into the drama of it all. They'd reenact these stories for the public, and believe me, they loved the spectacle."

He was in the middle of explaining more when Rebecca glanced at her watch. "Oh! I've got a lecture in half an hour. I should probably go."

Alex watched her leave, then turned back to Ellen's phone, feeling a renewed sense of purpose. He scrolled through her emails again, this time checking the Trash folder. One message caught his attention—it was addressed to Professor Thompson at Oxford about Lord Carnarvon's death and the items from Tutankhamun's tomb. Alex noted the professor's email and quickly fired off a message.

He dug further, logging into a site Ellen had registered on called *EgyptConfidential*. There, he found some exchanges between her and users named Sinuhe, Khaemhet, and Mutnodjemet. Their messages were filled with theories and speculation, but none seemed relevant to the case at hand.

Then, just as he was about to give up, another email arrived. It was from The Griffith Institute at St Anthony's College, Oxford. The message stated that Professor Thompson was no longer at the institute.

Alex paused, staring at the screen. A dead end? Or was it just another clue waiting to be uncovered? Either way, he knew he couldn't stop now. The truth was buried somewhere in these mysteries, and he was determined to find it.

Chapter 19

Razor, the man who'd worn the blue-mirrored Aviator sunglasses, was hunched over a table at The Pie Crust café in London's East End. The café was the gang's unofficial HQ—a place where they could think, plan, and blend in. Razor's plate held the remnants of a greasy all-day breakfast, the kind that clogged arteries but satisfied his craving for something real. None of that overpriced American franchise rubbish at American franchise prices. It was late afternoon, but the dark winter sky made it feel like midnight. Razor's mind drifted to the warehouse where they'd stashed the loot from Highclere Castle. The plan had been airtight until it wasn't. His job had been simple: manage their inside man. But the gas explosion had thrown everything off course. Lemmy was supposed to trace the missing item, but now he was tailing MacLure. And Gazza? Gazza was sorting the real from the fake, prepping the goods for the market.

Razor pulled out his phone, dialling Lemmy. Straight to voicemail. Typical. Gazza was unreachable too, and you didn't call the boss. He called you.

Frustrated, Razor doodled on the back page of The Sun. Lemmy had last checked in from Hammersmith, tracking MacLure, but now he was radio silent. Had something happened? Or had Lemmy fallen off the wagon again? Gazza always said Lemmy was unreliable, but Razor wasn't so sure.

The boss had reassigned him to follow MacLure. They'd tracked him to Putney Bridge, and Razor had tailed him. The guy didn't seem to know he was being followed—maybe there was nothing to find. What if their source had been wrong? Or worse, lying?

Razor's thoughts circled back to the source. No reason to lie—he wanted his share of the treasure. The Champion girl had solved something, but what? And who had shot at him by the river? Razor touched the graze on his shoulder, a reminder of how close things had come.

He scribbled on the newspaper: *Gang, Lemmy, Source, MacLure.* He circled *Gang* until the pen tore through the paper. Another gang? The source playing both sides? Razor couldn't shake the questions.

They had found the girl's notes in her briefcase: drawings of an item that looked like a box with Egyptian writing. Gazza called it an artifact, but without a sense of scale, Razor imagined it as a shallow music box.

With no new ideas, he decided to contact the source. It was his plan from the start; maybe he had more answers. Razor left the café, heading towards West Ham. A car horn blared—a black BMW cut across traffic. Razor swore under his breath, shaking his head. As he walked, something made him turn. The BMW cruised by slowly. Two men inside, both glancing his way.

"What the fuck?" Razor muttered, glaring at the driver—a guy with dark skin, probably Arab. The car disappeared around a corner, leaving Razor on edge.

"Excuse me, I'm lost."

Razor snapped back to reality. The BMW was beside him, the driver leaning out the window.

"Can you help us find the Olympic Park?"

Razor stepped closer, ready to unleash some abuse, but the passenger seat was empty. Too late, he heard a sound behind him. As he turned, a cosh connected with his face.

When Razor came to, pain radiated from his shoulders. He was hanging from a rope tied around his wrists, naked. Blood trickled down his leg. The smell of oil and the cold metal of a tyre-iron brought his focus back. The Arab from the BMW stood in front of him, eyes cold.

Razor knew then that survival wasn't the question. It was a matter of how long he could hold out.

Rebecca returned with a pizza takeaway menu. As they waited for their order, she asked. "Any closer to finding what Ellen's research at Highclere was about?"

"No. Did I tell you about the scrap of paper I found?"

"In the book?"

"At Highclere Castle—the exhibition where she was researching. There were some doodles and I think she tossed it as rubbish."

"Ah," she said with a knowing smile, "there's a but coming."

"I could see the indentation of numbers. Three in particular: eight, twelve and forty."

"Interesting. Does it relate to your book, like before?"

Alex had thought of that, but nothing leapt out as relevant.

"What about her phone?"

Alex shook his head. "I found a web forum she was on, discussing mysteries and theories."

"Like?"

"Where Akhenaten's body is buried and what happened to his queen—Nefertiti."

"Oh, I've heard of her!"

"Strange, isn't it? People know Nefertiti, but not Akhenaten."

"She was supposed to be beautiful, wasn't she? What happened to her?"

"She vanished from the records two-thirds through his reign. There's an unidentified mummy that could be her. Some think she became co-regent and changed her name. There's a bust of her in Berlin that looks like an older woman."

"That's fascinating. So, she might not have died young... Why pretend to die at thirty?"

"Maybe someone wanted to erase her legacy."

Rebecca nodded. "Did she believe in one god like Akhenaten?"

"She had a gate at Karnak with references to many gods. It's unlikely she believed in just one."

The pizzas arrived, and Alex's eyes lit up with curiosity. He couldn't resist diving into one of his favourite topics. "You know," he started, tapping his finger thoughtfully on the table, "God has many names. The sun god Ra had many titles, just like the God of Judaism: Jehovah, Elohim, Yahweh..."

Rebecca raised an eyebrow, intrigued. "Well, there's also Tzevaot, El, Elyon, Avinu, Adonai, and Shaddai. But many of those are more like titles than actual names," she added, her voice thoughtful.

Alex nodded eagerly, his voice taking on the excitement of someone who couldn't help but talk about something he loved. "Exactly! When a pharaoh died, the priests would chant the Litany of Ra, calling on the sun god in all seventy-five of his names. Aten was one of those names. Akhenaten's father even called Him Ra-Horakhty."

Rebecca tilted her head slightly, processing the information. "So, Akhenaten didn't necessarily believe in just one god?"

"Right," Alex replied, his hands animated as he explained. "He erased the god Amun's name from Karnak, but that was probably more political than religious. He didn't get rid of the other gods' names—those temples were still supported. In fact, at Amarna, they found evidence of multiple gods and even plans for a bull cemetery linked to the god Ptah. That doesn't exactly scream monotheism."

"Interesting and confusing. So, you don't think Akhenaten was the founder of monotheism?" Rebecca asked, genuinely curious.

Alex gave a soft chuckle. "Even though Freud thought so, but the evidence doesn't back it up. It's more complicated than that."

Rebecca considered this for a moment, looking at him with a mix of curiosity and scepticism. "Then why push the idea that he believed in one god?"

Alex leaned forward slightly, his voice lowering as if revealing a hidden thought. "It's almost like someone's trying to convince people that the idea of one God came from an Egyptian pharaoh, as if it somehow started there."

Rebecca's expression softened, the gears in her mind turning. "I see," she said, nodding slowly. "That's... strange. Like rewriting history."

"Exactly," Alex said with a grin, pleased with how the conversation had unfolded. "Maybe like the myths of pre-dynastic Egypt. It's one of those fascinating puzzles."

As they wrapped up their conversation, Rebecca stood up, grabbing her jacket. "Before you go, two things for tomorrow. First, we're getting you outside. I mean, you haven't even looked at the sky in days. No sign of Mr Blue-Sunglasses yet, so I'm leaving it up to you. Deal?"

Alex laughed softly. "All right, deal. And the second thing?"

Rebecca's smile became more knowing. "Those numbers you mentioned earlier—eight, twelve, and...?"

"Forty," Alex replied, his curiosity piqued again.

Rebecca nodded. "Numbers are crucial in Judaism, and if her research ties into it... understanding those numbers could be key."

"Hmm, that's not a bad idea," Alex mused, tapping his fingers against his cup. "I'll take a closer look at those."

"Great," Rebecca said, already heading to the door. "I'll see if I can introduce you to my uncle."

Alex raised an eyebrow. "Your uncle?" he asked, intrigued. Then realised. "Oh, the flat. You mean about the rent?"

"No, dummy," she said laughing. "He knows a lot more about Judaism than me. He'll know what those numbers mean."

Chapter 20

Jackson and Belmarsh flashed their IDs at the constable, who lifted the cordon without a word. They stood outside a decrepit warehouse in the East End of London, the early morning light casting everything in a dreary grey.

"I don't get it." Belmarsh stifled a yawn. "Who called this in?"

"Anonymous tip-off during the night," Jackson replied. He spotted the Metropolitan Police officer in charge and waved. The detective, DI Spears, walked over with a sour look.

"What the hell is this?" Spears demanded.

Jackson introduced himself and Belmarsh. "We understand you've found the Highclere Castle stolen goods."

Spears grunted. "This is more than just stolen goods. We've got a triple murder investigation on our hands." He paused. "Follow me. I'll show you."

The warehouse was a graveyard of disused crates and rusting forklift equipment. Massive lights hung from the rafters alongside old chains and pulleys. Dust and rust coated everything. A partition divided the warehouse, the rear half shrouded in shadow except for a glow from the far right.

"No power," Spears explained as he led them towards the darkness. At the back were a series of offices. The one on the right was lit by portable lights, blue-suited CSI officers bustling inside.

Spears pointed. "Three bodies in there. The goods are over here." An officer stood by three piles of boxes.

She nodded to Spears and shone a torch on the nearest box, lifting the flaps with a pen. Inside was a six-inch stone figure. "Genuine," she declared.

Belmarsh raised an eyebrow. "Are you an expert?"

The officer grinned.

Spears explained, "We have a list. The thieves typed up an inventory and divided it into genuine, fake, and appears genuine. We think it was to assess market potential."

Jackson nodded. "We have our own list." He turned to Belmarsh. "Check their list against ours." To Spears, he said, "Tell me about the bodies."

Leaving Belmarsh with the Met officer, Spears led Jackson to the end office. They peered through a grimy window. The spotlights revealed three bodies: one shot execution-style with blood pooling around his head, another with no visible marks, and the third, naked, covered in cuts and burns.

"They were under the tarpaulin," Spears said. "Initial assessment is that we have one killed here, the naked one appears to have been tortured and dumped here. The middle one was shot once in the head, once in the torso. Classic double tap. No blood on site so, again, he was killed elsewhere and dumped."

Jackson frowned. "If these are the Highclere burglars, why are they dead?"

"Maybe a fourth man killed the others," Spears suggested.

"Possible." Jackson stared at the bodies. "Someone wanted information. They tortured the naked guy, tracked down the others, and brought them here.

Whoever did this wasn't after the stolen goods; they wanted us to find them." He shook his head. "This is a weird case."

"Sir…" Belmarsh approached with papers in hand. She glanced at the grim scene inside the office. "Jesus! Do you think they're the burglars?"

Jackson nodded.

"And responsible for Ellen Champion's death?"

"Possible. I'd even say highly probable." To Spears, he said, "We need to link up with your investigators. There could be a connection to the girl killed by the gas explosion near where the goods were stolen."

Belmarsh added, "Everything the Estate and museum reported missing matches the records here, except for one item—a ceremonial funerary block."

"A what?" Spears asked.

Fox sipped his coffee in a nearby café, watching the commotion at the warehouse through the window. The Met police had arrived within twenty minutes of his anonymous call, and the scene of crimes van shortly after. Jackson and Belmarsh pulled up in their silver Vauxhall an hour later, likely delayed by rush hour.

Perfect.

Fox pressed speed-dial. "All gone according to plan," he reported.

The smoker's voice crackled through. "Did they know?"

"Some, but not all. Not nearly enough."

Relief in the other man's silence. Fox added: "I've got the girl's papers from her briefcase—drawings of the artifact and notes on the hieroglyphs."

"Enough for us to work from?" The smoker's excitement was palpable.

"I think so. Now that we know this is the map, it's just a matter of time."

"Good."

"One thing bothers me. We know about the communications, but there's nothing in her notes. Most of the research is missing."

"Let's hope it's just a matter of us solving this and putting it to bed once and for all."

Fox nodded at his reflection. This mystery had loomed over them for nearly a century. It would be an honour to end it.

Jackson and Belmarsh emerged from the warehouse, ducked under the cordon, and got into the Vauxhall.

"Fox?" The smoker's voice brought him back.

"Yes?"

"What about the rabbit?"

"He should be in the clear now. The evidence will wrap this up."

The other man's breathing rasped before he spoke again. "Keep him in play. He might find the missing research."

"I'll use the reporter again. Feed her info linking the rabbit to the Polish mafia. She'll lap it up and it'll support their theories."

"Good."

"And if the rabbit doesn't find the research?"

"Eliminate him."

Chapter 21

In the morning, Alex received an email. Not an Oxford University email address, but it was from the professor.

Dear Mr MacLure

Please accept my apologies for not picking up your email straight away. I have retired from my post at The Griffith Institute, St Anthony's College, Oxford. The email address is still active, but I have to log on to the computer to check for messages.

Regarding your query, it has been some considerable time since I reviewed the private papers collection, and I am sure you appreciate that the suggestion of missing papyri from the tomb of Tutankhamun is nothing new. However, I found your enquiry intriguing.

I would greatly enjoy revisiting the old documents and have reviewed a communication with the curator at New York's Metropolitan Museum of Arts.

I would enjoy discussing my findings with you and will be able to arrange for you to view the collection as requested.

I look forward to hearing from you again.

Yours sincerely

Emeritus Professor Christopher L Thompson

There was a phone number at the bottom and Alex immediately called it.

"Professor Thompson," a deep, slightly amused voice answered after the eighth ring.

"Professor, it's Alex MacLure," Alex replied, a touch of nervous excitement in his voice.

"Goodness gracious, I only sent you a message earlier this morning!" There was a brief pause, then the voice chuckled. "Ah, my apologies. You must forgive an old man, Alex. I'm still getting the hang of this Internet business. My daughter insists I use a computer and this 'electronic post', but perhaps I should stick to good old pen and paper. There's something satisfying about ink on parchment, don't you think?"

Alex grinned, momentarily distracted. "I understand, Professor. I'm just grateful for your time. I'd like to arrange that visit."

"Oh, yes, of course. The visit to see Howard Carter's original notes. Very intriguing, indeed. And as I mentioned in my email, I think there's possibly something to the theory you're suggesting. Actually, I've obtained—"

"Could I come tomorrow?" Alex interjected, his eagerness palpable. "If it's possible, I mean."

"Tomorrow?" Thompson's voice faltered slightly. "That's rather quick. I was under the impression you might need a little more time to prepare—"

"I would really appreciate it, sir, if you could arrange to meet tomorrow," Alex said, trying to keep his tone respectful but urgent.

"Goodness, you young people are always in such a hurry. Everything has to happen right this instant, doesn't it?" Thompson laughed softly. "All right, all right. I suppose I can accommodate. Meet me at the institute at 11 am sharp, and I'll make sure you have access to everything you need."

"Thank you, Professor. I really appreciate it." Alex's voice was full of quiet determination as he hung up.

With a sense of renewed purpose, Alex turned back to his computer. His fingers moved quickly over the keyboard, scrolling through notes and documents about the discovery of Tutankhamun's tomb. Ellen's original email to the professor had pointed out certain inconsistencies in the records—the way events surrounding the discovery and the death of Lord Carnarvon were handled.

The scrap of paper Alex had found, included Carnarvon tablet. Maybe that didn't mean a stela. Maybe it meant something else. One thing was for sure, the series of events leading up to Carnarvon's death didn't add up, and Alex was determined to find out whether it was relevant.

Chapter 22

It was mid-morning when Rebecca finally walked in, her presence immediately brightening the room.

"How are you feeling about going out? Still up for it?" she asked, flashing her trademark crooked smile.

Alex looked up from the papers spread in front of him, pushing his glasses up with one finger. "Ready and willing," he said, his voice steady, though his eyes betrayed a flicker of nerves.

"Great! Sorry I'm later than planned. I had a few things to finish up." She pulled a small black tube from her purse, an impish gleam in her eye. "Before we go," she said, holding it out toward him, "I need to fix those eyebrows."

Alex sighed, half amused, but didn't protest. He sat down as she worked on darkening his eyebrows. Her perfume was subtle but unmistakable, a mix of jasmine and something he couldn't quite place. Then he found his mind switching to the puzzles he'd been thinking about: Numbers, Carnarvon's death, Ellen's research. Were the words 'Block' and 'Stone' relevant.

When she finished, he glanced in the mirror, surprised to see how much better it looked.

"Not bad, I'll admit," he said, lifting an eyebrow.

"See? I told you." Rebecca grinned. "All right, let's get moving."

Stepping outside, Alex glanced around nervously, his gaze darting up and down the street, instinctively checking for anyone who might be following them.

Rebecca, ever the picture of calm, pointed to a small black and purple Smart car parked across the street. "I've brought my car," she said, sounding reassuring.

Alex climbed into the passenger seat, feeling a slight wave of relief wash over him. As they pulled away, Rebecca turned to him briefly. "I had to finish an essay this morning. Took a little longer than I expected, but don't worry, I'm sure no one's following us."

He nodded, though his fingers absently traced the edge of his notebook. "So, we're going to see your uncle?"

"Yes," she said, keeping her attention on the road. "Then we'll have a picnic in Richmond Park."

Alex adjusted his position, trying to relax. The quiet hum of the car was oddly soothing. As they stopped in traffic, Rebecca glanced over at him. "You know, if you adjust the side mirror, you'll have a better view."

Alex gave her a grateful smile and adjusted it accordingly. "Thanks."

By the time they reached Fitzroy Square, Alex had calmed down. There hadn't been any signs of a tail. The square was as serene as it was upscale, with its well-maintained garden and elegant Regency-style properties.

Rebecca led him up to a black door, which they entered through. Inside, they were greeted by a receptionist, who guided them to a meeting room. Alex was taken aback when they entered: instead of a formal setup, the room had comfortable leather armchairs surrounding a low coffee table stacked with biscuits and coffee cups.

The receptionist smiled. "Please, help yourselves. I'll inform Mr Abrahams you're here."

Rebecca poured the coffee while Alex settled into one of the chairs. They sat in quiet anticipation. Twenty minutes later, Alex checked his watch.

Rebecca shrugged. "Sorry, he's a busy man. He'll be here soon."

At that moment, the door swung open, and a large man entered, his voice warm but a bit raspy. "Rebecca! How nice of you to call on me." He had a cane in his hand, and his thick frame, though aged, still held a powerful presence.

"Uncle Seth," Rebecca said, standing quickly. She walked up to him and gave him a hug, kissing his cheek in greeting.

Abrahams eyed Alex carefully before offering a hand. "So, this is the young man."

Alex stood, shaking his hand. "Alex MacLure," he introduced himself, offering a friendly smile. "Thank you so much for… for the use of the flat."

"Temporary use," Abrahams clarified and motioned for them to sit down. He checked his watch with a sigh. "I've not got long, I'm afraid."

"I know, Uncle," Rebecca said, settling back into her seat with a grin. "Alex has been telling me about ancient Egypt, gods, and all sorts of things. Thought you might find it interesting."

Abrahams raised an eyebrow but looked intrigued. "I'm always happy to be of service. So, Alex, this PhD you're working on—what's the research about?"

Alex smiled nervously, adjusting his glasses. "My current focus is on the pre-dynastic period, particularly the boats of Abydos. But… this isn't about me."

Abrahams glanced between them. "Oh? Then what's it about?"

Alex hesitated for a moment. "It's about my friend's research."

Abrahams gave him a puzzled look. "Your friend? But why can't they do their own research?"

Rebecca stepped in smoothly. "It's complicated, Uncle. But we thought you might be able to help."

"All right then, what's your friend researching?"

Alex took a deep breath. "I don't know exactly... not all of it, but generally it's about communication during the New Kingdom—specifically hidden messages, and some things that could be relevant to our discussion." He glanced over at Rebecca.

She added, "Especially numbers. I thought you might have some insight there."

Abrahams leaned forward slightly. "Numbers? You're talking about gematria, aren't you? The practice of interpreting words as numbers?" He gave a small chuckle. "Like the famous 'number of the beast'—666 for Nero Caesar."

Alex nodded eagerly, then glanced at Rebecca for support. She smiled. "Yes, sir. Exactly. But I understand there's more to it than just the common interpretations. What do you think about certain numbers in the Torah?"

Abrahams shifted in his chair. "Well, there's certainly a lot to unpack. What numbers are you particularly interested in?"

"How about forty?"

Abrahams looked thoughtful. "Forty is significant. There were forty days and nights of rain in Genesis. The Israelites wandered for forty years. Moses spent forty days on Mount Sinai. Elijah fasted for forty days..." He paused and glanced at Alex, as if testing his reaction. "But forty isn't always literal, you know."

Alex nodded slowly. "So, it's symbolic."

"Exactly." Abrahams smiled. "What other numbers are on your mind?"

Alex thought about the numbers he'd identified for Ellen and ticked them off one by one. "Three, four, and five?"

"Ah, well, three represents completeness, stability. Five symbolises the same. And of course, the Torah is often referred to as the five books of Moses. Four is more... subtle. It's everywhere though—questions, angels, the matriarchs, the kingdoms of the eschaton."

"Interesting," Alex murmured. "And twelve?"

"Ah, twelve. The tribes of Israel. It's totality in gematria. That's a significant number."

Alex thought for a moment, then asked, "What about eight?"

Abrahams smiled, clearly warming to the topic. "Eight represents Shleimus—completion. It's the number of circumcision, the eighth day. Chanukah lasts for eight days. The Mishkan—the Tabernacle—was dedicated on the eighth day."

Just then, a knock on the door interrupted the conversation. A young man poked his head inside. "Sir, the Goldmans are on the line. It's urgent."

Abrahams stood, using his cane to push himself up. He extended a hand to Alex with surprising strength. "It's been a pleasure meeting you, Alex. If you ever want to discuss these numbers further, don't hesitate to get in touch."

"A quick question, if I may..." Alex said as Abrahams moved towards the door. "When was the first Hebrew text written?"

"The tenth century BCE, I believe. The first substantial sections of the Hebrew Bible have been dated two to three hundred years later. Now, I'm sorry... I really must take this call."

As the door closed behind him, Alex sat back disappointed.

Chapter 23

Rebecca drove out of the city, navigating the busy roads with practiced ease. Thirty minutes later, she pulled into Richmond Park, cut the engine, and turned to face Alex. Her intense gaze, so close, sent an unexpected current through him. He shifted slightly, adjusting his glasses, unsure whether to meet her eyes or look away.

"Do you think my uncle helped?" she asked, her voice quiet but insistent.

Alex exhaled, considering. "It's... definitely something to think about. I mean, I certainly understand gematria better now, though if there's a hidden code in the Bible, it seems to be tied to a later period than what Ellen was interested in. By at least 300 years. But it was generous of your uncle to offer his help if I come across anything specific."

She studied him a moment longer before nodding and getting out of the car. The moment of intensity passed, leaving Alex feeling slightly off-balance. She retrieved a small hamper from the trunk. "Lunch. Come on, I know a great spot."

She refused his offer to carry the hamper, leading him across the grassy expanse. As they walked, she said, "I watched a documentary last night about a pharaoh queen."

"Cleopatra or Hatshepsut?" he asked immediately.

"Hatshepsut. It was fascinating. She must have been remarkable. Do you know much about her?"

Alex's eyes lit up. "Quite a bit, actually. She ruled as a pharaoh in her own right—not just as a queen consort. In fact, for part of her reign, she was the senior ruler. Some of her statues even depict her with a false beard."

Rebecca frowned. "Why would she wear a fake beard?"

"It was symbolic," he explained, warming to the topic. "The false beard was a key part of the pharaoh's regalia— like the crook and flail. It wasn't about gender, but legitimacy. She had to present herself in a way that reinforced her authority. Her reign was marked by prosperity, massive building projects, and even some military campaigns."

Rebecca spread a picnic blanket on a grassy slope, offering a view of a shimmering lake. "And what happened to her?"

Alex sat down, crossing his legs as he thought. "She ruled for a long time, but after she died, her stepson, Thutmose III, took over. Later, he had her monuments defaced, her statues destroyed, and her name erased from records."

"Why would he do that?"

"Historians debate that. Some think he wanted to reassert his authority. Others believe it was more about reinforcing the idea that female pharaohs were exceptions rather than legitimate rulers." He accepted a sandwich from her with a nod of thanks. "It's incredible how much history is lost or rewritten. Makes you wonder what they'll say about us in a thousand years."

She smirked. "Probably that we had great sandwiches."

He chuckled, and they ate in a comfortable silence, enjoying the crisp air and the quiet of the park. After

115

lunch, they wandered through the trees, their conversation ranging from ancient history to classic films. Rebecca's enthusiasm was infectious, and Alex found himself relaxing in a way he hadn't expected.

When they reached Pen Pond, they found a bench. Rebecca turned the conversation back to Hatshepsut. "The documentary called her story one of the last great mysteries. Is that true?"

Alex adjusted his glasses. "Not really. There are plenty of unresolved questions in Egyptology. Her mummy was only identified in the last couple of decades, even though she was the first royal mummy found since Tutankhamun's in 1922. But a lot of royal tombs are still missing, either stolen or deliberately hidden from grave robbers." He sat on the tartan rug she had laid down. "Ellen was fascinated by that—especially the fates of Akhenaten and Nefertiti."

Rebecca's eyes sharpened. "So, that's another piece of her research?"

"I suppose, though she never mentioned making any breakthroughs with that."

Rebecca held up a hand, stopping him before he could continue. "But if she was onto something big, she might have kept it to herself, right?"

Alex hesitated, then shrugged. "Possibly."

She caught the teasing note in his voice. "You've made progress, haven't you?"

"I've been in touch with a professor at Oxford," he admitted. "Ellen was particularly interested in some private papers linked to Carter, Carnarvon, and the early 20th-century digs."

Rebecca's excitement flared. "Ah, so that explains why she was so determined to work at Highclere."

"More significant than going on an excavation, yes."

She leaned in, eyes gleaming. "So…?"

He hesitated, then said lightly, "It's probably just me, but speaking of numbers, Lord Carnarvon died in 1923. April 5th." He raised an eyebrow. "Two... three... four... five."

She groaned, laughing. "Yes, that's probably just you. I know he supposedly died because of the mummy's curse."

Alex grinned. "And he had a mark on his cheek in the same place as Tutankhamun's. But the whole 'mummy's curse' thing? A media invention. No actual tomb curses existed. Carter and the others played along for publicity—and money."

"But why? Carter must have been rich after finding all that treasure."

Alex shook his head. "You'd be surprised. Carnarvon was the financier; Carter was just the archaeologist. They spent thirteen years looking for the tomb. By 1922, they were out of money. Carnarvon had already given up, but Carter convinced him to fund one last season. Fortunately, they found the tomb in November."

Rebecca handed him a juice carton, looking intrigued. "So, Carter didn't get rich?"

"Not from the discovery itself. The Egyptian government changed the law and claimed everything. Carter made his fortune later—selling his story, touring the world, and capitalising on the curse myth."

Alex's phone rang. He ignored it.

Rebecca opened another sandwich. "So, you're going to Oxford?"

"Tomorrow. I'm hoping the trip will turn up something useful."

"Shame," she said. "I'd have come with you, but I have plans."

His phone rang again. This time, he glanced at the screen. Number withheld. He sighed and answered. "Alex MacLure."

A voice said, "You're not at the address in Hammersmith."

Alex's tone shifted. "Detective Dixit, how nice of you to call."

Dixit ignored his sarcasm. "Where are you, Mr MacLure?"

"At this moment? Having a picnic in Richmond Park with a fascinating conversationalist."

Rebecca arched an eyebrow, amused.

"Tell me exactly where you are. I need to speak with you."

Alex smiled. "Meet me where I'm staying. Simon's café, Putney. One hour."

Dixit hesitated, then said, "Fine. We need to talk. It's about the missing item."

❧

Chapter 24

Detective Constable Dixit looked like a man on the edge as he pushed through the door of Simon's café. He scanned the room, zeroing in on Alex at a corner table, and without a word, he sat down.

"What's going on?" Alex prompted, sensing the tension.

"Why didn't you tell us you had moved?" Dixit's voice was laced with frustration.

Alex leaned back, studying the detective. "It's only been a couple of days. I was told not to leave the country. I wasn't hiding from you. I was hiding..." he stopped himself. "I was hiding from the press. You called me, I answered, and here I am. Available for your questioning."

Dixit grunted, not satisfied. "Have you seen the latest article by your friend Milwanee?" When Alex shook his head, the detective continued. "She's asserting that you have ties to the Polish mafia. Care to comment?"

"Absolutely not!" Alex's denial was immediate and firm.

Silence hung between them as Alex pulled out his smartphone, reading Aysha Milwanee's article. She claimed Alex was involved in the Highclere break-in, planning to sell the stolen items to the Polish. The article detailed the crime scene in East End, where the stolen artifacts and three bodies were found, all executed.

"That triple murder in West Ham… is it linked?" Alex asked, his voice low.

Dixit nodded. "It looks like that's the gang who stole everything."

"I don't get it," Alex muttered.

"Frankly, I don't care if you do," Dixit snapped. "More importantly, the case is now with the NCA. Organised crime, gang war, you get the picture."

Alex took a deep breath, reigning in his frustration. "So, Detective, if the NCA has taken over, why are you here?"

Dixit's eyes twitched, and he forced a smile. "We've identified the person responsible for Ellen Champion's death."

"Who?" Alex's voice was a harsh whisper.

"One of the victims in West Ham. His DNA was found on the… on Ellen."

Alex's mind raced, imagining the scene. He wanted details but feared them too. "That's good news, I guess."

"Yes."

The pieces didn't fit. If the case was solved and the NCA was handling the gang war, what did Dixit want? "There's something else, isn't there?"

Dixit's eyes twitched again. Alex waited for a customer to pass before leaning in. "Let's stop playing games. What's this really about?"

"Stolen goods."

Alex's frustration bubbled up. "You still think I was involved in the burglary?"

Dixit hesitated. "No, *I* don't." The emphasis on I, Alex noted. "Let me run this by you. The gang disabled the cameras and entered through the emergency exit. They took items from the main exhibit but left obvious fakes like King Tut's bust and the golden statue of Isis."

"Of course. They weren't stupid. The real statue would've had much tighter security."

"They had some knowledge of what was genuine," Dixit acknowledged, his tone serious. "There's a small room after the black curtains with small artifacts in display cabinets. They took everything from that room."

Alex nodded, his expression matching Dixit's seriousness. "Detective, get to the point... Please."

Dixit sighed. "They took all the stuff in that small room. The British Museum identified everything, but the Highclere Estate reported one item missing."

A chill ran down Alex's spine. The thug with the blue sunglasses had asked about another item. "There was something else missing?"

"Looks that way."

"What is it?"

Dixit checked his notebook. "The Estate describes it as a ceremonial funerary block, about a foot square and a hand's grip deep. Not particularly valuable but genuine."

Alex's breath caught. That was it! Ellen had written 'Block' on the note paper. His mind spun, then he realised the detective was talking to him.

"Mr MacLure, are you all right?"

"Er yes... just visualising the item. It was used in the embalming process to separate bodily fluids. A religious artifact. Ceremonial and practical..."

Dixit grimaced. "Sounds right."

"Could the gang have taken it, and it just hasn't been found?" Alex asked, knowing it didn't add up. "Or... could the Estate be mistaken?"

Dixit shook his head. "We're pretty sure the gang never had it. And the Estate doesn't seem to be mistaken."

Alex's heart pounded. "Are you suggesting I took it when I visited before the robbery?"

Dixit's body language betrayed him. "No, I don't believe that."

The detective's demeanour softened. "By the way, the coroner has released Ellen's body. The funeral is at 1pm on Monday, near Southampton."

Dixit stood to leave and, surprising Alex, extended his hand. "Good luck."

Alex watched him go, the weight of new questions settling over him. The missing funerary block was more than just a piece of history—it was a clue, and potentially the key to everything.

Chapter 25

After Dixit left, Alex felt a gnawing sense of unease. He needed to call Nadja. She picked up on the first ring, her voice brittle with stress.

"They're saying I'm prostitute," she said on the verge of tears. "And I don't know this Slimowicz man. They say he is criminal."

"I'm sorry for dragging you into this," Alex said, guilt weighing heavy in his words. After the call, he rang his mother to arrange for her to pick up Topsy.

"How long are you going to stay in hiding?" his mother asked, concern evident in her tone.

"As long as it takes for this to blow over."

"Will you go to Ellen's funeral?"

He wanted to, but the media circus around him would only add fuel to the fire. He sighed, realising he couldn't.

Alex booted up his laptop and searched for images of the ceremonial block. The more he looked, the more questions he had.

That evening, he didn't see Rebecca, but they exchanged texts. Her goodnight message, ending with a kiss emoji, brought a slight comfort.

In the morning, Alex donned a beanie and sunglasses, deciding disguise was favourable to twenty-twenty vision. He could see well enough as he walked to the underground and caught the tube to Paddington. He bought a ticket for the 9:35 to Oxford, keeping his head down and avoiding eye contact.

The journey was supposed to take an hour, but at Didcot Parkway, they were all asked to leave the train due to signal work. The final stretch to Oxford was by coach, which arrived later than the train would have. Eyeglasses back on, Alex jogged the half-mile to a row of Georgian houses that didn't match his expectations of an Oxford academic building.

A small brass plaque confirmed he was in the right place. The Griffiths Institute. He knocked on the white front door, which was promptly opened by a young man in a navy sweater.

"Alex MacLure to see Professor Thompson."

"Yes, come in." The young man gestured Alex inside. "Up two flights. First room on the left."

Alex ascended the stairs, each creak reminding him of old galleons on high seas. At the top, he knocked on the door, then entered a reading room with tables and chairs. Six cardboard boxes awaited him, marked with *Howard Carter's Diaries* and other documents.

He waited for five minutes, expecting the professor to join him, but no one came. Alex sat down and began reading the first folder. The notes grew sketchy after the initial exploration of Tutankhamun's tomb. When Lord Carnarvon fell ill, Carter's entry reported that Carnarvon had an 'acute attack of erysipelas and blood poisoning'. But what drew Alex's attention was a code and date.

973 750 and Oct. 3 11 4 7 35.

Alex puzzled over this, but no inspiration struck. He moved on. The documents detailed the cataloguing and shipping of items to the Cairo Museum, interspersed with more codes and initials that might refer to ships or something else entirely.

A creak of floorboards made Alex look up. The door opened, and an elderly man with a twinkle in his silver-grey eyes entered the room.

"Professor Thompson?" Alex stood.

The professor, using a walking stick in each hand, smiled. He had an unlit pipe protruding from the side of his mouth. Alex met him halfway and shook his hand, noticing a faint smell like burnt toast.

They sat and Thompson removed the pipe. Enthusiasm sparkled in his eyes. "How are you getting along?"

"I've just got to the end of 1925."

"Good, good. So, what do you think?"

"I was hoping you would tell me what my friend Ellen Champion discovered."

"All in good time. First, I'd like to know what you've discovered today." The professor reinserted the pipe and clamped down hard on it.

"I knew Lord Carnarvon took items for his collection at Highclere Castle. But Carter uses codes in his diary. I couldn't interpret them, but it suggests he was hiding the truth. Was he smuggling antiquities out of Egypt?"

"Of course he was!" The professor's eyes gleamed. "They caught him at it in February 1924. The *Service des Antiquities* found Fortnum and Mason packing cases in Ramses XI's tomb, used as a storeroom by Carter. One case contained a beautiful wooden statue of Tutankhamun's head emerging from a lotus flower, clearly intended for England since there was no catalogue entry for it. Many items Carter held back for 'scientific purposes' are now in New York's Metropolitan Museum of Art."

Alex nodded.

The professor said, "What else did you discover?"

"I think he entered the tomb before he was officially allowed."

The professor pointed at Alex with his pipe. "He was supposed to be accompanied by a government official, but it certainly looks like they went in and re-closed the entrance. They claimed it was a robber's hole from antiquity, but the repairs look too new and disguised." The professor's eyes creased with a smile. He bit down on his pipe again before resuming. "Anyway, that's not why you're here. You want to know what Ellen was investigating. Sometimes you should look for what is *not* there."

"What does that mean?"

"Have you eaten?"

Alex glanced at his watch, surprised to see it was almost five o'clock.

"The institute will be closing soon. Why don't we get a bite to eat and talk about the missing papyri?" the professor suggested.

Alex nodded, his heart thumping with anticipation, as they left the institute together.

Chapter 26

They settled in a bijou café off Broad Street, the air thick with the clatter of crockery and the hum of conversation. The two men sat close, their voices low, looking like conspirators plotting something monumental.

The professor leaned in, his breath sour with the smell of strong tobacco. "What do you know about the missing papyri?"

"Nothing."

"Lord Carnarvon wrote to a friend and later to the British Museum about a box of papyri." Thompson nodded to himself. "He even mentioned it in an interview with The Times: 'One of the boxes contains rolls of papyri which may shed much light on the history of the period.' Yet, Carter said nothing about them."

Alex ears pricked up. Did the professor what was in them? "Were they in code?" he asked.

"We'll never know. They vanished. And no one knows if they really existed."

"You're saying Carnarvon could have been mistaken?"

"In Carter's book, published in late 1923, he goes out of his way to stress there were no papyri, only rolls of linen. He blamed the mix-up on dim candlelight."

"That's not true! They had power from the tomb above and set up electric lights. It's in his notes."

"Exactly! Such an exciting find would have been checked immediately," the professor nodded. "Carnarvon would have known straight away."

"So, do you think Carter or Carnarvon kept the papyri?"

"Something undoubtedly happened," Thompson said eventually. "Papyri were expected because of what we now call the Book of the Dead—the instructions for reaching the afterlife. The directions and spells were written on the walls and bindings of the mummy. Allegedly, no Book of the Dead was found."

Alex's fingers tapped the table excitedly. "What did Ellen think?"

"She agreed there should have been documents, and they're missing."

"Did she ask you about a ceremonial funerary block?"

Thompson thought. "Yes... We confirmed that Lord Carnarvon had taken a funerary block found in Amarna."

"Did she ask about its interpretation?"

"She was excited about it but..."

Alex waited expectantly.

Thompson shook his head. "I'm afraid it didn't mean anything to me... something about codes and translations. I couldn't find anything suggesting it meant anything other than its designated purpose."

"She'd been working on the Amarna Letters. Did you talk about those?"

"Ah yes. The diplomatic correspondence found on hundreds of clay tablets. They appear to tell of secrets being smuggled into Tutankhamun's tomb." The professor stared into space for a minute, lost in thought, before he said, "It is perfectly possible that it describes the item or items Carter and Carnarvon fell out about."

"The alleged papyri?"

"I believe Carter and Carnarvon discovered something sensitive. Carnarvon couldn't keep it to himself and died a few months later. Carter denied finding papyri, even explained them away as rolls of linen. Carter stayed silent—until he lost his temper over his treatment. Remember, he was out of money, and the Egyptian government was taking all the artifacts. He went to the British High Consulate in Cairo and threatened to expose the truth."

"The truth? Secrets?"

The professor sighed. "In the papyri? We don't know. Ellen told me what she'd translated, but... as secrets from the New Kingdom period? I don't think they would be enough to use against a modern government... and certainly no reason to murder."

Alex had been holding his breath, desperate to hear the secrets Ellen had learned. But the last word froze his spinning mind.

"Murder?"

Thompson said, "How did Carnarvon die?"

"Septicaemia after a mosquito bite on his cheek got infected."

"He cut himself shaving," Thompson said, "but there are many issues with that version. Most notably, there were no mosquitos in the Valley of the Kings at that time of year! He allegedly failed to disinfect the cut but had antiseptic in his medicine cabinet. Private notes held by the Metropolitan Museum indicate Carnarvon had trouble with his teeth before he died. They chipped and fell out. That suggests rare-metal poisoning, like mercury."

"Why—?"

"Why is this not public knowledge, Mr MacLure?" The professor leaned closer. "Let me tell you something... the same thing I told your friend. There are

129

powerful people involved in this conspiracy. And they will do anything to keep the secrets that were in Tutankhamun's tomb. They will suppress information, provide misinformation, and they will think nothing of murder if it's necessary."

Alex's chest constricted. "It looks like Ellen was murdered." The words came out strained and hoarse.

Thompson's eyes flew wide. He took a sip of water and Alex noticed the man's hands were shaking.

When he composed himself, the professor said, "You've noticed I'm no longer with the institute? I pushed, and someone pushed back. I asked certain questions, and it was easier for them to let me go than acknowledge my legitimate enquiries. I stopped looking into the papyri and I think I'm only alive because I found nothing before I stopped. Your friend Dr Champion learned something from her research, and I suspect it unnerved them."

"Who... who are they?" Alex asked.

"Better that you don't ask," the professor said. Then his parting words were a stern, dark warning. "You should stop now. Some secrets are not worth dying for."

Chapter 26

As the countryside blurred past the train window, Alex felt a chill. Had Ellen been murdered by that East End gang or was there another group?

He remembered DC Dixit telling him that the DNA on Ellen matched to one of the gang members found murdered. And the man in blue aviator sunglasses who'd attacked him by the river seemed to be from east London. So, who were the others? His mind went back to the gunshot. Had that been the other group? Shooting at him... or the thug?

His later thoughts were about the professor's warnings. Maybe it *was* tied to the missing papyri. But another possibility nagged at him—perhaps the professor was simply covering for his dismissal, blaming it on his controversial research.

When Alex arrived back at the flat, Rebecca was waiting for him.

"I'm not sure what I found out," he said after she asked. "Ellen believed she was onto something big. And maybe she was looking into a connection with items missing from Tutankhamun's tomb."

"Really?"

"Howard Carter threatened to reveal the truth and was seemingly paid off to keep quiet."

"Did the professor have any evidence?" Rebecca asked, raising an eyebrow.

"That's the frustrating part. We're in the realm of speculation. If there was evidence, it's either lost or destroyed. The professor believes Lord Carnarvon was killed for what he knew. Carter kept silent, but Carnarvon was willing to talk."

"Wow! Do you think Ellen found something about that at Highclere Castle?"

"I don't know, but after you dropped me off yesterday, I had an interesting meeting with the detective investigating her murder. He told me something was missing from the exhibition. The East End gang knew about it and wanted it."

Rebecca's eyes widened as she sat on the coffee table, her knees brushing against his. "What was it?"

Alex let the moment linger, enjoying her anticipation. "A ceremonial block used in the embalming process."

"A what?"

"I know, not as thrilling as missing papyri, but it's still missing. I think we're making progress."

Rebecca leaned forward and hugged him. Her hair smelled clean and fresh. "This is so exciting."

Alex smiled but couldn't shake the confusion. "If only I could understand the significance of the block. I've searched online but found nothing. Ellen must have pieced it together. Maybe the numbers come from the block, maybe she converted them using gematria."

"She was smart, your friend?"

"In ways most people wouldn't get." He described her personality, and Rebecca nodded knowingly.

"Bipolar?"

"Amongst other things. High-functioning autistic, too."

"Did she have therapy?"

"As a teenager, but not recently."

132

Rebecca's eyes softened with concern. "Ever attempt suicide?"

"She overdosed at seventeen, but her parents found her in time. A few years ago, she went camping in the Arctic with inadequate gear, expecting to die of hypothermia."

"What happened?"

"She came to her senses." He laughed wryly. "Said it was too damn cold." Despite his chuckle, Rebecca's serious eyes didn't waver.

"Sad. Sounds like a troubled genius."

Alex sighed. "Now I need cheering up. Let's go out. I know a great place in Primrose Hill."

The dark sky cast an eerie glow that reflected in the window of the Thai restaurant Alex had chosen.

"How did you know Thai is my favourite?" Rebecca asked as he held the door open for her.

"Call me psychic." He laughed, pleased to have impressed her. "Actually, you told me your favourite place was in Thailand. I figured you wouldn't have stayed four months if you didn't like the food."

They settled into a table at the rear, and Rebecca chuckled at his attempts to pronounce the dishes, though she ultimately ordered by number.

"Languages aren't my thing," she confessed. "I survived in Thailand by pointing and using a handful of words. I ate a lot of rice and fruit."

Her light laughter made him suspect she was joking, but then she suddenly turned serious. "Can I ask another question about Ellen?"

"Okay," Alex said, bracing himself.

"Was she on medication?"

"Venlafaxine."

"How did it make her feel?"

"She hated it—said it confined her. Off the meds, she thought faster, though sometimes too fast."

"You're pretty smart yourself—and that thing with the numbers." Rebecca gave a coquettish smile. "Tell me something interesting."

Alex laughed. "Nothing like putting a guy on the spot. Let's see... Take three consecutive numbers where the largest is a multiple of three. Say ten, eleven, and twelve. Add them together—thirty-three. Three plus three equals six. Always six."

"Any consecutive numbers?" Rebecca's eyes lit up. "Six! What's the explanation for that?"

"The magic of numbers," he said.

"You know that's a special skill, seeing numbers like that."

He shrugged, unsure how to respond.

Rebecca hesitated, but then asked, "Why did you stay with Pete when you couldn't stay in your flat? Why not go home to your mum?"

"It's complicated. Mum struggled after Dad died. She never worked, and he left debts. My brother has Duchenne muscular dystrophy."

She looked uncomfortable. "Oh, I didn't know."

"It's fine. Of course you didn't. Home is difficult, and there's no spare room. I send money home every month, but I can't live there. And I'm a Londoner now. I'd feel lost out there."

"I know what you mean."

After a while and a relaxing glass of red, Rebecca confided, "I had a terrible phobia of spiders as a child. I'd see them even when they weren't there—cobwebs closing in, suffocating me."

"Sounds awful."

"It was. Therapy sorted me out. I'm fine now, though I still hate spiders!" She squeezed his hand. "When everything settles down, you should try counselling again."

"You think it'll help?"

She leaned over and gave him a peck on the cheek. "It might."

On the way back, Alex asked to stop by his house in Maida Vale. "I'm going crazy with so little stuff in Simon's flat. I need clothes and some books that might help solve what Ellen was doing."

Rebecca suggested she go in while Alex waited in the car to avoid the paparazzi. She was only gone a few minutes when his phone rang.

"Alex… Oh my God. You need to get here. You need to see this!"

Chapter 27

Alex didn't take any chances. Instead of approaching the front of his house, he slipped through the backyards, moving stealthily toward the rear of his property. His heart thudded as he noticed the kitchen window was open.

Carefully, he stepped on a garden pot to get a better view inside. Chaos greeted him—his flat, a war zone.

Rebecca met him at the back door, her face ashen. "Don't touch anything," she warned, leading him inside. "Looks like they came in through the kitchen window."

Inside, the curtains were drawn and the lights off, making the darkness feel more oppressive. Yet, enough light seeped through the gaps for him to see the mess. The kitchen was a disaster: every cupboard door open, every drawer upended. Utensils, paper, cans of food, packets, and an array of odds and ends littered the floor. Even Topsy's dry dog food had been tipped out. Nothing was left untouched, unturned or unemptied.

The fridge and freezer doors hung open, a large pool of water gathering at the base.

"They look for fake tins," Rebecca explained. "People hide valuables in tins in the cupboards. Like food. In the fridge or freezer too."

Alex moved past the mess into the lounge. The sofa was slashed, white cotton wool stuffing spilling out. The TV lay on its side, the back pried open. Books were flung into a corner. His only plant, a twisted fig tree, had been yanked from its pot, the compost scattered.

"I'm so sorry," Rebecca said, her eyes full of concern. "This is awful."

He shook his head, speechless. When he finally found his voice, he asked, "The rest of the flat?"

"Just the same. Floorboards pulled up. Everything thoroughly searched."

"What were they looking for? Valuables? They didn't take the TV." His voice sounded strained even to him.

"The TV was probably too big."

He walked into the second bedroom—Ellen's room. It was devastated. Floorboards were dislodged or broken. The bedside cabinet lay on its side, drawers emptied. He picked up the Isis puzzle-ball he'd bought for Ellen and placed it back on the windowsill.

Rebecca asked, "Can you tell if anything's missing?"

He shrugged. They returned to the lounge.

"Surely it wasn't valuables," he said, pointing to the sofa. "They were looking for something hidden."

"What did they think I had hidden, for Christ's sake?" He shook his head and sank onto the sofa. Rebecca moved some books, dusted off a seat, and sat beside him.

"Maybe it's linked to Ellen's research. Someone else thinks it's important."

He rubbed his temples, trying to ease the headache forming there. "Who else would know about her research?"

"Think," she urged softly.

"I really have no idea." He covered his eyes with his hands.

After a while, he said, "The people who murdered the East End gang. Who were they?"

"I know you don't want to believe it..." Rebecca's voice was gentle but firm. "What if it is linked to your

137

dog walker—the Polish woman? What if she really does have connections to organised crime?"

He shook his head, unable to accept it could be Nadja. She had seemed genuinely distressed when they spoke.

"Should we call the police?" Rebecca asked, her arm around him.

"Do you think there's any point? All I can see coming from this is more media attention. There's no way the police will find anything—and if it is linked to the East End murders, they'll think I'm involved."

They sat in silence until Rebecca suggested a drink. As he began to rise, she stopped him. "Rest a while. You've had a shock. My grandmother always made a sweet cup of tea at times like these. You stay here and I'll make us some."

He watched her in the kitchen, finding the kettle, filling it, and sorting through the mess. She replaced drawers and put things away, not perfectly but enough to restore some order.

When they finished tidying, the flat looked presentable at a glance, but Alex still sensed the violation. The window latch was broken but closed enough to feel somewhat secure. He left the house through the back door, retracing his route through the backyards. Rebecca was already in the car, and they headed back to Putney. Near Hammersmith, she tensed.

"What's up?" Alex asked.

"I think we're being followed."

He turned to look. Halogen headlights loomed behind them.

"It's a BMW," she said. "He's been keeping the same distance. I'm sure it's the same car that jumped a red light earlier."

"Do you know the back streets around here? Can we lose him?"

"Let's try."

At the Hammersmith gyratory, Rebecca took King Street, then a sharp right. The BMW stayed with them. She sped up, taking turns quickly, but the BMW closed in.

After another corner, the BMW bumped them. Rebecca screamed.

As they entered the next street, Rebecca hesitated, her hands visibly shaking.

"Go!" Alex yelled. "Drive, don't think!"

She reacted, but the rear window was now ablaze with the BMW's full beam. They took three more corners and each time there was a jolt as the BMW rear-ended them.

"Slow down," Alex said. "We can't shake them like this. Take the next left and stop before the right turn. Keep the engine running."

She complied, and the BMW pulled back, stopping with dipped headlights. Two men got out.

"They've got guns!" Rebecca's voice trembled.

"Go!" Alex shouted. "Right, then immediately left."

The Smart car's tyres squealed as she slammed her foot down. They sped through the turns. Alex glanced back. No BMW.

"Now right again." Alex pointed to a car park entrance. "In there."

Rebecca took it, bumping over a concrete strip separating the entrance lane from the exit. The lane curved into a dark well before opening up into the orange glow of a multi-storey.

"Slow down and turn into that car park," Alex instructed. Rebecca did, parking in the dark well of a multi-storey. They waited, barely breathing. A car roared past.

After forty minutes, Rebecca restarted the car, heading west to avoid Hammersmith. They took a long detour, finally arriving in Putney, where she parked away from the flat as a precaution.

Inside, Rebecca opened a bottle of red wine. They sat in silence, lit by a streetlamp. Rebecca broke the silence: "Maybe Ellen's research was about something bigger. What if she left you more clues?"

Alex nodded, though his mind was foggy. "Maybe. But where would another clue be?"

They pondered in silence, finishing the wine. Rebecca offered to sleep on the sofa, but Alex insisted she take the bed. He settled on the sofa, drifting into uneasy sleep.

In his dream, he was at Highclere Castle with Rebecca, showing her Carnarvon's secret cupboard. She whispered something he couldn't hear. Her scent lingered, and then she was really there, standing over him in his shirt, unbuttoned.

"Rebecca?" he murmured, half asleep.

She silenced him with a finger on his lips, leaning down to kiss him. Her touches sent a charge through his body. He pulled her down, fumbling and then ripping off the shirt.

Chapter 28

When Alex woke up, they were on the floor. Somehow, during the night, they'd improvised with the sofa cushions, creating a makeshift bed. It was early, and his neck ached from being at an odd angle. Rebecca was still asleep, so he carefully slipped from under her arm. Groggy with tiredness and the after-effects of the wine but still tingling with the excitement of a new relationship, he went into the bathroom, flicked the lock shut, and turned on the shower.

Rebecca had left her handbag on the table beside the bath. He moved it so it wouldn't get splashed, pulled back the shower curtain, and stepped over the edge of the bath. He started with the shower on cold, like he always did—a jolt to stimulate the body and brain first thing in the morning. After the initial shock, he turned up the temperature and enjoyed the hot torrent as it pummelled his head and shoulders. He felt the fuzz of a hangover being washed away.

As he rubbed shampoo into his hair, there was a knock on the bathroom door, and he heard Rebecca call something. He turned to say, "One minute," and slipped, grabbing for the towel rail. The towel pulled off, knocking some things to the floor, including Rebecca's handbag. She knocked again, more urgently this time.

"One minute," he repeated. He climbed out of the bath and bent down for Rebecca's handbag. A few things had tumbled out, and he replaced her purse and a laminated card. Then he stopped. His veins froze.

She knocked again. "Alex?"

He held the card and studied it—an ID card with her photo. But the name was different. She'd told him her name was Rebecca Reece. The name on the card was Talyia Vance.

He wrapped the towel around his waist and unlocked the door. Rebecca glanced at Alex, the ID, the handbag open on the floor, and then looked back at him.

She snapped, "You've been through my bag!"

"What is this?"

"How dare you go through my things?"

"Who are you?"

She quietened then and her anger melted. After a beat, she said, "My name really *is* Rebecca."

He waved the card at her like it was damning evidence. "So, who is Talyia? Why have this ID?"

"Alex, I…" Her eyes went from side to side as though searching for a script to provide the right words.

"So, you've been lying to me, haven't you?"

Her eyes stopped their flicker and fixed on his. Her face became calmer. "It's not like that." She stepped back from the door. "Let's get dressed and have a cup of tea, and I'll explain everything."

Ten minutes later, they were sitting in the lounge facing one another. Rebecca held a mug in both hands, almost as if praying with it.

Alex said, "So?"

She looked up from the mug. "Talyia Vance is my pen name. I'm a writer—a freelance writer. If I had told you what I did, you wouldn't have trusted me." She paused, took a sip and added, "I wanted to tell you. I just hadn't found the right moment."

"Tell me one thing. When I met you on the embankment, was that by chance?"

She said nothing.

Alex shook his head and started to rise.

"No, it wasn't," she said quietly. "I followed you there."

"And the incident with the thug—the fight—that was a set-up, right?"

"No!" She put down her mug and looked at him with earnest eyes. "That was for real. I have no idea who he was or what he wanted. I was as scared as you, remember? You have to believe me!"

"Actually, I don't!" He sighed and looked out of the window. "In fact, I don't know why I'm sitting here giving you this chance."

"But you are, and that says a lot. Alex, look at me."

He looked into her deep brown eyes. They seemed genuine.

She said, "Yes, I'm a writer and yes, I was following you. But since I've got to know you, I've realised there's a much better story. Probably two. One is the story of Ellen's research and what you've found. That doesn't deserve to be in some stuffy specialist magazine. With your celebrity, with the crime at Highclere, the whole King Tut thing, this is mainstream—certainly Sunday papers. Maybe even a book."

"And the second?"

"The human-interest angle—about you—about Ellen. Wouldn't you like to set the record straight?"

"There's a lot you don't know." It was all he could think to say.

"I'd like to find out."

Alex stood and walked around the room. He could hear the sounds from the street. His own thoughts seemed less distinct.

143

She said, "Give me a chance."

Eventually, he said, "I need time."

"I'll give you time. Search for my work—under my pen name—see the sort of thing I write. I'll start writing something on you, but I won't publish it, because I want us to work on it together. I want you to be happy with it."

He said, "Maybe. I should find somewhere else to stay no matter what."

"That's really not—"

"Yes, it is."

"Look. I'm going up to York to a hen party and then the wedding. Let's get together when I get back. Okay?"

"Sure," he said with little conviction.

Alex opened the door for her to leave. There was a moment of awkwardness as she said goodbye, and he closed the door with her still looking at him. He stared at the back of the door, a cascade of thoughts running through his mind. After a while, he realised he was just staring at the paintwork that needed touching up.

He picked up his phone and rang Pete.

Chapter 29

Alex said, "Pete, I need your help."

"Why am I not surprised? You've fallen out with that tart, I'm sure. What was it? Did she find out about the real you?"

"Yeah, something like that. Are you in? Can I come over?"

Thirty minutes later, Alex was standing on Pete's doorstep. Pete eyed him with suspicion and glanced down the stairwell. "I hope no one followed you here!"

"The guys who followed me before, and the one who attacked me by the river. They're all dead. I'm not scared of them anymore. It's a bunch of other guys I'm worried about now. They're probably the ones who killed the first guys." Alex removed his beanie to show his dyed hair. "And I've got a disguise."

"What about the press?"

Alex nodded. "It's okay, no one has followed me."

"You look weird. The hair I mean."

"No change there then. Can I come in?"

Pete moved inside and Alex followed, dropping his bag on the floor.

Pete said, "So what's happened now?"

They stood in the lounge and Alex told him about Rebecca, about how she was actually a reporter. Freelance or not, she was still a reporter. She earned her living as a writer and he was her subject.

"Oh great!" Pete moaned. "Shit, she met me. She's been in my apartment!"

"She promised… Anyway, why are you so paranoid? She won't connect you to your old conviction. Your job's safe, if that's what you're worried about."

Pete visibly relaxed. "So, what progress have you made with Ellen's research?"

Alex told him about going to Oxford and the mystery about missing documents from Tutankhamun's tomb, how it was connected to Exodus and the uncertainty surrounding Lord Carnarvon's death.

"Shit! It's big then." Pete went through to the kitchen. "Cup of tea?" he asked, and then, as the kettle boiled, shouted, "So where do you go from here?"

Alex said, "I have no idea."

Pete returned with two steaming mugs of tea. "But where's Ellen's research if it wasn't in her briefcase?"

Alex shrugged and then pulled out his book. "The only clue was in here. These numbers." He opened the book and showed his friend.

"Any idea what they mean?"

"Yes. Isis is the key. I converted Isis into 1515—numbers not letters—and it was the code for Ellen's phone. What I didn't finish telling you before was Ellen wasn't just interested in Lord Carnarvon's death, but also missing artifacts from when he and Carter found Tutankhamun's tomb."

Pete looked excited. "Missing artifacts? Like the missing one from Highclere Castle?"

"What? How did you know about that?" Alex glared. Suddenly, his head throbbed from too much wine the night before.

Pete held up his hands. "Hey, steady. Now who's getting paranoid? It's in the papers. That's how I know. They found the stolen stuff with the guys who were murdered in West Ham. A funny block was missing. I think they called it the mummy stone."

Alex shook his head and explained what the ceremonial block was.

"There you go then," Pete said. "Missing artifact."

Alex sank into an armchair and nursed the mug. He thought about what Rebecca had said: Maybe the clue wasn't about the phone.

"Scary about that other gang then," Pete said.

"What?"

"The people responsible for the triple murder. Executions, for Christ's sake. They're saying serious organised crime."

"Yeah, I suspect it was them who chased us last night."

Pete looked shocked. "What?"

"Last night we had a car chase like something out of the movies. Only it wasn't good. The guys had some sort of sub-machine guns."

"Shit man!"

Pete was talking but Alex's mind was back in his home, seeing the devastation. The way everything seemed turned upside down and inside out. He pictured the spare room and how he'd picked up the puzzle that he'd bought for Ellen. A wave of sadness washed over him. The room had almost been like a shrine to his friend. All he had was the book she'd given him and the phone he'd found. The only other thing to remind him of her was the puzzle. At least he still had that.

"What?" Pete said. "What are you thinking about? You've been miles away and haven't heard a thing I've said."

"Oh my God!" Alex said. He stood but suddenly felt lightheaded. The room spun. "Oh my God!" he said again.

"What, for Christ's sake?"

"Isis is the key."

Pete looked expectant, said nothing.

"My God, Isis is the key!"

"I get that, but what does that mean?"

Alex was laughing. "It's a puzzle."

"Yeah, I know that, but—"

"No, not a mystery. I mean literally a puzzle. Isis is the name of a puzzle. It's in my spare bedroom. I have a puzzle called Isis in my house." He clapped his hands. "I need to go home." Then he stopped. He thought about last night and being chased by the BMW through Hammersmith, about the men with guns who had probably been in his home.

Pete said, "What?"

"I need another favour." Alex smiled hopefully. "I need you to get it for me."

Fox's phone rang. The old man said, "Where's the rabbit now?"

"He's back at the Hammersmith flat." Fox let that message sink in, milking the news. He could hear the smoker's rattling breath.

Fox filled the silence: "I've got him. He's going nowhere without me knowing."

"You made a mess of his apartment and found nothing."

"I had to know for sure that the item wasn't there."

"You spooked him."

Fox knew there was no point in arguing. It had been the plan. The other man's tar-filled breathing sounded like he was building up to something. Fox said, "Give me time. We have some of the bird's papers but it's only part of them. She must have done something with her research. It's out there somewhere, and if we don't get it, we run the risk of someone finding it."

"All right," the old man said. "The longer this goes on, the bigger the risk that the police pick up on us. We'll give the rabbit a few more days."

"And if he makes no progress, I end it."

"No," the old man said, surprising Fox. "Change of plan. You won't kill him."

The call ended and Fox shook his head. The old man was going senile. If he could no longer make the hard decisions, then it was time for someone else to do it for him.

Chapter 30

"Shit, your place... it's..."

Pete's words on the phone cut through Alex like a knife, dragging him back to the chaos he'd tried to forget. They'd waited until dark to avoid any reporters lurking around, but Alex hadn't mentioned the break-in, the devastation—it was bad, but not as bad as before.

"Yeah, I know." He hadn't mentioned it in case Pete didn't want to go.

"You had a break-in, and you didn't think I needed to know? You arsehole. If I'd known—"

"Pete, you're looking for a metal ball the size of your fist. Silver with turquoise-blue rings. It's in the spare bedroom on the window ledge."

A few minutes later Pete called back. "I can't find it."

"It's sitting in its open box—a wood-effect cube. By the window. It should be obvious."

Pete snapped, "It would be obvious if I saw it. But I haven't!"

"You're in the smaller bedroom at the back? On the window ledge..."

"It's not here."

Alex ended the call and threw himself on the single mattress in Pete's spare room. So, the burglars must have come back and taken his Isis puzzle. Did that make sense? Why had they trashed the house and left the puzzle, only to return for it? How did they know?

He heard Pete come back, but didn't get up. The guy was annoyed, and there was nothing to say. A short time later, he heard Pete leave again, probably off for the night shift.

Alex kept his clothes on to keep warm, but sleep wouldn't come. He fired up Ellen's old phone and went through everything, checking all the apps for any more notes or clues. When the first strains of morning lightened the night sky, Alex got up and headed for the kitchen and caffeine.

As he waited for the steaming mug to cool, he sat at the kitchen table with the phone and looked at the email again. Then he realised something. It hadn't updated for a couple of weeks—the last email in the *Trash* folder was dated the Sunday she'd left his house early. He went into *Settings* and *Mail, Contacts, Calendars*, and touched the email account. It was off.

Alex swiped it on.

A moment later the phone pinged with incoming mail. Alex checked it. Thirty emails, all junk, it looked like. He selected each one in turn, just to be sure before deleting them. And then he saw it: an email from someone with the Cairo Museum as the domain. Intriguing.

Not heard from you. Is everything all right?
Yours – Marek

Alex sorted his emails but found no others from Marek at the Cairo Museum. He went back to the new one and stared at it, wondering whether to reply. Wondering what to reply. He could pretend to be Ellen but that didn't seem right. If he said Ellen was dead, that might frighten this guy away before Alex had managed to make proper contact. But then how could he say he was replying on Ellen's phone?

151

While he was thinking, an event came up. Ellen's mum's birthday. Alex stared at the calendar reminder. Why hadn't he seen that before? Okay, so it was her birthday today, but he should have seen it in the calendar as a scheduled event. Shouldn't he? Were there any other events he hadn't seen? The birthday event was in *Tasks*. Alex went into *Organiser* then *Tools* and then selected *Tasks*. There were two. The birthday reminder and one other.

A message. It had a reminder date of the day before she had died.

A dead chill ran though Alex's bones. There was no mistaking the meaning of the note. It was a message to him, like a warning from the grave.

Do not trust Pete.

Pete had been very strange when Alex had first turned up after the meeting with the police. He'd said he'd been interviewed by the police, but they never mentioned him. And Pete didn't want them to know where he lived. He also virtually blackmailed Alex with the rent into his bank account. What had he said? *Don't mention me being involved. It looks bad for both of us. Worse for you because of the money.*

So, they had never interviewed him. They didn't know he existed. Pete said he was concerned about his history, about losing his job. But was he really? What did he have to hide? Was he somehow involved? Ellen didn't trust him. She was warning Alex not to trust him.

Damn, he should have known there was something wrong. Pete had hinted at a relationship between him and Ellen. Alex should have known it wasn't true.

And then there was the research. It had been Pete's idea to find out what Ellen had been doing. He kept mentioning treasure. God! It was so clear now. The guy thought Ellen had discovered something valuable and wanted it for himself.

Alex went into the lounge, located Pete's laptop and switched it on.

Password required.

Pete was probably one of those people who used the same password for everything. Alex had seen his lazy swipe of the keyboard: *qwerty*. He hit the keys and was in. Internet Explorer was open. Alex looked at the history. For the past few days, Pete had mainly searched for information about the ceremonial block. Then last night he had been on the Isis puzzle website and had checked forums for hints about how to unlock the puzzle.

There was only one conclusion.

Pete had the Isis puzzle.

Alex began to search the apartment, starting with Pete's bedroom. After two hours of looking, first randomly and then methodically checking every possible site, he sank down at the kitchen table again.

Where would Pete hide it? He thought over and over. He got up again and prowled around the flat. In Pete's bedroom he found a loose skirting board, but there was just the wall behind it. In the bathroom he unscrewed the side panel. Here there was nothing but cobwebs and dust debris from when the bathroom had been constructed.

Where would I hide it? If it's here, it'll be inside something. No new inspiration came, and he found himself thinking: What had Rebecca said? *People hide valuables in tins in the cupboards. Like food. In the fridge or freezer.*

The kitchen had a single unit fridge with a freezer compartment. The fridge wasn't well stocked—the usual minimalist guy-things, including a four-pack of beer bottles. He opened the freezer compartment door.

Embedded in excessive frost was a box of fish and frozen mixed vegetables. He pulled them out. Behind were some burgers that looked like they'd been there since the last ice age, and next to them, a packet of peas. Only, the packet was more of a large lump than Alex would have expected. He pulled it out. Heavy.

Inside, surrounded by peas, was the Isis puzzle.

Chapter 31

Alex waited for Pete to return home, his glare fixed on the door. He sat in the lounge, clutching the Isis puzzle like a weapon, ready to hurl it across the room. The moment Pete walked in, Alex's fury erupted.

"You bastard!"

Pete's eyes flicked to the puzzle, and he took a cautious step back toward the door. Alex sprang up, blocking Pete's exit, his hand slamming against the door just as Pete reached for the handle. He shoved Pete into the room, cornering him.

"You're going nowhere, pal," Alex growled. "Not until you've told me what's going on."

"I didn't wreck your flat!" Pete protested.

"You were looking for the Isis."

"Yes, but honestly it *was* in the spare bedroom. It was where you said it'd be. I was in and out quickly."

Alex advanced until Pete stumbled back into a chair. Alex loomed over him, eyes blazing. "So, you took the puzzle. Did you open it?"

Pete shook his head. "I couldn't work it out." He tried to look hopeful. "How about you? Can you open it?"

"Of course."

Turning his back, Alex fiddled with the puzzle, keeping his actions hidden. After a couple of minutes, he faced Pete again, holding the puzzle's two halves apart. The hollow space inside was empty.

"There's nothing inside," Alex said.

Pete blinked rapidly. "You're joking?"

"What was in it, Pete?"

"I don't know. I honestly didn't know how to get it open!"

Alex's glare intensified. "I don't believe you!"

"It's the God's honest truth!"

In one smooth motion, Alex reassembled the puzzle, still fuming. "You really didn't find anything?"

"No."

"Damn! All that effort and there's nothing in the bloody thing. Mustn't be the clue I thought it was."

Spinning around, Alex stormed to the spare room, grabbed his bag, and headed for the door. As he left, he shot one last venomous look at Pete. "I never, ever want to see you again. Is that understood?"

Pete's silence was all the answer he needed. Alex slammed the door behind him, the sound echoing like a final verdict.

Chapter 32

Two hours earlier

Alex waited Pete's flat until the Isis was warm-up enough to handle comfortably. He solved the puzzle and opened it up. Inside was a slip of paper like something out of a fortune cookie, only pink. On it was written: PAD140Δ

He was sure Pete didn't know how to open the ball. He was certain Pete hadn't seen the note. It was clear that Pete wasn't to be trusted, however, and so the strategy formed in Alex's mind: He would make Pete believe there was no clue—that the trail had ended.

While he waited, Alex went through his emails again looking for anything from Marek. He searched for the name rather than the email address.

He got one hit: Marek Borevsek. This time the domain was the Berlin University and had been sent just before Ellen had applied for work at Highclere Castle. It said:

Switching to the webmail and deleting emails

It was signed *Sinuhe*—one of the names from the EgyptConfidential forum.

Alex had been searching through the browser history on Ellen's phone for a sign of a webmail address when an email arrived on his phone from Rebecca.

The subject: *an apology*.

Alex—I'm so sorry about what happened yesterday. It was wrong of me to lie to you. If you'll never see me again, my only consolation will be that I would not have discovered the real you otherwise. If I'd told you upfront that I write for a living, you wouldn't have let me help you, you wouldn't have opened up to me. Alex, I've attached a working draft of an article about you. The problems of your past make you more human and add a dimension to the story that will endear the readers to you. Especially when they understand you've been working on Ellen's research. Nothing could be more exciting and intriguing than a secret about Tutankhamun. Anyway, read it and let me know what you think. If you don't want me to, I won't publish.

Take care

Rebecca

Alex read the article. It was the kind of thing that he'd originally expected the other reporter to write. It was positive and interesting without the scandal. She'd woven in the information they'd discovered about Ellen's research. The piece was clearly unfinished. She ended with a note about adding a conclusion and wrapping back to the start.

Could he give her another chance? He couldn't stay with Pete. Where else could he go? And she was rather nice and good company.

Yes, he could give her another chance, though this time he'd have his eyes open.

He sent a text: **Got another clue!**

Moments later she was on the phone, breathless and without preamble: "Isis is the key?"

He explained that Isis was the puzzle from his spare bedroom. The one he'd given to Ellen. He also told her about Pete going to the flat and pretending he hadn't found it.

"I *thought* he was untrustworthy," Rebecca said.

Alex coughed. "That's a bit rich coming from you!"

She said, "Fair point."

"I opened it and there was a slip of paper inside with six characters: P-A-D-1-4-0 and then a triangle or the Greek letter delta."

She was quiet for a second. "Could this be a page reference again? Or is there a pad as in pad of paper? Perhaps it's line or page 140? Or pad as in apartment. Maybe it's an address?"

"I don't think it's a page reference, and if it's an address... well, there's not enough information."

"And what about the delta?"

"Well, it's often used as a mathematical symbol to mean difference."

"And what does that mean?"

He heard someone coming up the stairs. "Gotta go!" he said, and ended the call.

Alex prepared himself. Now to get Pete off the trail and out of the picture. A key turned in the lock and Pete entered the flat.

Chapter 33

After confronting Pete and pretending to storm out of the flat, Alex checked the street. All clear. He headed for Fulham underground station, retracing the convoluted tube journey he'd taken to get to Pete's the day before. On the way, he typed a message to Rebecca.

Sorry for cutting you off. It was about Pete. I'll explain later. Heading back to the flat over Simon's café. Hope that's okay.

The message didn't go through immediately due to the lack of signal. By the time he reached Putney, Rebecca's reply had arrived.

>Pleased to hear it.

Throughout the afternoon and evening, Alex scoured the Internet for any clue about PAD140. He also searched for a webmail service Ellen might have used. Though he made no progress, his mind felt agile and charged.

He wanted to send Rebecca a text wishing her a nice evening. After considering a few options, he settled on:
Looking 4ward 2 cing u sunday

She replied later.

>I get into KGX at 15:44. Will come straight over

The next morning, Alex awoke with a clarity he hadn't felt since learning of Ellen's death. He re-read Rebecca's text. She'd gone to York by train, and she was arriving back at King's Cross station. KGX was a three-letter acronym for the station. The realisation made him spring out of bed. PAD wasn't the reference to a pad of paper or apartment. It was a place. KGX was short for King's Cross station. PAD was the abbreviation for Paddington station. It was so obvious now he thought about it, especially since Paddington was the closest main line station to his home in Maida Vale.

Checking his watch—just after 5:30—he decided it was too early to call Rebecca. Instead, he sent her a text.

I think I've cracked it. Off to investigate

Within the hour, he was at the station. He had expected it to be deserted early on a Sunday, but the main concourse buzzed with people in yellow charity T-shirts, some holding placards, a giant banner announcing a mass fundraising event.

A text arrived from Rebecca.

>Amazing! If you're going out, be careful

Alex confirmed that he would, then looked around. Spotting a man behind the information desk, he weaved his way through the crowd. "Are there lockers at the station?" he asked.

The man looked up from his papers. "Sorry, sir?"

"Lockers? Is there somewhere at the station to store something?"

"Not lockers," the man shook his head. "But if you have luggage you want to leave, there's the Excess Baggage Company at the end of platform twelve."

Alex thanked him and headed towards platform twelve. He saw a glass-fronted shop with a blue sign—beyond the ticket barriers. A railway employee stood by the barriers, and Alex approached him with a shrug. "I need to go to the left luggage place," he said, "but I don't have a train ticket."

161

"Not open yet." The man checked his watch. "You've got twenty minutes, mate. Come back after seven and I'll let you through."

A nearby coffee bar caught Alex's eye. The long counter ran on both sides of the barriers. He ordered a double espresso and a Danish pastry, making a comment to the attractive barista about the absurdity of the barrier cutting off the café and Excess Baggage place. She responded with something unrelated in a thick Eastern European accent. Abandoning small talk, Alex found a seat and ate his breakfast.

At 6:59, he returned to the ticket barrier. The employee opened the panels for him. "Mind you, don't get on a train," he warned. "Big penalties for boarding without a ticket these days."

"Just going to the Excess Baggage Company place— really. Thanks."

Alex slipped through and rounded the platform's end, passing close to the coffee bar. Outside the left luggage place, he stood impatiently. The door was closed, but he could see staff inside. A knock went unnoticed. After four minutes, a spotty youth finally opened the door.

"You're supposed to open at seven," Alex said, regretting it immediately when the assistant gave him a strange look. He thought back to his attempted conversation with the barista and had to remind himself that these people saw a million people a day, most of whom were in a hurry. There was no time to talk and interact, just do your job and get paid.

Alex took a breath and smiled. "Sorry, I'm just a bit... agitated today."

"A bit!" the youth snapped back, then mellowed as though his training was just kicking in. "Hey, it's okay. What can I do you for?" He lifted the counter and moved to the far side.

"I've come to collect something."

"Okay. Give me your ticket and we'll get it right to you."

Alex handed over the pink slip of paper.

"If that's a ticket, it's not from here."

Alex decided to bluff. "Ah. I mean this is the reference, but I've lost the actual ticket."

"No problem. There's a £15 charge for a lost ticket. All we need is your ID and a description."

"Ah. You see… I'm not really sure."

The youth eyed him suspiciously, then rolled his eyes. "Someone left your luggage for you?"

"Right."

"What's your name and address?"

Alex hesitated, wondering if it would be in his name or Ellen's. Since he didn't have ID for Ellen, he provided his own name, fearing the assistant might connect him with recent publicity. The youth showed no recognition, casually pulling a form from under the counter.

"Address here," he pointed to the form. Then again at the bottom. "Sign here and show me some form of ID please."

"A credit card do?"

"Nicely."

Alex signed an indemnity, paid £15 in cash, and the assistant took a photocopy of his card and checked the signature.

"All righty," the youth said. "Now, what am I looking for?"

"A package, I guess."

Another odd look, but the young man disappeared for a while. Alex saw him return and place something under the counter.

"I see now. It wasn't left here but sent for collection. You need to give me a three-digit code…"

"Okay. How about 140?"

"Cool." The youth pulled a black leather briefcase from under the counter and slid it over.

As Alex swung the briefcase to his side, he noticed another man in the shop. Their eyes met briefly, but then the man held out a ticket for the assistant. False alarm.

Clutching the handles tightly, Alex moved into the flow of passengers heading for the barriers. He waited for the station employee to be unoccupied and held up the bag. "Collected this from the luggage place—you let me through."

The man opened the barrier with the most fleeting of acknowledgements, and Alex followed the crowd towards the entrance to the tube station.

Something grazed his arm. No, not a graze. A grip

"Hey!" Alex tried to pull away and looked into the face of a stern man in a brown suit.

"Alex MacLure," the man said in a monotone, "you are under arrest."

Chapter 34

Alex instinctively gripped the briefcase tighter. The man in the brown suit leaned in, his voice low and controlled, as if masking an accent. "You are believed to be in possession, or have been in possession, of stolen goods," he said, flashing a warrant card open then closed. "Police."

Alex's mind raced, but he said nothing, surveying his surroundings.

The man spoke again. "What's in the bag, sir?"

Alex's thoughts cleared just enough. "Did Jackson send you?" he asked.

"Yes," the man replied, but there was a hesitation, something off in his eyes.

"Okay, take me to him," Alex said, trying not to sound challenging.

The policeman didn't react to his tone, maintaining a firm grip on Alex's arm just above the elbow.

Alex nodded and moved toward the escalator descending into the tube station. With a brief tug, the man pulled alongside and steered him down the steps rather than the narrow escalator.

To the right was a small shop selling papers, books, and snacks. To the left, ticket machines. A queue of yellow shirts spilled across the foyer; groups clustered in the centre—the fundraisers.

Alex made his way through the bodies, the policeman jammed against his side. A board with the map of the underground split the crowd in two. Alex headed right, close to the map. At the last moment, he jerked left, causing the man's arm to strike the board's metal post.

The grip broke. Alex took off, reaching the ticket barriers and waving his card over the reader. As he darted through, he glanced back. The policeman was following but had no pass or ticket. No way he could jump the barriers. Alex saw the man force someone aside and charge through.

Alex ran down the first escalator, turning onto the Circle Line platform. He knew another exit led to the Bakerloo Line. Before reaching it, he passed an exit route and sprinted along it to the escalators. These took him to the other side of the station with three exit options. At the top of the final escalator, he looked back. No sign of the pursuer. He passed through the barrier, turned right, and emerged on the Paddington station concourse near the platform twelve coffee bar. Without stopping, he scooted left and up the ramp, through a wall of cigarette smoke, to the street.

A red bus was moving through the crossroads. He jumped on and sat down, panting. Near the smoke-enshrouded entrance, he saw the brown-suited man emerge, look around, and disappear again.

Alex stepped off at Edgware Road, heading to a Costa Coffee with a quiet basement. He ordered a double espresso and went downstairs; his heart rate finally calm again.

The room had seats for thirty, but only two were occupied. Neither person looked up as he found a chair opposite a TV showing the view of the upstairs bar and entrance.

He placed the briefcase on the table, running his hands over its surface and along the edges, sensing what was inside. It was fastened with combination locks, one on each side, three dials each.

First things first. He took out his phone and called DI Jackson.

"Did you send someone to arrest me?" Alex asked without preamble.

"It's Sunday morning, Mr MacLure—"

"You picked me up last week on a Sunday."

"Fair point, but Highclere Castle had been burgled overnight. We were working. I am not working this morning."

"Did you send someone to arrest me?"

"No." There was hesitancy in Jackson's response. "What makes you ask that?"

"The latest rubbish from that reporter, saying I was definitely responsible for the break-in at Highclere Castle and was working with a Polish gang. It's nonsense. You know that, don't you?"

Jackson paused before responding. "Yes."

Who the hell was the guy in the brown suit? If not Jackson's man, then maybe another force. "Could it be someone from the Met?"

"Could who be? Are you saying a policeman is there to arrest you?"

So, not the Met police. Who then? The other gang? The guys from the car chase with the guns, the ones who trashed his flat, responsible for the triple murder of the other gang.

"Mr MacLure?"

"Oh, yes. Sorry to have disturbed you this morning, Inspector. It must have been a reporter, someone trying it on. Just wanted to check it wasn't a policeman I gave the slip."

167

"You sound a little strange. Is there anything you need to tell me?"

"Just the adrenaline and out of breath."

"Are you in trouble?"

Alex hesitated. Would it help to tell Jackson about the other gang? Maybe, but that might lead to the briefcase. He ran his hand over it again. Too small to hold the missing ceremonial block. No, this contained Ellen's research.

"Sorry," Alex said again and ended the call.

He knocked back the coffee, staring at the combination lock. Two sets of three numbers. He tried 140 on each, knowing it was too obvious. Anyone collecting the case would know the reference number and try 140.

What would Ellen choose? No! What would Ellen think he would choose? It had to be significant.

She knew he'd won the lottery. Would she remember the numbers he'd chosen: 2, 5, 10, 17, 28, 41? Six numbers, ten digits. He tried 251 and 017 but knew it wasn't right.

What were the numbers she'd written in his book? She used Isis twice. Why not use those numbers for multiple purposes? He tried recalling the sequence. He was pretty sure the first page number was 256. Quite interesting. The lowest number that's the product of eight prime numbers. Four to the power of four. Relevant in computing as two to the power of eight. Maybe…

256 didn't unlock either combination.

Alex steepled his hands in front of his mouth, staring at the locks, hoping for inspiration. Come on, Ellen, what would you choose for me?

After several wild guesses and growing frustration, Alex decided to get more coffee. He checked upstairs before returning to the counter, ordering a long black this time.

As he paid, he saw the pink slip of paper in his wallet. He'd put it there with the credit card he used as ID at the baggage place.

He pulled it out.

"Sir?" The barista asked again for payment.

"Oh my God!" Alex whispered. "Oh my God! Ellen, you're a wicked genius."

In his haste to get downstairs to try the numbers that had just struck him, Alex forgot his coffee and had to be called back.

The number on the paper was 140. He'd tried that, but 140 was special. A pyramid number. That's why there was the symbol. An extra clue. Not a delta but a pyramid!

Start with a square base of balls and build up. Not counting one ball alone, the first pyramid was a base of four balls with one on top. The second was a base of nine balls followed by four, then one, making fourteen for the second pyramid number. The sixth pyramid number was 140. And the number of balls in a pyramid with a base of 140 by 140 was a six-digit number: 924,490.

With trembling fingers, Alex dialled 924 on the first combination lock.

Click.

He dialled 490 on the second lock.

Click.

He lifted the lid.

Chapter 35

Alex scanned the café, his eyes darting from one face to another. Four people sat scattered around the basement, none paying him any mind. He glanced up at the TV monitor, half expecting to see the fake policeman appear. A minute passed, and nothing suspicious happened. He exhaled, tearing his eyes away.

Inside the briefcase was a bundle of papers in a red folder bound by string. Alex's hands trembled slightly as he lifted the bundle from the briefcase, feeling a mix of anticipation and dread. He worked the string free, revealing the first few pages—emails from Marek.

We've solved it. You were right about the code in the cuneiform messages.

Alex smiled because Ellen replied saying that he had been instrumental in decoding it. But then assured Marek that she wasn't sharing their research.

She could have trusted him, but Alex understood— especially since she was working with someone else.

He flipped through the pages, seeing images of clay tablets that resembled dog biscuits etched with arrows and lines—cuneiform script, cramped and barely legible. The translations followed, interspersed with scribbles and corrections. He recognised the translation as an Amarna Letter, a record found at Tell el-Amarna, the site of

Pharaoh Akhenaten's city. It was a strange message formally translated as:

To Napkhuria, King of Egypt, my brother, my son-in-law, who loves me and whom I love, thus speaks Tushratta, King of Mitanni, your father-in-law who loves you, your brother. I am well. May you be well too. Your houses, Tiye your mother, Lady of Egypt, Tadu-Heba, my daughter, your wife, your other wives, your sons, your noblemen, your chariots, your horses, your soldiers, your country and everything belonging to you, may they all enjoy excellent health.

Ellen had interpreted this as being a coded communique suggesting that the pharaoh (probably Ay) had declared war.

Marek had interpreted passages from the tablets held in Berlin. Dry stuff.

Then he started questioning whether there was another coded message, something deeper and included in the most mundane records.

That's what they had solved, and Alex skimmed through notes and emails with identified words, phrases and messages.

Then the emails from Marek painted a picture of urgency and danger. He included a comment that Howard Carter wrote of papyri rather than the clay tablets they were translating. He wondered whether the papyri related to something else entirely.

Marek's final email was dated just over a week before Ellen had been murdered.

I'm becoming worried. How close are you to getting it? We need to be extra careful and cover our tracks. I think you are right that they have killed—maybe even Lord C—and will not hesitate to kill to stop this information from going public. Let's not communicate until you have the information.

Alex continued reading Ellen's notes and diagrams. It was all there, what she'd been doing at Highclere Castle and why she'd taken the ceremonial block. The realisation struck him hard: he had to destroy the notes.

The last page caught his eye—a handwritten letter from Ellen.

Alex, if you are reading this, then I know my worst fears have happened. Please take care. This discovery is huge but it is also very dangerous. We are convinced there are people who do not want this information to come to light.

She directed him to find Professor Thompson at the Oxford institute. He would help understand the importance of what Carter and Lord Carnarvon discovered and died for.

There are two parts to this. The first is the ceremonial block. The second is the hidden message. You'll find Marek's details in the bundle. He's done a lot of the decoding and translations. I've been looking for the stone that the tablets refer to. It must be the ceremonial block and I think it's a map. You'll understand when you read the notes. I think the missing papyri included information too, maybe all of it. Maybe the map has already been worked out and there's nothing at the end. But I am absolutely convinced that whatever it is, or was, has immense consequences. Solve it, Alex. Solve it for me and, if it really is as huge as I think, find the truth that someone wants buried.

She included secure URLs and passwords, urging him to destroy the hard copies once he'd gone through them and not to print anything else.

I'm not sure what you'll find, but in the wrong hands, maybe this could be used in a damaging way. I don't know. Or perhaps the map was solved decades ago, and we'll never know what lay at the end. But I know for sure that if it hasn't, then this information could lead the wrong people to the solution.

She repeated herself a few times, and he found himself imagining her state of mind. He figured she'd written this in the early hours of Sunday, bundling up the papers and leaving his house. She'd almost told him on Saturday night. He was sure of it. Maybe the fear that someone was watching stopped her. But he reckoned she'd left the phone and put the code in the Isis puzzle before leaving. She'd have bought the briefcase, possibly from one of the stores down from the café he was now in. She'd left him the research at the baggage reclaim and then gone back home. And two days later she was dead.

Her final words made him choke up:

Thank you for being my friend. If there is an afterlife, a Field of Reeds, our hearts are not heavy. The gods will welcome us, and I will see you again. Until then, I remain your—Ellen.

By the time he finished, it was almost lunchtime. Alex stuffed the papers back into the briefcase and locked it. After a quick glance at the CCTV monitor, he left the coffee shop, crossing Edgware Road and heading towards Paddington station. He reached a deserted plaza, buying a cigarette lighter from a convenience store on the way.

In a secluded corner behind some blue boarding, he kicked open a loose panel and stepped through. He opened the briefcase, piling the papers into a makeshift pyre. He lit the bottom, watching as the flames consumed months of work, reduced to ashes in moments.

When he was sure the papers were destroyed, he scooped the remains into the briefcase and flung it into the construction site. As he walked back to Edgware Road, heading for the Circle Line station, he stared at his hands, grey with ash, and thought about Ellen and Marek's work, now gone forever.

Chapter 36

On the secure site, Ellen had included the decoded passages. There wasn't a clear sequence, and many words didn't seem to fit. Perhaps there were more, either missing or deliberately excluded.

Marek had detailed the alleged secrets. They provided information about Pharaohs Tutankhamun's and Ay's deaths. The fleeing of Nefertiti after Ay took charge and how Horemheb, Ay's successor had lied about being of royal decent. There was also an explanation that Tutankhamun's queen had no choice but to marry Horemheb. She'd attempted to get support from abroad, but her secret communiques had been intercepted.

The author, who appeared to be called either Meryra or Yanhamu, also referred to building a secret tomb for Akhenaten and later for his queen, Nefertiti. He said that each would have an innocent-looking map. The Map-Stone.

There was also talk of treasure with the author saying he had rescued it. There were also passages about a chest which possibly contained treasure. However, these decoded sentences were incomplete.

It appeared that the maps would lead to the tombs, whether there was a specific treasure, Alex couldn't interpret. However, the discovery of undisturbed tombs from the period 1300 BCE was mouth-wateringly exciting.

Maybe the treasure was worth killing for, but were the secrets? Alex thought not. There was some evidence supporting these disclosures and he couldn't imagine anyone being harmed by their publication.

Carter had threatened to tell the truth. Perhaps the papyri and the Map-Stone were unconnected.

Alex pondered the words that had been identified in isolation: The names Yanhamu, Meryra, Laret and Akhetaten – Akhenaten's fabled city. He also noted: Serq, which Marek interpreted as a man called Scorpion.

Why would the author embed odd words, scattered about on the tablets. That made no sense. Unless...

Glasses off, Alex studied the picture of a tablet with the name Yanhamu on it. The code Marek and Ellen had identified wasn't here and yet...

Alex's heart fluttered. There was a different code, one more complex than the other.

Excitedly, Alex began to extract the hidden information and then translate it.

My name is Yanhamu. I was born a peasant, and this is my story.

It was evening when a knock on his door disturbed his work. He'd lost track of time with paper scattered all around with partial translation and summaries, so that he could piece it together like a jigsaw puzzle.

Rebecca stood in the doorway, her silhouette casting a shadow across the dimly lit room. "Can I come in?"

Alex stepped aside.

"Are we good?" she asked.

He'd been eager to share his news with her and yet... "I trusted you," he said, the accusation sharp.

Her shoulders slumped. "I'm sorry." She took a tentative step forward, reaching out as if to touch him, then hesitated and withdrew her hand. "But if you'd known my initial interest, you would never have let me close, would you?"

Her scent, a mix of musk and something sweet, reached him. He fought to maintain his composure, his face an impassive mask. "No."

She sighed, a mix of regret and resolve in her eyes. "But I've gotten to know you, Alex. Aside from the penname—"

"The deception."

She winced as if struck. "Apart from that, you've gotten to know me. I like you, Alex. I really like you. It's genuine."

Despite himself, a smile broke through his stern façade. "I'm glad you're back."

She grinned, relief washing over her, and pulled him into a hug. "Me too."

They moved to the sofa, the tension slowly easing.

She prompted: "You found a clue…"

"Yes." He grinned, unable to stop himself.

"What?... Wait! You found Ellen's research?"

"It's amazing," he said breathlessly.

"Can I see it?"

"No."

Her face fell. "Oh, I thought—"

"I destroyed it." Alex explained Ellen's letter and her plea to ensure the research never fell into the wrong hands. He recounted the encounter with the man in the brown suit, the fake policeman. "That gang is determined to get their hands on the research. I had to erase any evidence. I burned it."

Her eyes widened. "Oh my God! So do you remember everything, or have you got some kind of photographic memory you haven't told me about?"

"I've a good memory, but nothing like Ellen's. I reviewed the pack, which was a jumble of her notes. That's what I burned. There were a couple of secure web addresses and passwords. They decrypted messages embedded in the mundane text of clay tablets. It needed decoding and…" He knew he was becoming animated as he explained, but the thrill was almost too great. "Amazingly, it all stemmed from my interpretation of numbers. Ellen and Marek used them to identify the hidden message. But they only got the simple ones. While I was staring at a tablet, I started to see numbers they hadn't… started to decode another message."

"The story of a young boy named Yanhamu. From the notes, it looks like he becomes a royal scribe called Meryra. He's also seeking revenge for the death of his sister."

"Interesting… probably," she said, "but worth killing for?"

"Maybe or maybe it's the first part or maybe it's the the ceremonial block. Ellen thought the ceremonial funerary block was what's referred to as the *Map-Stone*. Which may lead to a tomb or tombs. And maybe Lord Carnarvon… maybe others have been killed because of it."

Alex was breathless and realised he'd been going too fast, maybe not making a lot of sense.

She said, "But what were the secrets? Did they decode those?"

"Yes… no… maybe. They decoded truths about the change in pharaohs… murder, suicide, betrayal…"

She frowned. "Worth killing over? Today, I mean."

He shook his head. It seemed unlikely.

Rebecca appeared to be thinking but Alex's mind was now moving on, filling in other information. "Ellen was collaborating with an Egyptian PhD student called Marek Borevsek. He was originally in Berlin and then moved to Cairo."

"Berlin? Why Berlin?"

"Berlin Museum has a vast Egyptian collection, including the majority of the Amarna Letters—the clay tablets. There are nearly four hundred of them from that period. They had a big piece of the puzzle with the letters but didn't know what they were looking for until Ellen figured it was the ceremonial block."

"So much information," she said seeming overwhelmed by it and Alex's breathless enthusiasm. "I'm trying to make sense of this, Alex. You're saying it all comes down to that missing block…."

"Ellen was at Highclere looking for the *Map-Stone*—it was separate from the missing papyri that Lord Carnarvon probably took. And perhaps it holds other secrets."

"But you don't know what it's for or what it leads to?"

"Tombs. I think tombs although I don't know what's buried. But you can bet it's significant."

She nodded thoughtfully. "Had she interpreted the map?"

"Not as far as I can tell – or at least she didn't include it in her notes.

"If only we could find it. Do you think Ellen hid it? Do you know where it might be?"

"I have no idea, but I'm not sure I need it."

"You don't?"

"There's another secure site with photos and sketches of the block. Look."

Alex opened his laptop, logged onto the site, and hit enter. "Best that you don't know the password. If those BMW men…" He trailed off, and she nodded.

"It doesn't look very special," she said as he flicked through the images. "It doesn't look like a map. It's more like a breeze block."

Alex nodded. "There are lines and symbols—unexpected ones."

"Can you interpret it?"

"I don't know. I've been more excited by the other hidden messages."

"Other—"

"There's a separate… a story that's coded differently and I don't think that either Ellen or Marek realised. I'm good with number codes."

"More sudoku than crosswords." She smiled.

He pointed to the papers scattered around. "That's what I've been working on… the story of a boy called Yanhamu."

Alex snapped the laptop lid shut. "I'm starving. Have you eaten?"

They went to a nearby Lebanese restaurant, their conversation bouncing between what Alex had learned and the story of Yanhamu, the young boy from the same period as Akhenaten.

"Yes. It's emotional stuff. I think I've made sense of the start. His sister, Laret, has been abducted and he's gone looking for her. I've got later sections in the highly religious area we now know as Karnak and also it sounds like the boy became a soldier. I've come across other names: Lord Khety, Scorpion and Ani but think there's much more to decode."

"Does the boy find his sister?"

"I haven't got that far. But finding and translating secret messages in clay tablets is an incredible thrill."

As they walked back, she said, "One burning question remains."

"Which is?"

"It looks like that brick, that lump of rock, is this so-called Map-Stone. If it's indeed a map… can you read it?"

He stopped, shaking his head. "No."

"But Ellen worked it out?"

"I don't think so. She figured out it was what they were looking for, but understanding how to interpret it…? I'm hoping inspiration will come."

"What about her colleague… Marek? Can he help?"

"I emailed him this afternoon. No reply yet."

Alex took her hand as they approached his flat. He opened the door, turning to her with a question laced with innuendo. "Are you staying tonight?"

"Let's take it slow. We need to rebuild our friendship first. And I want you to trust me again." She kissed him lightly on both cheeks. "Sleep well. Let's see what tomorrow brings."

Chapter 37

Alex couldn't sleep. The glow of his laptop cast an eerie light as he poured over the Map-Stone site, hours slipping away as he sketched what he saw. His eyes burned, and when he couldn't think anymore, he switched to the other site, immersing himself in the story of the boy Yanhamu. Eventually, he succumbed to sleep, waking up with Ellen on his mind. Her funeral was today at 1pm. Could he go? He desperately wanted to, but the risks loomed large. Reporters would be there, and if Milwanee still believed he was linked to a gang—maybe Polish—she wouldn't miss the chance to corner him.

The BMW guys with guns could also show up. They wouldn't give up on the Map-Stone. The fake policeman in the brown suit had seen him collect the briefcase. It must have looked suspicious: collecting a briefcase on a Sunday. Did they know what the Map-Stone looked like? Did they think the ceremonial block was in his case? No, no matter how much he wanted to go to the funeral, he couldn't risk it.

"You have to go," Rebecca insisted over the phone. She had lectures in the morning but called to arrange a meeting later. "She was your best friend. You have to—"

"I'll be spotted," he said despondently. "I daren't."

"Screw the lectures. I'll be over within the hour. You are going!"

When Rebecca arrived, she was carrying a bag. She opened it with a flourish, revealing a wig and makeup kit. "I've got an actor friend," she explained. "We'll give you a proper disguise so not even your mother would recognise you."

Thirty minutes later, Alex had to admit it was an incredible transformation. With grey hair and a beard, he looked like an old man. Rebecca had lightened his skin and made his eyes look sallow.

She transformed her image too, then pulled an old suit and tasteless dress from the bag. "Now we're an old married couple," she announced. "Let's find you a walking stick, and we'll be in and out again, and no one will be any the wiser."

At the Southampton crematorium, Alex spotted Milwanee lurking outside. The six people around her were either part of her team or more reporters. He kept an eye out for the BMW or anyone who looked like a gang member but saw no one suspicious.

Once inside the east chapel, he relaxed. The room was packed, and they blended into the crowd seamlessly. Ellen's brother gave the eulogy, ending with a poem she had written as a teenager about the wonder of life and her bright future. He choked up at the end, leaving the podium with tears streaming down his face.

Alex found himself shaking with emotion. "Thank you," he said as they left. "I did need that. I guess it's what the Americans call closure."

"Cognitive closure," Rebecca said, "is a gestalt principle of perceptual organisation that explains how humans fill in visual gaps to perceive disconnected parts as a whole object." She shrugged. "Sorry, we just covered it in my course."

He nodded. "I have no idea what you said, but I'm sure it's true. I do feel ready to move on."

In her car, she studied him. "Are you telling me you won't be pursuing Ellen's research?"

"Of course I will! I've not got this close to stop now."

She laughed. "Phew! Okay, let's get home and solve this thing."

On the way to the M3, they stopped at a service station. Rebecca helped him remove the wig and beard, a relief to get the itchy things off. Back in the car, she put on some rock music, and he sank into the seat, finally relaxing.

He must have been dozing when she spoke. "I got expelled from ballet," she said.

"Sorry, what?"

"I used to go to ballet lessons, but by eight, I was asked not to return. At least, Uncle Seth was asked not to bring me back."

"What did you do?"

"Ridiculously, it was just because I was a free spirit. A bit too independent."

"You mean you didn't do what you were told?"

"I guess you could see it like that. I just wanted to dance, so they decided it was best I did it in my own time."

"And did you?"

"Of course not."

He stared out of the window until she asked what he was thinking.

"Why did you tell me that?"

"Busted," she said. "I wanted to rebuild our relationship. I was a bit too blatant, wasn't I?"

"A bit. So why are you doing a politics and psychology degree now? Didn't you do a degree after school?"

She sighed as though this wasn't a story she expected to tell. "I was brought up by Uncle Seth and Aunt Atara.

My whole life in Hendon. My whole life pretty controlled and dull. I guess that's why I rebelled when I could. As soon as I passed my A-levels, I was off to Israel. Like a rite of passage, I suppose. Amazingly, I got accepted into Tel Aviv University. However, I dropped out after the first year. Too much of a free spirit again, I suppose."

Alex had seen the news about the troubles: the West Bank and Gaza Strip. "Was Tel Aviv safe? What was it like?"

"It's like California. Beautiful beaches where people surf all day. Guys go to work in shorts and flip-flops. It's a chilled place."

"And the bombs?"

She shook her head. "It's not like that. Israel is very well protected. There's a defence system called Iron Dome. While I was there, Hamas fired tons of missiles and mortars from Gaza. Not one of them caused any damage. I remember sitting on a balcony with friends. It was like a firework party. Missiles soared into the night sky only to be met by a defence missile in an explosion of light and colour. Literally."

"So why leave if it's such a cool place?"

"Uncle Seth. He came to get me and took me home."

Alex waited. He could tell there was more to the story and saw her face flush.

Quietly, she said, "I got into trouble. I was working less and less, drinking more, and doing some drugs. I was in with the wrong crowd. My aunt and uncle found out— someone they knew in Tel Aviv told them. One minute I was partying in one of the coolest cities in the world, and the next I was in Dullsville and grounded. Shit! I was twenty-two and treated like a kid."

"Must have been tough."

"It was the right thing, though," she said with a half-smile. "Uncle Seth is always right. He made sure I got

185

myself sorted. In Israel, I'd worked for a paper—clerical stuff, not editorial—and they didn't let me write anything. Anyway, the job experience got me into the Evening Standard, and although I'm still officially clerical, they do accept articles I write. I also sell pieces to other publications."

"So why the degree?"

"Because my boss says it's the easiest way into proper journalism. Politics provides a great foundation, and psychology is just so I don't go out of my mind with boredom." She coughed. "Speaking of which, am I boring you?"

Alex had been looking at his phone. "Oh my God!" he said.

"My story wasn't that dramatic."

Alex held up his phone. "I've had a reply from Marek, Ellen's colleague from Berlin. He's suggested I get a flight out tomorrow. He's sent a list of flights from Heathrow to Egypt. God, he's keen. He's checked out all the details. He's hoping to meet me tomorrow in Cairo!"

That evening, over a takeaway pizza, Rebecca asked, "Is Egypt safe? It wasn't long ago that they had riots and forced President Mubarak to resign. They've also had hijackings and terrorists blowing up planes."

"It's safe enough." Even as he said it, Alex knew he didn't sound convincing.

"What does the Foreign Office say?" She was on her phone, checking as she spoke.

"High threat from terrorism."

"Then you can't go."

"The tourist areas are fine. Along the Nile and Sharm el-Sheikh aren't included in the warning."

They ate their pizza in silence for a while. She continued to check the Internet.

Finally, she said, "So you will only go to the safe areas. Nowhere else."

"Just the safe areas, I promise." Her concern made him feel good. "Thanks," he said. "I'm touched that you care."

"It's more than that, Alex." She shook her head. "If you're going to Egypt, then I'm coming with you."

Chapter 38

Uncle Seth's Bentley glided to a halt at Heathrow, the scent of new leather mingling with the lingering aroma of old cigars. He stepped out and hugged his niece, murmuring something in Yiddish that Alex couldn't catch. When he turned to Alex, his face was a portrait of concern.

"Take good care of her, young man," he said, shaking Alex's hand. "She's my only niece and means the world to me."

Alex nodded, promising he would. Only then did Uncle Seth release his grip, get in his car and drive away.

After they checked in, Alex confessed, "Your uncle scares me a little."

Rebecca laughed. "He's just protective. I spent hours convincing him to let me come." She shrugged. "You'd hardly believe I was old enough to make my own decisions!"

They navigated through security, Rebecca still chatting about her uncle. "You know," Alex said, "it's funny he's called Seth. Seth was an Egyptian god."

"Really?"

"Yeah, the second son of Ra, the sun god. Cain and Abel's story was likely derived from the myth of Seth and Osiris."

She gave him a sceptical look. "Seriously? People have been killing their brothers for ages. Doesn't mean the stories are the same."

"Well, Lucifer's story has similarities too. Cast out of Heaven for being jealous, wanting to take over. Seth again."

"Thank goodness you didn't say that in front of my uncle. He'd never have let me come!"

The British Airways Boeing 787 taxied down the runway. Rebecca gripped Alex's hand as the plane took off, her knuckles white.

"I deal with this by knocking myself out using sleeping pills and diazepam. Took the diazepam half an hour ago, otherwise I wouldn't be calmly sitting here."

"Afraid of flying?"

"No, it's the old joke."

"What?"

"I'm afraid of crashing."

Alex tried to reassure her, but she wasn't interested. Instead, she handed him a piece of paper. "It's a contract. I won't publish anything unless you agree. Sign it."

Alex tried to protest but ended up signing. "Good," she said, satisfied. "Now talk to me. You told me the other night that I didn't know you."

"What would you like to know?"

"Tell me about your dad."

"He was from Aberdeen, a big football fan. I never showed any interest in football."

"Fond memories?"

Alex thought for a moment. "Giving me shoulder-carries. He used to make me put my arms in the air. He'd hold on tight to my legs and run really fast."

She smiled. "That's a trust thing."

Alex was remembering now and something he had forgotten popped into his mind. "One birthday I got a bike. I'd wanted a new bike for ages and had been shown the second-hand one I was going to get. But on my birthday, I was amazed to see a brand new one. It had front and back suspension. I was beside myself with joy. Dad also had a thing for castles, and we liked nothing more than finding a new castle to explore. Of course, his interest was historical whereas I used to play at being Highlander: Alex MacLure of the clan MacLure!"

"So, you were close, you and your dad?"

"Not really. Shortly after that we moved to Surrey. Dad was the accountant for a firm whose head office was in London. They needed him there, so we moved. It was a tough time. Money was short. Dad worked long hours and seemed to get more and more uptight. I didn't understand it at the time, how the stress can change you. I just remember him going from a fun dad to a grumpy old man with no time for his family. I was eleven. I went from a small, friendly school in Aberdeen to a huge comprehensive in Woking."

When the meal arrived, it included quails' eggs, and the flight attendant informed them it was a traditional Egyptian meal: quail meat and eggs were as common as chicken in the UK.

As they ate, Rebecca said, "You felt lost and alone."

He looked at her as though she could read his mind. Then he realised. Of course she'd understand. She was a student of psychology.

He said, "And then Andrew was born with muscular dystrophy. Unplanned too. It put a strain on everything. My parents started arguing a lot. Then Dad's company had financial troubles. They blamed him for everything. He was an honest man, couldn't take it. He hanged himself."

190

He took a slug of wine and looked at Rebecca. By the time he'd finished talking, the sleeping pills had kicked in.

She woke up with the landing announcement, gripping his hand again. They arrived in Cairo around 1am, stepping into the warm night air. They joined the queue for currency and visas, a smooth process except for the long wait for Rebecca's luggage.

At the exit, Alex spotted a wiry man with quick eyes. He held a sign bearing Alex's name.

"I am Marek, your friend," the man said, beaming as they approached. He shook their hands, then led them outside.

As they loaded their bags into a battered Hyundai, Alex thought he glimpsed a familiar face.

"Quick, in the car!" he urged. "There's a man by the exit. He just ducked back inside as our eyes met."

Marek jolted the car out of the space and sped around towards the barriers. To get there, they had to pass the airport exit.

Alex instinctively ducked down. "He's still there, watching!"

"Who is he?" Marek asked.

"I don't know. There's something familiar." Alex paused in thought and then looked at Rebecca. "My God, I think it's the man from the BMW!"

Rebecca stared back at the exit. "I think I see who you mean. Are you sure it's him?"

"No, but there's something—"

Doubt crossed her face. "Okay, maybe you're right, but if he's watching, then he's not following us."

"And I'll drive us very fast," Marek said rather too cheerfully for Alex's liking.

The car sped away from the airport and picked up a dual carriageway. Alex glanced behind twice, but realised it was impossible for him to judge if anyone was following. The way Marek drove, Alex guessed they were travelling at between 80 and 100 miles an hour. He tried to read the speedometer and was shocked to see it wasn't working. Marek began to chat like a tourist guide. He said something about the name of the road and that it went straight through Cairo and ended at the pyramids. Alex also heard him say something about a special hotel and then Muhammad Ali. Alex looked out of the window into the darkness. He made out the vague shape of a giant mosque and, straining to make sense of the dim images he could see, he began to relax. Perhaps it wasn't the BMW man. Perhaps he hadn't been watching them. Perhaps he was innocently waiting for someone or looking for a taxi.

Rebecca broke into his thoughts by saying, "So, Marek, do you have Arabic blood?"

"I am from Hungary, where my father's family come from, but my mother's side is originally from Egypt. I think this is why I became an Egyptologist. The Egyptian people are very friendly, but you must stay aware. Do not have your Western expectations." He looked over his shoulder at Alex and nodded as though he was saying something very significant. The road became more congested and Marek was forced to slow. As they came off the carriageway, a car with no lights cut them up. Marek did not react, and Alex quickly realised this style of driving was to be expected. A cyclist, with nothing but a torch in one hand, passed them on the kerbside, squeezing between parked cars and the moving traffic.

"Crazy!" Rebecca gasped.

Marek said, "There are almost twenty million people in Cairo. It is a big problem."

"What, do you mean it's all right for some to get killed?" A figure in black ran across the road, weaving between cars. "Whoa!"

Marek chuckled, "No, no, no! I mean there are so many people that it is very crowded, and drivers are very aware."

The roads became even more tangled with traffic and Alex noted that horns were sounded as single, short blasts as a warning rather than in anger. More people dodged between the cars, and he tried not to worry about them or the other vehicles that looked like they would hit but amazingly didn't.

Just when Alex felt like the journey would never end, Marek announced, "Ah, we're here."

He pulled up outside Hotel Victoria. From the outside the building was a five-storey block of salmon-pink. "I hope it is all right," he said, taking their bags out and again carrying Rebecca's. "The tourist hotels are very cheap, but I don't think you would like to stay there. There are, of course, the five-star hotels, but I don't think you would like to stay there either!"

From the outside, the hotel looked tired and dirty. If the tourist hotels were worse, then Alex judged they must be terrible. Yet, his concerns vanished when they entered the foyer: transported from a bygone era, stylish and not at all shabby.

Rebecca confirmed his impression. "It looks lovely… inside."

They checked in, Rebecca on the first floor, Alex on the opposite side, higher up.

Alex was desperate to talk about the research and joined Marek who had waited in the foyer.

"I've been through all the notes," Alex said. "It's an amazing discovery. Just incredible. You should get a prize for what you both found."

"Thank you, but let us find what it leads to first, Alex." Marek cleared his throat. "I think you have an expression in England: do not count your chickens until they are catched."

"Something like that," Alex acknowledged. "I'd like to go through your translations line by line. Not now, of course, but when you're ready."

"Of course. Tomorrow morning. Perhaps on the way."

"Where are we going?"

Marek looked across at him, confusion on his face. "I thought—"

"That I'd know where to look? To be honest, I don't know. I'm hoping that being here makes sense of the Map-Stone."

No one spoke for a moment and Alex felt awkward for whipping up the excitement without having a plan. "The clay tablets were found in Amarna, in Akhenaten's ancient city."

Marek nodded. "Yes, but the Map-Stone probably came from Tutankhamun's tomb in the Valley of the Kings."

Things suddenly crystallised in Alex's mind. The map led somewhere else. It wasn't a map to the Valley of the Kings. "The starting point has to be Amarna," he said assuredly.

Marek reached across and patted his shoulder. "Tell el-Amarna it is. I will book us a train for tomorrow afternoon. I'll book a train to Dairut. The trains are very bad, but don't worry, I will get a first-class train, and it will be very comfortable." He grinned. "We'll stay in Deir Mawas which is near the ancient city. We should have time in the morning and then perhaps on the train to look at the images from the funerary block, no?"

After Marek left, Alex accompanied Rebecca to her room.

"Double-lock your door and jam a chair up against it," he advised her. When she looked curious, he added: "I'm making sure you're safe—I promised your uncle."

In his room, Alex followed his own advice. He settled down but couldn't sleep, his mind racing. Should he call Rebecca?

Before he could decide, there was a knock on the door.

"Who is it?" he asked.

"Me," Rebecca whispered.

He let her in. She'd brought wine, and they drank from plastic cups.

"Nervous? Excited?" she asked.

"Excited but uneasy. Meeting Marek wasn't what I expected."

"I meant about me being here." She laughed awkwardly. "I'm sorry about what happened between us," she said, placing a hand on his thigh. "It's best we remain friends."

"Yes," he agreed, but their lips met anyway. Minutes later, she was out of her clothes, and he discovered she wore nothing underneath.

Chapter 39

The cigarette-smoke-filled room produced dim blue-grey patches of light. There were three chairs and two men. The young man in one of the chairs made animated gestures between rapid puffs on his cigarette. The other man was impassive and had a walking stick propped against the arm of his chair. He wore a hat and his cigar smoke curled around its brim.

He shook his head at a complaint and was about to interrupt the younger man when there was a knock on the door.

After a hesitation, the younger of the two stood and answered it.

"Yes?"

"Brotherhood."

Recognising the password, the young man opened the door. "Joachim," he said in polite greeting, although both men knew it was merely out of necessity. This new man was the one codenamed Fox but there was no need for secret names here.

"Hello, Wael," Joachim acknowledged the younger man, then walked to the chairs and stood behind one.

The senior man leaned on his cane as though about to rise. But it was just for show and he simply nodded, welcome.

He said, "Please sit." His voice was thick with an accent, which Joachim reckoned the old man put on for effect. He could speak good English when he wanted to. The gruff accent gave him gravitas.

When they were all seated, Joachim said, "Our friend is nervous."

"I was just talking about that," Wael said. "It's no wonder he's nervous after you arranged for him to be chased and have his house burgled." He looked from Joachim to the old man and back. "And you scared him with guns!"

"It's worked, hasn't it?" Joachim shrugged dismissively. "And do you have any information about the map?"

"No, but—"

"Then stop criticising me and do your job, you idiot."

"How dare you? You insult my family…"

"Enough!" For the first time, the old man showed anger by gripping his walking stick and banging it on the floor. "You,"—he pointed the stick at Wael—"what do we need to do to convince the Englishman?"

Wael shook his head. "I have no idea."

Phlegm rattled in the old man's throat and he sat forward. "Do you have access to the map?"

"No. I think it's in his head."

Joachim groaned.

Wael said, "What we need to do is get him to draw it."

The old man nodded thoughtfully. "This is what we will do. Joachim, you will travel with them to Dairut."

Wael began to protest but was silenced by a look before the old man continued: "To be clear, Mr MacLure must not feel threatened. He needs to be at ease and solve the map. Is that understood?"

Wael immediately said, "Yes."

"Joachim?"

"Yes, sir. But if I can't get the map?"

The old man lit a fresh cigar with rapid sucks and then a long draw. After he had blown out the flame, phlegm rattled as he spoke. "Then we will use your original plan." He looked at the young man, nodding slowly. "If we can't obtain the map from Mr MacLure using peaceful means, then I think you are quite capable of extracting the information."

Chapter 40

The stories of Yanhamu swirled around Alex's head all night, like restless phantoms refusing to let him sleep. In his dreams, he was the ancient Egyptian, wandering through corridors of sand and time, seeking his sister.

When Alex finally awoke, the sun was piercing through a gap in the curtains. Rebecca wasn't beside him, though he had no memory of her leaving. His head pounded like he had jetlag, even though the time difference was only two hours. With a groan, he stumbled into the bathroom and stepped into the shower, letting the water pummel him back to life. By the time he was dressed, it was already midday.

He picked up the phone and called Rebecca's room. No answer.

As he finished buttoning his shirt, he noticed an envelope slipped under the door. Expecting a message from Rebecca, he was surprised to find a note from Marek.

I need to finish a review of an MRI scan for my professor, so I'll be delayed a day or so.

Inside the envelope were two train tickets and the address of a hotel in Deir Mawas.

Alex found Rebecca in the lobby, nursing a miniature cup of what looked like black mud. He leaned over to kiss her, but she turned at the last moment, his kiss landing on her cheek.

"It's a Muslim country," she said, raising an eyebrow. "We must be discreet."

"How are you feeling?" Alex asked, rubbing his temples.

"I didn't sleep much. You?"

"Too well, I think." He grimaced. "I don't know whether it's jetlag or what, but I only just woke up and I feel like the walking dead."

She poured more of the mud-like coffee into her cup and handed it to him. "Drink this. You'll feel better."

He swallowed the glutinous liquid with effort. After a few gulps, he told Rebecca about Marek's note and showed her the tickets. "We have three and a half hours before our train leaves. After we eat, I want to go to the Egyptian Museum."

"Oh?" She raised an eyebrow.

"I think we should check out our friend—just as a precaution."

"You're suspicious about something?"

Alex pressed his fingers around his right eye socket where the headache seemed to have found a home. "There was the thing about the research... he seemed nervous. And he had shifty eyes, didn't you think?"

"Oh, Alex, you're being paranoid! He was Ellen's colleague... And did you see his teeth?"

"His teeth?"

"They were discoloured. Heavy smoker, and we didn't see him smoke once. Probably nicotine withdrawal— being kind to us non-smokers."

They grabbed a map of the city from the concierge and headed out. The acrid air hit them immediately, and the road was packed with slow-moving cars. After a short walk, they found a café bustling with locals and a sprinkling of tourists and sat at a table beside the road. Rebecca randomly picked a plate of falafel and crudités, which Alex was relieved to find looked edible.

After another strong cup of coffee, washed down with a bottle of water, Alex began to feel human again. The waiter quoted a price that seemed unsure, much more than Alex expected. He handed over the cash, reminding himself to agree on prices beforehand.

They located the museum on the map, near the Nile.

"Too far to walk," Rebecca noted.

They flagged down a taxi.

"How much to the museum?" Alex asked.

"Fifty," the driver replied.

"Twenty Egyptian," Alex countered.

The driver shook his head. "Forty is best price."

"Thirty is *my* best price."

The driver shook his head. "Forty."

Alex turned away. "Let's try another."

The driver called after them, "Okay. Okay. Thirty."

As they climbed into the backseat, the driver added, "To the museum, thirty each."

"No! Thirty total."

"Okay. Okay."

The ride was slow, weaving through side streets. Alex glanced at Rebecca, who seemed perfectly content. He tried to shake off the worry they were being taken somewhere to be mugged. Finally, they reached Tahrir Square and saw the imposing museum building. The driver stopped by security barriers guarded by armed soldiers.

"Forty," the driver said, grinning cheekily.

Alex handed over thirty pounds.

"Tip?"

Alex laughed and gave him another ten.

"You need a guide?" the driver asked as they climbed out.

"No thanks," Alex replied, and they walked away to join the queue for tickets.

The adjacent road was crammed with coaches, and security men shouted at the drivers, who shouted back. Alex wondered if they were being told to move along but didn't seem to be friendly exchanges.

"Is it safe?" Rebecca asked.

Alex shrugged. "I hope so! Let's just keep out of the way of anyone with a gun."

They filed through a detector, Rebecca's handbag checked, and then queued for entry tickets. The path through the garden was littered with remnants of statues and broken temple blocks.

A few drops of rain made them look up.

"Now that's one thing I didn't expect," Alex said, then immediately felt foolish. *Of course it rains in Egypt—just not very often.* He smiled awkwardly. "I mean, let's hope it isn't a downpour."

They approached the entrance, blocked by turnstiles. Alex asked someone checking tickets. "Excuse me, I'm looking for a researcher called Marek Borevsek. The man didn't look up from his task.

"Could you tell me where I might find…?"

Still no response.

Rebecca spoke to a vendor selling bottled drinks. Then called Alex over. "The offices are underneath. There's an admin entrance at the end." She pointed to the third entrance.

They walked past the second entrance and found the admin entrance. At the top of the steps, through an open door, was a full-body turnstile with a security man at a podium.

"I'm here to see Marek Borevsek," Alex said.

The man squinted, cigarette in his mouth, then looked down, presumably at a register. "He's not here."

"What? Not here at all?" Rebecca asked.

"No. Not here today. He works at the hospital."

Alex passed the map through the bars. "Could you show us where?"

The man marked a spot with a red pen. "Cleopatra Hospital," he said, pointing to Arabic writing.

They thanked him, exited the museum grounds, and immediately caught a taxi.

The driver spoke little English but understood the slip of paper from the security man. Forty minutes later, they were outside the hospital.

"That was cheaper than the first taxi and more than twice the distance!" Alex marvelled.

Rebecca said, "Let's hope this is the right place."

Inside the hospital, they saw signs in English and followed directions to the radiology department.

They found a door labelled "Ancient Egyptian Research Department, Cairo Museum." Rebecca and Alex exchanged glances and pushed it open. Inside, another sign above a door read "C.T. Unit." They rang for attention, and a young woman in blue scrubs answered.

"We're looking for Marek Borevsek," Alex said.

"Oh yes," she smiled and disappeared through the door.

"My friends!" Marek appeared, shaking their hands warmly. "Sorry to keep you waiting."

Alex glanced over Marek's shoulder, but saw nothing. "What are you working on? Can we take a look?"

Marek shook his head. "I'm sorry, but it's sensitive. We're lucky to have this access." He gestured to a room with an MRI scanner and a body on a table. A man with a machine gun stood to the side.

203

"Security," Marek explained. "We're scanning unnamed mummies, trying to identify them. I'm sorry I can't join you on the train. I'll catch up later tomorrow."

"Wow!" Rebecca said. "I told you I'd seen the Queen Hatshepsut documentary, right?"

"Shame we couldn't have a closer look," Alex said as they left.

"But you're happier now?"

"Yeah. I felt a bit unnerved by his appearance. I expected someone who looked eastern European." He held up a hand when she started to speak. "Yes, I know that's unreasonable. Names don't necessarily explain appearances, but yesterday... yesterday, I didn't like how he didn't acknowledge my involvement in the breakthrough with the Amarna Letters. I'm sure Ellen will have told him."

Rebecca grinned. "In history, how often do researchers complain that someone stole their idea or didn't acknowledge them?"

"All the time."

"And you're guilty of pride, Alex MacLure. Don't worry, I'll tell the true story."

"It's what we find that matters." Alex pushed his glasses up with one finger and nodded to himself. "Come on. Back to the hotel, freshen up, and then we've got a train to catch."

Chapter 41

Ramses Station pulsed with the barely contained chaos that only Cairo could muster. The twenty platforms were a storm of movement, people crisscrossing in every direction, shouting, bartering, embracing. No one checked tickets at the entrance—an observation Alex found fascinating.

"You know, historically, train stations were always liminal spaces," he mused, dodging a man carrying a precariously stacked crate of chickens. "Places of transition. People come and go, identities shift. It's—"

"Alex," Rebecca cut in, adjusting her bag, "now is not the time for a lecture."

"Right, sorry," Alex said, blinking and refocusing. "Platform eight. That's where we need to be."

They navigated the throng, finally arriving at their platform just in time to see a train roll in. It was solid blue, unmarked, its metal body scarred with dents. The windows were so coated in grime they were nearly opaque. Something felt… off.

Alex tilted his head, studying the train. "That's interesting. The lack of identification suggests it's not a commercial passenger train. And those window bars—wait, are those cells?"

Through the filth, glimpses of metal benches, chains, and shadowy figures came into view. A prison transport.

The train stopped only briefly, doors never opening, then rattled away into the heat haze.

Alex exhaled. "Well, that was unsettling."

Rebecca gave him a look. "We're sure that wasn't our train, right?"

"Unless we've been secretly sentenced to hard labour, I think we're safe."

Ten minutes later, another train arrived. This time, an armed porter barked at them, "Second class!"

The doors swung inward, releasing a blast of heat and cigarette smoke. Faces were pressed against the windows, passengers crammed in so tightly some were still clinging to the door handles as the train started moving. The doors didn't close. They couldn't. More people were trying to board.

Alex adjusted his glasses and grimaced. "You know, the structural integrity of that entryway is—"

Rebecca groaned. "Shall we just get on?"

"Not our train," Alex said, then stiffened. His gaze flicked to a vending cabinet near the platform wall. A man standing, his posture overly casual. When Alex glanced his way, the man deliberately looked away. Not suspicious on its own—but the grey hoodie he wore was. In Cairo? In this heat?

"We're being watched," he murmured.

Rebecca frowned. "Where?"

"Behind you. Wall. Grey hoodie."

She risked a glance, then turned back, eyes widening slightly. "Definitely out of place."

Alex chewed his lip. "Stay with the bags. I need to confirm something."

He moved, not with the confident stride of a spy, but with the kind of awkward deliberation of someone mentally mapping every exit. He circled the platform, using the crowd as cover, then doubled back. The man in the hoodie was shifting position, scanning from Rebecca to the exit.

Watching her. Looking for me.

Alex took a breath, edged around a waiting room, and caught a flash of pale skin under the hood. Familiar. Too familiar. His mind connected the dots in a sudden, blinding realisation.

He lunged, grabbing the hood and yanking it back. "Pete?!"

Pete's face twisted from shock to something resembling guilty resignation. "Hey... er... hi, Alex."

Alex gaped. "What the hell are you doing here?"

"Er… watching you?"

"Following!"

"Fine, yes. Following you."

Alex's brain kicked into overdrive. Pete had been involved in the break-in. He'd helped forge the plan. He'd taken the Isis puzzle. And now—

"You know Ellen hid the ceremonial block, don't you?" Alex challenged. "It's at Highclere, not Egypt."

Pete gave a humourless chuckle. "Oh, Alex. I know it's not just about a missing chunk of stone."

Alex swallowed. "How? How do you know this?"

Pete's smirk deepened. "I know more than you think."

Rebecca appeared at Alex's side, eyes narrowing at Pete. "You!"

"Yes, me," Pete said breezily. "Following you two across continents. Honestly, I deserve some credit."

"He's been following us. He must know," Alex said.

Pete grinned wolfishly at Rebecca. "More than Alex realises. I'm part of the team."

Alex stared. "What?"

Another train pulled up. Rebecca and Alex grabbed their bags. As they moved, Pete followed.

"You don't think that East End gang really planned the burglary, do you? Ha! I did that when Ellen told me she'd found something. Here's the deal: let me in on this treasure hunt, or I tell the police you arranged the break-in and forced me to help."

They eyed the train—it was another second-class one. Still not theirs.

Rebecca said, "I'm confused. Did you just confess to organising the burglary?"

"Yes, but the police won't know that, and my statement will make them question everything again." He jerked his hood from Alex's grip.

Rebecca looked at Alex. "What do you think? Is he telling the truth?"

Alex rubbed his temples, thinking. "So, was it you or your thugs who trashed my flat?"

Guards called and waved people to board. Rebecca pointed along the platform. "Look over there."

A tall man in a black suit stood near the exit, staring straight at them. "The guy from the BMW. You were right, he *was* at the airport!"

Rebecca nodded. "One of yours then, Pete?"

"What? Who?"

The man started walking quickly towards them. Alex felt a shiver. Pete was staring too. "Pete?"

"Never seen him before!"

The man started moving. Then running towards them.

"Oh, this is bad," Alex muttered.

Rebecca shoved him toward the train. "Get on!"

Alex hesitated, transfixed by the approaching figure. A gun? Did he have a gun? Why wasn't he running in a more—

Rebecca jumped onto the train, forcing her way through the crush of passengers. The train started moving. Alex was still trying to grasp the situation when Rebecca yelled, "For God's sake, Alex!"

That snapped him into motion. He grabbed the rail, swung himself up. Pete threw his bag in and leapt for the opposite handle.

A woman on the platform screamed.

"Alex!" Pete yelled.

Alex turned—Pete was dangling by one hand. The man in the suit had reached him, gripping his collar, trying to yank him off the train.

Pete's eyes bulged with desperation. His fingers slipped, and he let go. Alex lunged, grabbed Pete's jacket, and pulled.

The train jerked, the man lost his grip, and Pete tumbled inside.

Alex pushed to a window, gasping for breath, watching the man on the platform. He wasn't chasing. Just... staring after them, as if he had all the time in the world.

Alex shivered. "Well, that's unnerving."

Pete groaned from the floor. "I hate Cairo."

Rebecca shook her head at Alex. "Next time, less thinking, more reacting."

Alex nodded, still catching his breath. "Right," he said. "Got it." Although, his mind was still spinning with Pete's involvement and BMW man and…

"You," Rebecca said glaring at Pete and snapping Alex back to their situation. "You are *not* coming with us!"

Chapter 42

The train rumbled on tracks that creaked and groaned as it slowly picked up speed. Rebecca's eyes bored into Pete. "We get off at the next station," she declared, her voice cold and final. "You, on the other hand, are staying on board."

Pete laughed, a harsh, mirthless sound. "As I said, lady, I know too much. I can make Alex look guilty. In fact, for all you know, he *is* guilty. I'm part of this whether you like it or not."

"You've got nothing," Alex shot back.

Pete shoved a fellow passenger aside, reaching into his bag. "It's all in my notebook. The whole sordid truth."

Next time, less thinking, more reacting. Alex moved to grab the bag, but Pete's hand whipped out, striking Alex across the face. At the same moment, the train jolted and began to slow. Rebecca seized the opportunity, spinning Pete around and slamming him against the carriage wall, twisting his arm behind him.

The other passengers scattered as she muscled him into the lavatory. Moments later, she emerged alone.

The train was now pulling alongside platforms at Giza, Cairo's second station.

"We need to get off and switch trains," Rebecca said. "Our train is bound to stop here as well."

Alex nodded dumbly.

"Are you okay?" she asked, looking into his eyes.

He took a deep breath, feeling the weight of many eyes on him. "Yes."

"Do you have the notebook?"

He held up Pete's bag.

The train stopped, and Rebecca motioned for Alex to follow her, saying, "Keep an eye out for BMW-man."

They moved along the platform, hugging the wall until they found a spot with a good view, yet shielded from most onlookers. Only one security guard could see them clearly.

Alex clutched his chest. "God, my heart's racing."

A minute later, another train arrived at their platform. The engine was the same dirty petrol blue as the others, but the first-class carriages were cream with green stripes.

An announcement blared in Arabic, followed by a list of places in English, ending with "Dairut."

"Our train? Only an hour late."

Most of the passengers boarding were backpackers. Alex and Rebecca waited until the crowd thinned, then ran to the open door, jumped in, and shut it behind them. Rebecca watched the platform until the train started moving.

"No sign of anyone suspicious," she said.

They found their seats in a compartment. Alex had to ask a fellow passenger to identify seats twenty-five and twenty-six, as the numbers were handwritten in Arabic.

Alex held up Pete's bag. "What did you do to him?"

"Helped him sleep for thirty minutes or so." When Alex frowned, she added: "Like you, I had some martial arts training. Uncle Seth insisted before I was allowed to go to Israel alone. Self-defence, really, but I know how to make someone go to sleep." She shook her head at Alex's concerned look. "Don't worry about him. He wasn't your friend. He was using you."

"I guess."

211

"There's no guessing about it."

Alex opened the bag, revealing mostly clothes, Pete's passport, and a tatty black notebook.

Rebecca held out her hand. "Let me see."

Alex handed it to her and tucked Pete's bag under the seat. He'd point it out to a guard and say someone left it behind. Hopefully, Pete would get his passport back.

The train finally pulled away. Through a window that looked sandblasted, they watched Cairo's outskirts fade. Unfinished houses with concrete-encased metal rods on their roofs passed by. Rugs dangled from windows, and a bicycle hung from a ledge.

"Look at that!" Alex pointed out. "Saves space, I suppose."

Rebecca didn't look up; she was engrossed in the notebook.

Soon, they were in the countryside, running alongside an irrigation channel, heading south. Fields, occasional buildings, palm trees, and distant sandstone mountains flashed by. Sugar cane seemed to be the principal crop. Alex noticed pickups overloaded with cane, and bony donkeys struggling under heavy loads. A dead donkey lay in a ditch, and Alex was glad Rebecca wasn't looking.

The train alternated between bursts of speed and inexplicable stops. An Australian passenger remarked that the track's poor condition caused the slow sections to avoid derailment.

Rebecca finally set the notebook down. "Well," she said, a strange glint in her eyes.

"Well what?"

"All has been revealed." She tapped the book. "Your friend Pete kept detailed notes. Lucky for you."

"Stop being cryptic and tell me what you've learned."

She smiled. "First, it confirms you weren't involved in the break-in at Highclere. Pete planned everything, even hiring a gang for the job. He used his contacts from the security firm he works for. He was playing both sides—working on Ellen to find out about the treasure while hoping for a payoff from the burglars if they succeeded."

"You said 'first'. Is there more?"

"There's a list of items from the exhibition. He marked which were genuine and which were fake, like Tutankhamun's headdress."

Alex reached for the book. Rebecca handed it over, but didn't immediately let go. "This is gold dust. Great news for you—it proves Pete, not you, planned the burglary. And for me, it's a story with a different angle. It might even be award-winning." As he opened the book, she added, "So let me have it back because I'm guarding it with my life."

He grinned and began reading Pete's meticulous plans and notes. Then he decided to look at the tablets again and decode more of Yanhamu's story.

He found a section about Yanhamu, an officer in the Black Egyptian army. He was a young man now, working on interpreting enemy communications. He also found a section where Yanhamu had the opportunity to poison the man known as Scorpion.

Alex's breath caught as he translated: 'the man had spoiled and killed my sister'.

"She died," Alex said.

"Sorry? Who died?" Rebecca asked. She looked like she'd been sleeping. Hours had flown by, and the sun was now low in the sky.

He gave Rebecca an update—the fragments of Yanhamu's story that he'd decoded.

A waiter interrupted and offered dinner. Which turned out to be various breads and a cup of Nescafé. Alex asked for wine and earned a scowl from the waiter.

"No sense of humour, that one."

"Muslim country with strict rules. But you did it because of the story. You were right before. It is emotional."

As they ate, Rebecca said, "So tell me again. This story is hidden in the text of the clay tablets?"

"The Amarna Letters, yes. It was diplomatic correspondence between Egypt and its vassal states from the 14th century BCE. See, most people assume they'd be in hieroglyphs, because, well—Egypt—but they're actually written in cuneiform, Akkadian script."

Rebecca frowned. "Why cuneiform?"

Alex grinned, delighted by the question. "Because Akkadian was the diplomatic lingua franca of the time. Egyptian officials had to learn it to communicate with foreign rulers. It's like how Latin was used in European diplomacy for centuries."

She gave him a sceptical look as he scrawled a series of wedge-like symbols. "And the code?"

"Ah! That's the fun part." He tapped the napkin. "Look here—these seemingly random numbers along the side? They aren't just scribal notations. They're positioning markers, guiding the reader to specific words within the text, creating a hidden message. Kind of like an ancient book cipher."

Rebecca studied the napkin, brow furrowed. "Numbers? I have no idea what I'm looking at."

Alex deflated slightly. "Right. Okay. Imagine taking the first letter of every third word in a letter, but only if a certain marginal note is present. It's a layered system, like encoding within encoding."

Rebecca groaned. "I think my brain just melted."

Alex gave her a sheepish smile. "It makes more sense if you see the full text." He started writing animatedly and she placed a hand over his, stopping him.

"Another time."

"*This* is interesting," he said persisting as he drew an upside-down pyramid. "It showed up in some marginalia on a few Amarna texts."

"Okay?" she said uncertainly.

He continued by drawing a right-side-up pyramid over the first.

"The Sar of David," she said.

"A pyramid symbolises God's power coming down to Earth, and an inverted pyramid is man reaching up to Heaven. Together, they form the Star of David. Ancient Egyptians used the hexagram to represent Sirius, aligned with the pyramids of Giza. One of the Great Pyramid's shafts points to Sirius, guiding the pharaoh to the afterlife, believed to be in the night sky, in the constellation of Orion, where Osiris dwelt. The belt aligns with Sirius, linked to Isis."

"It's all very interesting, but there's a long gap before becoming a Jewish symbol."

"Exactly!" Alex beamed. "Which is why it's so weird that it's on the clay tablets. Some scholars think it might have been added much later by a medieval scribe. Others theorise it was just a geometric motif that meant something else entirely at the time. Either way, it's a mystery."

Rebecca shook her head. "You really do get excited about this stuff, don't you?"

"More than is socially acceptable, I suppose." Alex grinned and leaned back. "But come on—what's life without a little ancient intrigue?"

She poured water into their cups. "Let's not talk about something else. Something I can follow... If you become famous, what will you do?"

"Famous?"

"For solving an ancient puzzle. I don't just mean decoding an ancient Egyptian's story about losing his sister. That's all incredible but... I sense you'll crack a big mystery of some kind, someday. Maybe find what the map leads to."

He smiled. "I don't know. I hadn't thought that far. I don't think I'll make a fortune. If there's anything valuable at the end of this, I'm happy for it to stay in Egypt. I'll be proud to see it in the Cairo Museum." He pondered. "I guess fame is its own reward."

She checked her watch. "Almost three hours to go. I could sleep for England!"

He removed his glasses and rubbed his face, suddenly feeling fatigued.

Rebecca said, "We arrive after ten. I'm going to catch a few more zeds."

Explaining the encryption to Rebecca had enthused him again. There were other tablets that he hadn't started on, that probably included Yanhamu's story. Alex opened his laptop and began.

A man standing over the table made Alex jump. Just a waiter clearing the tables. Alex nodded politely at the man and resumed his translation.

Chapter 43

After the waiter had cleared the trays, he stopped at the next compartment and nodded at a watchful passenger. Joachim stood and looked through the waste on the trays. He lifted the napkin with the symbols and walked to the next carriage. Pulling out his mobile phone, he pressed a speed-dial number.

"Yes," a gravelly voice answered.

"They've been discussing symbols," Joachim said, his voice expressing his excitement. "And I'm looking at some right now. MacLure wrote them on a napkin."

"And just left them for you to find?"

"You're dubious?"

"I'm realistic. What are the symbols?"

Joachim described what he was looking at.

The old man was silent.

"Gershom?" He used the old man's fraternal name and prepared for a rebuke.

The old man either didn't pick up on it or didn't mind. He said, "The last one worries me... the Star of David."

"If it is from the map, then the clue may not be as cryptic as we suspected."

Gershom scoffed, "It is not from the map. The star symbol is far too modern to have come from ancient Egypt. No, my worry is that if it came from the artifact then it may be a fake."

"Or perhaps MacLure has made a mistake."

"Perhaps." The old man coughed and Joachim waited for him to speak again.

Gershom said, "There is another possibility—Mr MacLure is on to us and playing a silly game."

"Then I will put a gun to his head and just get him to tell me the truth."

"No. You know we promised no killing, Joachim."

"I won't kill him, just threaten."

"And if the threat doesn't work? No, Joachim, you will wait and only use that as a last resort. You will follow him again tomorrow and let me know as soon as you learn something more."

They ended the connection. Joachim stared at the row of symbols and thought about what the old man had said. Tomorrow, he decided. Tomorrow is a day that could change the world.

Chapter 44

"Alex, we're here." Rebecca's voice cut through his concentration. He tore his eyes from the laptop screen to the dimly lit train carriage.

"We've arrived in Dairut. Time to get off," she said.

He straightened his seat with a jerk and put his head in his hands for a moment. The quick movements had caused a throb behind his right eye. He should have used the journey to sleep rather than get engrossed in the translation.

Rebecca was already standing, urging him to hurry. Alex rose gingerly, collecting his bag, and followed her onto the platform.

"What next?" Rebecca asked as they watched the last passengers disembark. The train pulled away, leaving them alone in the dim light.

Alex unfolded a note from Marek. "We're to take a taxi to Deir Mawas. Nefertiti hotel. We'll have to find a taxi—"

A man, who had been reading a newspaper, sprang to his feet.

"MacLure?"

"Yes."

The man grinned, folding his paper. "I driver. I take you and wife."

"Not wife," Alex corrected, but the man only looked confused. "Fine. Deir Mawas?"

The driver nodded eagerly and led them to an old silver Nissan estate, loading their bags into the back. Alex hesitated.

"How much?"

"No, no. No price. All paid."

Rebecca shrugged and climbed in. They buckled up, exchanging relieved glances as the seat belts clicked into place.

The driver glanced back. "English? Where from?"

"London," they replied in unison.

"Yes, London. Arsenal. Chelsea. Manchester United! Lovely jubbly."

Alex found himself nodded off in the car. Fortunately, within ten minutes they were stopping outside a small hotel. Despite the grand name—the Nefertiti—it appeared old and quiet. Off the main tourist trail, Alex figured that only serious explorers ventured this way.

He planned to get back to the translations, but once he had checked in and was in his room, Alex flopped on the bed. Within minutes he was dreaming about an ancient Egyptian called Yanhamu.

Over breakfast, Rebecca had found Tell el-Amarna on the map. They were almost there—a mile or so, then across the Nile.

"We don't need to wait for Marek to visit the ruins, right?" she had asked as they ate. The atmosphere seemed strange: no other residents and at least five staff for each of them.

"No. He's already organised our trip here."

"So what was on the block that Lord Carnarvon took—the one Ellen hid?"

"Symbols that form a kind of map."

"Right, I get that, but if I'm to help..."

Alex rubbed his eyes. She was right. Of course she was. Ellen had identified what she thought was important and he felt sure it wouldn't make sense until they were here.

He sketched a rectangle, adding sides to give it dimension. "This is the funerary block."

"Yes."

"The ancient Egyptians mastered disguising language and double meaning. They hid messages in pictures too: their two-dimensional drawings could often mean three-dimensions." He drew a square with concentric lines. "I think this represents the tomb, with steps here and here, and a hidden section."

"The tomb we're looking for?"

"Yes, that's my assumption. And the other markings will lead us there. This map needs a starting point which we may not realise until we see it. Which is why it's so important that we're here."

"You asked my uncle about special numbers."

"Ellen was looking for them, I think. And they feature on the stone." Separately, Alex drew what looked like a portcullis. "It's the number eight in cuneiform. And this"—he drew a line with twelve dots along it—"is twelve. Ancient Egyptian builders used a rope with twelve equally spaced knots. Twelve is made up of three, four, five which forms triangle."

"What about forty?"

"Interesting that your uncle said it was often used to imply a large number or period... which could be the case, but for a map, I think it would need to be very specific." He drew four hoops. "A hoop would symbolise the number ten and there are four of them, one each vertical side. There are also right-angled triangles which appear to have sides three, four and five—the smallest and most well-known Pythagorean triple, and as I said, it can be formed from the builders twelve knotted rope. There's another triangle... different, but it might just be an ancient imperfection. It's impossible to know what's an original marking and any subsequent scratches and dents... Sorry am I going too fast?"

Rebecca smiled. "A little. So I'm to look out for anything that might symbolise those numbers. Anything else? You mentioned gold and treasure."

"The Amarna Letters secret message includes 'treasure' but the block has the symbol for gold." He drew and arch with droplets below.

"Looks like a pearl neckless," she said.

"Right! And there's this..." Alex sketched a bird in flight.

"An airplane?"

He tried again. "A bird. There are four of them. They're geese, I suspect. Which can symbolise Geb, the god of the earth. Also, wealth..." Alex shrugged. "Fertility and prosperity, especially when relating to the afterlife. Also rebirth. So the birds fit with the idea that we're looking for a tomb. And the flag—"

"Flag?"

"The other triangle might be part of a pennant. Often the symbol of a god or royal authority. But more interestingly may be used to refer to a location. Although a flag on its own won't be very useful. So keep your eyes open for a the numbers in any form, a square with concentric lines—although I think this is the tomb—possibly right-angled triangles..."

"And four geese," she said but was looking away, towards reception. "Our drivers just arrived."

A moment later, the man walked into the breakfast room and greeted them with a worried expression. "Not good," he said, pointing upwards.

Alex wondered if he was suggesting the hotel wasn't up to scratch but Rebecca understood.

"The weather?" she guessed.

The driver nodded, hands mimicking the weighing of the air. "Wind. Not good."

Rebecca unfolded a map. "Can you take us to Tell el-Amarna?"

The driver's face was full of doubt.

"We've travelled a long way," Rebecca said. "Please."

"Okay." He waved for them to follow, and they were soon in his taxi, speeding out of the town.

"Anything else?" Rebecca asked. "Geese, the gold symbol, triangles, possibly flags, the gate thing that means eight. And the lines making a square with other squares inside?"

He shook his head. "Nothing that's clear. Bits of hieroglyphs... except... maybe a spoon." He shook his head. "Spoon-shaped but indistinct. Maybe part of something else. Maybe nothing."

The Nissan jolted as they left the main road, thundering along a potholed minor road. Alex half joked about their driver's racing skills.

From the front, the driver laughed. "Formula One. Hamilton. Yes, that is me. Ahmed Hamilton!" He over-steered around a bend and halted at a moored ferry.

A man in a galabia approached, face wrapped in a scarf. The wind howled as he spoke to the driver.

Ahmed Hamilton wound up the window after a brief animated conversation. He looked back at the passengers, weighed the air again and said, "Sand."

Alex pointed to the ferry. "Let's go."

The driver shrugged, pulled across the hardstanding and onto the ferry.

There were no gates at either end, just drive-on, drive-off ramps, and Alex estimated it would take eight cars, maybe four trucks. Their Nissan was the only vehicle and, as soon as they stopped, the diesel funnel belched smoke and they began to trundle across the hundred-metre gap.

They crossed the Nile, the town of Tell el-Amarna looming through the sandy blur.

In the town, Hamilton stopped and briefly scanned left and right as though looking or waiting for someone. No one appeared, and after a few seconds, he continued.

Alex handed the driver a note. "The Great Temple."

Before breakfast, Alex had managed to get on to the Internet and copied out the layout of the ruins that were once the great city of Akhetaten. It had been five kilometres long and housed over twenty thousand people. The modern town was just beyond the northern reaches of the old city and the taxi driver followed the road east out of town before turning south on a dusty track and following the boundary between farmland and desert. A large modern cemetery ran along their left and ended abruptly. Beyond were the ruins of a city destroyed more than three thousand years ago.

"Here." The driver stopped and handed them scarves for the wind and sand.

Alex and Rebecca braced against the hot, dry blast. The temple's enormity took Alex's breath away. Rebecca's eyes were wide with wonder.

She placed her head close to his so he could hear. "I never imagined I could feel this way about ruins," she shouted. "It's both awe-inspiring and devastatingly sad."

"This temple was vast and open," he said. They walked over walls and into sections, past offering tables, but nothing matched Alex's diagram.

They returned to the shelter of the Nissan. "Is there another palace?" Alex asked.

The driver beamed and drove them to another set of ruins. Alex quickly counted the pillar stumps.

"Forty. There are forty."

Excitedly, they looked around the site, searching for any of the other symbols they'd discussed over breakfast.

They found nothing.

There was also nothing to see at two other locations, one hidden now under a corn field.

Alex felt the tension knot in his shoulders as he stood in the last barren ruins, the wind whipping sand around them. He glanced at Rebecca, her eyes searching his face for reassurance.

"Let's go," he said, his voice barely audible over the howling wind.

The driver turned, his expression a mix of confusion and readiness. "Hotel?"

"No, the Royal Wadi." Alex pointed towards the distant hills. "Take us there."

Chapter 45

The driver grinned, the corners of his mouth twitching with an eager anticipation as he swung the Nissan around to head south once more.

Rebecca touched Alex's arm. "Are you all right?"

"Akhenaten's tomb," he muttered. "It may be too obvious, but we should check his tomb here. We have to see it. Since we're here, we absolutely must see it."

They drove back through the town, picked up the main road, and followed it towards the hills and into a winding valley. The road seemed newly paved, with drainage channels indicating recent improvements.

"Wadi means riverbed, right?" Rebecca asked, breaking the silence.

Alex nodded. "Yes, but it's been dry for centuries, even in Akhenaten's time. This was his version of the Valley of the Kings, radical for its eastern orientation to greet the rising sun rather than facing the underworld in the west. There are five royal tombs here, though only one was completed."

They drove deeper into the valley until the road ended in a small parking area. Four other cars were already there, their occupants milling about in the distance. Alex and Rebecca got out and followed a well-worn path into a side valley, where the wind's fury lessened, providing a momentary respite.

At the ticket booth, two men in black uniforms with carbines scowled at them. Alex couldn't help but comment, "The Antiquities Service—charming as ever. Carter must have loved dealing with them."

He paid for their tickets, and they moved towards the farthest tomb, a gated entrance barely visible in the rocky landscape. An Asian couple, escorted by what appeared to be a police officer, emerged from the tomb, nodding politely as they passed. Alex and Rebecca entered, stepping into a cool, dimly lit corridor carved from solid rock.

Rebecca ran her hand along the smooth surface. "How did they do this? It's so precise, like they used modern tools."

Alex didn't respond. He half-closed his eyes, breathing in the musty air, imagining the pharaoh's footsteps echoing through the stone halls three thousand years ago. To their right, a small opening led to a roughly cut tunnel, barricaded with a no entry sign. Alex continued straight, stopping where the corridor narrowed.

"This would be where the door to the outer chamber was," he said, stepping through an imagined threshold. Immediately to the right was another passageway, and ahead, twenty stone steps descended into the depths. Weak lights cast a pinkish glow, enhancing the ancient ambiance.

A male voice echoed from a side chamber. Alex and Rebecca followed the sound, finding an American guide explaining the tomb's history to a small group.

"This side chamber held the coffin of Meketaten, Akhenaten's and Nefertiti's second daughter," the guide said, pointing to the carved image of a young woman with a child. "Some say this is Meketaten with her child, but she died at ten, so it's unlikely."

The guide continued, detailing the plague that possibly claimed Queen Nefertiti's life. A tourist asked about her burial place.

"No one knows," the guide said with a hint of mystery. "Even Akhenaten's body is missing. Maybe it was never buried here."

Alex interjected, "Could it be the mummy from KV55?"

The guide smiled, enjoying the audience's curiosity. "Ah, KV55—a small, unadorned tomb in the Valley of the Kings. Many believe the mummy is from Akhenaten's royal house... but sadly no, not Akhenaten himself."

The guide led them further into the tomb.

They entered a room adorned with reliefs showing the royal family worshipping the Aten. Akhenaten wasn't here. But what if the map started here and then pointing to his real tomb?

He and Rebecca search for they symbols but finished disappointed again.

The group started to move on, ascending towards the main burial corridor. Alex was still studying the walls and happened to look back the way they'd come. He caught the glimpse of someone tall, silhouetted in the tunnel.

Alex grabbed Rebecca's arm, pulled her aside.

"This way," he hissed, darting for the barricaded side opening. He lifted the tape and pulled Rebecca after him.

"What's—" she questioned, but he raised a hand and pressed on. The light faded. After ten yards, they reached a small chamber, barely lit by the distant glow. Alex's breath echoed loudly in the confined space. He whispered into Rebecca's ear, "There was a tall man at the entrance—the BMW man!"

He eyes wide, she mouthed, "You're sure?"

He nodded.

They stood motionless, listening. Voices and footsteps echoed distantly. Five minutes passed. Then ten. New footsteps approached, accompanied by the beam of a flashlight.

Alex and Rebecca backed into the darkness, feeling their way through another passage. The flashlight's beam grew brighter, illuminating the chamber they had just left.

Alex pulled Rebecca to the side, crouching beside the entrance. He held her hand tightly, his heart pounding in his chest.

The light bobbed and swung towards them. The crunch of footsteps grew louder. Then a figure stepped into their chamber, the flashlight attached to a gun, its beam sweeping the room.

They were trapped.

Chapter 46

The beam of the flashlight revealed the figure of a security guard. He gestured with his weapon, ordering Alex and Rebecca to stand and step out. Into a walkie-talkie, he barked something in Arabic, receiving a burst of static in response. With a sharp snap of the gun, he motioned for them to lead the way out.

With the BMW man lurking somewhere behind them, they had no choice but to obey. They retraced their steps through the chambers and passages back to the main hall. The security guard tried the walkie-talkie again, exchanging terse words with someone on the other end. At the junction of the side passage and the main hall, he reattached the no entry barrier and sign, then prodded them forward.

Blinking against the blinding sunlight as they emerged from the tomb, the guard halted them once more to converse with another guard and then the walkie-talkie again.

"What do you think?" Rebecca asked as they sat on a stone bench in the shade.

Alex scanned the valley, trying to sound reassuring. "I don't think they know what to do with us. One good thing—the BMW guy isn't here." He knew the man was probably waiting somewhere, biding his time.

The guard, finished with his communications, waved his gun again, directing them down the track towards the parking area.

As they approached the road, Alex searched desperately for the Nissan and their driver. About a hundred yards ahead, he spotted Hamilton standing beside the car. Alex waved frantically, hoping to summon help. Instead, Hamilton got into the car, executed a casual K-turn, and drove away.

"Hey!" Alex shouted, only to be silenced by a rough shove from the guard.

At the parking area, they were made to wait. A few minutes later, a white Toyota van with 'Police' emblazoned in reverse on the front approached at speed. Two policemen, armed with long batons, climbed out.

The guard nudged Alex forward, causing him to stumble towards the van. A policeman by the side door commanded, "Get in… both of you."

They complied, climbing into the rear of the van. One of the policemen slid the door shut and took a seat opposite them.

Alex reached for his pocket, but the policeman rapped his stick against Alex's hand. "No."

"It's just my passport," Alex explained, slowly retrieving it and holding it out. "We're English."

The policeman took the passport but didn't bother to look at it. "You have been arrested. You were in a forbidden area."

Alex began to protest, but the policeman cut him off. "Why did you not have a police escort?"

"We had a local driver," Alex replied.

The policeman shook his head. "You will be taken to the station at Mallawi."

The van bypassed the ferry queue, and after a brief shout from the front, the flatbed began crossing the river.

On the other side, they turned north on the main road, away from Deir Mawas, away from their hotel.

In under ten minutes, they were at a shabby police station, providing their details to a disinterested desk sergeant. Rebecca handed over her passport with no argument. They were patted down and led to separate eight-by-ten-foot cells.

Alex sat on a hard wooden bench, uncomfortable, hot, and hungry. A toilet and sink behind a screen offered scant privacy. He thought wistfully about the luxury of their last hotel.

An hour later, the jailer opened Rebecca's cell, and she glanced at Alex as she passed by.

"Ask for the British embassy," Alex called after her.

She didn't look back as she returned to her cell twenty minutes later. The jailer then opened Alex's cell and motioned for him to follow.

"Where am I being taken?" Alex asked, but the jailer only grunted, "This way." He prodded Alex along a series of corridors to a room with a table. An officer with a pencil-thin moustache sat behind a desk.

"Sit down, please," the officer said in perfect English.

Alex complied. "I'm a British citizen and—"

"You are in my country, Mr MacLure. You do not make demands. Now, I would like to take your statement. Explain why you were wandering around the ruins at Tell el-Amarna without a tourist police escort."

"I didn't know we needed an escort."

"I do not believe you. I think you avoided an escort because you were looking for artifacts, or perhaps a trophy."

"No! We weren't looking to steal anything."

"Then why were you hiding in the tomb? You went into an area that was clearly forbidden."

"I thought I saw someone… someone I was afraid of. I thought we were being followed."

The officer rubbed his forehead, as if warding off a headache. Alex noted the man's wince, realising English wasn't his first language. He took a deep breath, speaking calmly.

"Let me start at the beginning," Alex said, recounting their journey from Cairo, mentioning Marek and their interest in Akhenaten. The officer took meticulous notes, occasionally interrupting for details like train times and the name of their hotel in Deir Mawas, the name of the taxi driver. When Alex mentioned Hamilton, the officer scoffed but continued writing.

Once Alex finished, the officer closed his notepad and said, "Go back to the cell."

Alex requested water upon his return. Moments later, he and Rebecca received bottles of water. The seals were broken, but thirst overruled caution.

As darkness fell, a plate was pushed into his cell. At first, he thought it was mashed potatoes, but the food was gritty and tasteless.

The next time the cell door opened, Alex sat up with a start. He massaged his stiff neck, rubbed his eyes and checked his watch. They'd been in custody for over seven hours. Rebecca stood in the corridor, looking equally dishevelled.

The jailer said, "You go now."

Uncertain, they followed him to the reception area where their passports were returned.

"Alex, my friend!"

Marek, who had been waiting, jumped up and gripped Alex's shoulders. "You are all right, yes?"

"I've been better… and worse," Alex replied. As they exited the station, he spotted the Nissan and driver. "That bloody driver!" Alex exclaimed to Marek. "He just left us at the tombs. He could have explained everything."

Marek shook his head. "Ahmed did the right thing. He risked arrest too. He returned to Deir Mawas, picked me up from Dairut, and we came straight here."

Ahmed, looking sheepish, opened the car door and bowed. "Hamilton is sorry," he said.

During the drive, Marek explained that their unauthorised presence in the restricted area raised alarms, especially since Ahmed hadn't registered with the tourist police. "You'd be amazed how much is still stolen from these sites."

Alex updated Marek on what they'd found at Amarna. "I expected to find something obvious, like a wall painting or an engraving of flying geese."

Marek thought for a moment. "Flying geese? There's a wall section in the Cairo Museum from the Royal Palace at Amarna with flying geese. Wild geese were symbols of an ideal life, and the accession of a new pharaoh was marked by releasing four wild geese to the four corners of the world. Perhaps we should review what we know before proceeding."

Rebecca interjected, "Before we do anything else, we need a bath and a decent meal!"

Chapter 47

The hotel's dining area was full and buzzing with quiet conversations. It transpired that the locals came to eat here in the evenings.

Alex and Marek's table had an intensity of its own. They'd started off by discussing what Alex had discovered during the day before moving on to the specifics of the Map-Stone. Alex learned that Ellen hadn't shared the Map-Stone images with him. Marek had simply worked on the translations. The news had been surprising due to their collaboration.

Alex said he'd draw the images after dinner when they couldn't be interrupted or overheard. He then moved the conversation onto the subject of tombs.

Marek said there was a tomb for someone who might be Meryra in Armana, but according to the wall paintings, that noble had died before Akhenaten.

Alex leaned forward, his eyes intense behind his glasses. "Unless the tomb was finished too soon... and never occupied. The higher classes of that period had multiple tombs."

Marek's face creased in thought. "True, and there was no evidence of funerary objects or his sarcophagus. You're certainly becoming an expert on the New Kingdom, Alex."

"Thank the Internet," Alex said with a wry smile.

Marek chuckled. "But remember, the Internet is full of unchecked information. We live in a time when gossip spreads faster than facts."

Alex's smile faded as he recalled Ellen's words about the New Kingdom's communications. Official records were often trivial, but the true messages—the facts—were hard to uncover.

"I've been translating the Amarna Letters every night."

"I don't understand... we already—"

"A different story," Alex said, and then explained that some of the tablets were encoded with the story of Yanhamu."

"Not the person who created the Map-Stone?"

"No, not Meryra."

Marek clapped his hands. "Incredible. The other name that kept appearing. I thought the Meryra and Yanhamu were the same person."

"Meryra was the scribe with secrets, but Yanhamu's story is the boy's tale."

Marek sipped his water, considering. Then he nodded. "When we have time, I'd like you to show me what you've translated."

"Of course," Alex said, although he was reluctant to disclose what he had before he'd published. He didn't sense that Marek would steal his work, but they had only just met. And there was the question that nagged him. Why hadn't Ellen shown Marek the Map-Stone markings?

Then before he realised it, Alex was voicing the concern. "Did Ellen ever discuss the likely location of the secret tomb?"

Marek shrugged, glancing around as though expecting someone. "We had many conversations. She was obsessed with the Amarna period."

"And you weren't?"

He grinned. "Not straight away. My doctorate started as the translation of partial stelae. There are hundreds and I thought... well I imagined being able to connect some and reconstruct a story. I had some success. Afterwards, working at Berlin University, I started translating the Amarna Letters."

"And that's how you met Ellen?"

"She was translating the ones in the British Museum."

Alex remembered something. "I found an email from you telling her to delete your communication and switch to a webmail account. I couldn't find that account."

Marek hesitated, then looked up as Rebecca walked in, her damp hair framing a fresh face. She joined them with a smile, charging the air with her presence.

"What are you discussing?" she asked.

"Ancient secrets," Marek explained. "Alex was telling me he's found a second story in the Amarna Letters."

"Yes," she said. "They're interesting... but partial?" She looked at Alex for confirmation.

"Probably. There are undoubtedly many more so-called Letters, as yet undiscovered. They were probably from the great library in Akhenaten's city—which was destroyed along with the city."

Rebecca picked up a menu. "Does it frustrate you that you'll never know the truth?" She looked from one to the other.

Both men shook their heads vigorously. "Oh no," Marek said. "That's the allure of Egyptology—the hope of finding answers one day."

"As long as there are clues and progress, there is hope," Alex added.

Their food arrived, and Marek explained he had ordered the special for everyone. "I hope you don't mind.

237

Always trust the recommendation," he said with a knowing nod.

As they ate, Rebecca said, "So, after Akhenaten died, what happened?"

"Nefertiti may have become pharaoh. The name Smenkhare replaces hers on a sarcophagus and one theory is that it was Nefertiti taking the role of a man."

Rebecca nodded. "Wearing a beard like Queen Hatshepsut?"

"That's right," Marek said. "Very good. Then Tutankhamun takes over with his uncle Ay as regent."

Alex said, "It's unclear what happened to Smenkhkare. Whether he was Nefertiti or not, Nefertiti appears to have fled when Tutankhamun and Ay took over. All mention of her vanishes."

After dinner, they sat huddled around a table. Alex had drawn the upper surface of the block and the symbols from the sides. They'd talked about the meaning of geese and the symbol, Alex thought was gold. Marek clarified that it was more specific. The arch, looking like a pearl neckless meant *gold*, but with a jar beneath, it meant *pure gold*.

They talked about other possible symbols before Marek asked, "How accurate is this? The originals would be better."

Alex shook his head. "Because of Ellen's concerns, I destroyed her work." Rebecca met his gaze but he looked away and continued. "These *are* the markings although it is impossible to know what's an original. It's been handled pretty roughly over the years."

Marek nodded, thinking. "Can you draw the whole thing... as a plan? I mean, flatten it out."

Marek fetched some scissors once Alex had finished. He cut out the image that looked like a thick, stretched cross.

"What are you doing?" Rebecca asked.

"Watch," Marek said, flipping the paper over then folding it back to reveal the images. They combined.

Alex got it. "Two dimensions into three!"

Marek nodded. "Four corners. Four directions. Items like the hoops facing different directions, and what might be partial hieros, made me think... what if..."

He finished folding.

"The lines... they don't join up but it looks... like a maze," Rebecca observed.

Alex realised she was right. There were lines that appeared to come together. The other marks might have formed pictures, but the only two they recognised, after some adjustment, were a bird and a broken horizontal rectangle that Marek said was a determinative for a building.

Alex agreed. "The throne can mean a god or pharaoh. But it looks like the flag combines with the building and that means—"

"A palace," Marek said.

Alex nodded enthusiastically, thinking of what they'd seen today.

"What about the triangles?" Rebecca asked. "Where do they fit in?"

"If you cut a pyramid and draw a line down the middle, you get two triangles with a base of three, height of four, and side of five," Alex said, thinking aloud.

Marek nodded. "If it is connected to the palace, we're looking for a building with dimensions of three, four and five."

Alex said, "But ruins don't reveal height. The other symbols will make sense at the right location." He pointed to the four hoops and a column. "Four hoops equal forty."

"And then a pillar. So, forty pillars?" Rebecca asked.

"Exactly," Alex confirmed, impressed that she was following. "And the flying geese next to that. The Northern Palace we saw used to have forty pillars. I didn't spot anywhere else that had forty of anything. But we saw no flying geese."

Marek said, "Geese were at the Royal Palace of Amarna."

"But the forty pillars were at the Northern Palace."

Marek frowned. "There's another possibility. Geese could symbolise the journey to the afterlife or the rise of a new pharaoh."

Rebecca sighed. "We're not getting anywhere."

Marek tried combining other marks but was soon frustrated. "There are too many possibilities. I'm convinced this folded solution is the right approach but I don't think it's accurate enough." He shook his head and Alex suspected the Egyptologist was frustrated with him for allegedly destroying the photographs Ellen had taken.

"I wonder..." Alex began. "I wonder if I can do a better job. I've an excellent memory. Now that I know how it fits together, I can spend time tonight..."

Rebecca's eyes narrowed at him, but Marek looked excited.

"Yes, yes," he said. "Please try. Let us meet again in the morning and try again."

Rebecca said, "Try now, Alex. Lock yourself in your room for a hour or two. Think of nothing else... see what you come up with."

He met her gaze. She knew he'd lied about destroying the information... after all, it was on a website. All he needed to do was log into it and draw more accurate pictures.

240

"You can do it," she said with an encouraging nod. "We've come so far…"

He took a deep breath. "All right, I'll see what I can come up with."

It took him less than an hour, but he delayed a little longer to make it seem more realistic.

When he returned, Rebecca was drinking mint tea in the lounge. Marek was outside smoking.

He returned with eager anticipation. "You've done it?"

Alex showed him the plan drawing. He'd already cut out his own version upstairs but let Marek do it this time then fold the edges to create a series of hieroglyphs.

"Oh my goodness!" Marek exclaimed.

Alex drew what he was looking at.

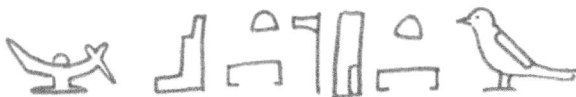

Rebecca looked at both men. "What does it mean? Can either of you translate this?"

Alex shook his head.

Marek said, "Is it possible this is incomplete?"

"Highly likely. I'm not even a hundred per cent sure about this."

"Relying on your good memory," Rebecca said with a hint of sarcasm.

Marek didn't appear to notice. Pointing to the first symbol, he said, "This is clearly a boat and could be a determinative—telling us the rest is the name of the boat. The next is a throne—it's not normally on its own, but it doesn't go with the rectangle." He was thinking out-loud. "No, that would make it a word. With the extra two symbols after the throne, the transliteration is *st*, meaning place. The flag is next to the rectangle and will mean temple. Not palace. The name will be something like *hw t ntr*. I think the bird is a swallow representing the sound *wr*."

Rebecca said, "So what does it all mean?"

"*Khd s t hw t ntr wr*—meaning: sails to the place of the Great Temple."

"That could refer to a tomb," Alex said, "rather than a temple."

"Yes, though it's oddly complex for a simple phrase." Marek shrugged. "But I know someone who might understand." He took the paper and stood, heading to find a fax machine.

Five minutes later, Marek returned, looking frustrated. "It is very late."

Alex had noted the lounge clock showed it was past midnight.

Continuing, Marek said, "My friend in Cairo isn't answering, but the fax went through. We'll have to wait. Meanwhile, tomorrow we should return to Amarna and check out the tombs of the nobles."

Chapter 48

Alex lay on the bed, but the day's activity and the whirlwind of thoughts kept sleep at bay. He went online and tried to make sense of the hieroglyphs they'd identified from the drawing he'd allegedly remembered. Although he'd not drawn two things from opposite sides. Deliberately. The four geese weren't alone. They were beside a throne. There was also another throne on its own. Why he'd not disclosed that, he couldn't explain. But it felt separate and also significant.

He was still wrestling with the interpretation when an email alert appeared. Neglecting his inbox since leaving the UK, Alex scrolled through a flood of marketing emails until he found one from his mother. It was a short note, checking in on him and letting him know that Topsy, his childhood dog, was fine. It wasn't sentimental, but he felt a pang of emotion. He removed his glasses and rubbed his face, realising he was exhausted. According to his watch, it was now 2:30am. He sent a quick reply to his mother and decided to scan through the rest of his emails.

One caught his attention. It was from Mutnodjemet, a name he recognised from the forum Ellen had been on.

Hi, Senemut. Thanks for your email. Been lying low after the warnings from Sinuhe. God, it's scary what happened to him. It can't be a coincidence, can it? Anyway, glad you're OK—are you coming back to the forum? Mutnodjemet x

Sinuhe was Marek. Mutnodjemet was a female name. If this person *was* female, why was she saying something had happened to Marek? A chill ran down Alex's spine. If something had happened to Marek, who was the man who picked them up at the airport and had dinner with them? It had to be him, didn't it?

Alex quickly replied, asking what had happened to Marek. He then searched for Marek Borevsek online, finding the usual references to his research. Nothing seemed amiss about his transfer to Cairo or his work on the cache of mummies found in Amenhotep II's tomb.

Alex returned to bed but left his laptop on in case Mutnodjemet replied. Sleep was still elusive. He replayed every conversation with Marek in his mind. The man seemed off. He hadn't acknowledged Alex's help in cracking Meryra's hidden message in the Amarna Letters. He didn't seem to remember telling Ellen to use a webmail account. He didn't know the details of the Map-Stone. Had Ellen really not shared them with her colleague?

Alex wrestled with his paranoia. Was he overreacting? Was he becoming like Ellen?

Ten minutes later, he made a decision. He picked up the phone and dialled Rebecca. After eight rings, she answered, her voice groggy with sleep.

"We've got to get out of here."

"Alex? What time is it?"

"Never mind that, just pack your things."

"What's wrong?" She was awake now.

He told her his suspicions about Marek.

"Are you sure? It sounds—"

"Paranoid, I know, but better safe than sorry. What if he's working for the bad guys?" He let that sink in, then added, "Get packed. We've got to go—now!"

"Okay, okay, I'll be at your room as soon as I can."

As soon as he hung up, Alex shut off his laptop, dressed, and stuffed everything into his bag. A couple of minutes later, there was a light knock on his door.

"Alex?" Rebecca whispered from the other side.

He opened the door, bag ready to go, but instead of leaving, Rebecca pushed him back inside and shut the door.

"Are you sure about this?"

"Yes!"

"Let me see the email."

He'd already packed, but reluctantly, he reopened the laptop. "We're wasting time."

She waited. When the email was open, she read it quickly. "It says nothing."

"But I was suspicious of him from the start, when he picked us up at the airport and seemed nervous."

Rebecca pointed to the bed. "Sit down and breathe." When he did, she continued, "He's a heavy smoker, addicted to nicotine. We discussed this, Alex."

"But I think he made mistakes about the letters. And when I asked about a webmail account, he acted like he knew nothing."

"What did he say?"

"He didn't. You arrived, and he changed the subject."

"Maybe my arrival distracted him. People sometimes forget what they're talking about. True?"

"I guess."

"Ask him again in the morning. I bet you haven't slept, have you? You're tired. It's been stressful, with being chased in the tombs and held overnight in prison."

"You think I'm paranoid."

"Just take slow, deep breaths and let's see how we feel."

Alex gradually calmed as Rebecca made him a cup of tea.

"So that's why you pretended to remember you could remember the Map-Stone images better. You didn't want him to know about the website."

He nodded. "I think Ellen would have involved him. It's too big a puzzle for her to have worked on alone. Why didn't she give him access to the website?"

"I think you're worried because of Ellen. What happened to her… anyone would be cautious after that." She handed him the tea. "And you're right to be. We need to stay vigilant. But Marek…? Anyway, you've told him everything now, so it's too late to worry. He knows what you know, so if he's not genuine, he won't be here in the morning."

Alex smiled. "Well, to be honest, he doesn't know everything."

"You didn't draw all the symbols?"

"I drew most." He put down his cup, feeling more relaxed, thinking he could and should sleep. "Except for two thrones. But—"

"See you in the morning," she said shaking her head. "I'm tired, and you've had less sleep than me. Get some rest. And let's hope Marek's friend comes back with a better interpretation of the message."

Alex nodded. He shut the door after her and settled in bed. Thoughts continued to swirl in his mind. Meryra had used code to embed the secrets in the Letters. Three, four five had been relevant. The numbers on the stone weren't just part of a map.

Chapter 49

"It's also a mathematical code," Alex whispered to Rebecca over breakfast. After thirty minutes, Rebecca stopped him talking.

"Tell me again why you think it's a mathematical code," she said. "And I don't mean to be rude, but slow it down this time."

Alex took a breath and tried not to charge through the explanation again. "I think there are three parts to the puzzle: the name of the building, the lines—which make up the map of a maze—and the code."

"Why a code?"

"Because I think Ellen worked it out. She was looking for numbers."

"But how—"

"Oh sorry. When ancient Egyptians wrote something that meant something other than the obvious, they would use modified hieroglyphs—ideograms that weren't hieroglyphs. Like the number eight in cuneiform."

"The grid-like thing you drew?"

"Yes. And the geese surrounding a throne."

"The throne you didn't show Marek?"

"Yes. It's unusual. Geese on their own, yes. Throne on its own, yes. But geese around a throne means something else."

"But you don't know what it means?"

"No."

"And there is another throne on the other side. Three thrones in total. Which seems significant." Three thrones triggered the thought about triangles. Three sides. Three, four, five…"

Rebecca said something.

"Sorry, what?"

She shook her head. "Then you should tell him. Tell Marek about the missing symbols."

"Not until I trust him."

"What about the name of the palace or temple? What does that mean?"

"I don't know."

"Then we do need Marek, whether you trust him or not. If he can work out the first part—"

"I'll work out the rest." Alex nodded.

She thought for a moment. "All right, when we've got the right building and location, we somehow ditch him."

Much to Alex's surprise, Marek returned in the morning. He'd still heard nothing from his expert friend.

As they stood at the front of the ferry to Amarna. Marek asked whether Alex had remembered anything else.

Alex shook his head and stared at the far shore, thinking about the ancient city.

Marek broke into his thoughts. "My best guess is that the symbols refer to the Great Palace somehow." The sun was over the ochre hills already shimmering in the heat. The Royal Wadi, the valley of his tomb, cut a V in the hill like the reverse pyramid—a supplication to the sun god.

Alex turned away from the view and looked at Marek. "So, the hieroglyph of the boat refers to the solar barque?"

"Exactly." Marek grinned. "We are thinking the same thing."

Alex glanced at Rebecca, who had stayed in the Nissan, then back at Marek, and said, "I've been wanting to ask you something."

"Oh?" Marek lit a cigarette and sucked long and hard before blowing a jet of smoke.

"You first met Ellen on the EgyptConfidential forum and then exchanged emails."

Marek inclined his head.

Alex continued: "But then you said to delete the emails and switch to a webmail account."

"Yes."

He couldn't help it. Maybe he wanted Marek to be genuine or maybe he wanted Marek to admit he was a fraud. Alex asked, "Why was that?"

Marek smiled. The ferry docked and he stepped ashore. Their driver, Ahmed, followed with Rebecca still in his Nissan.

Marek said, "We must register with the transport police this time, Alex, do you not think?"

"Marek!" Alex hurried after the wiry man, took hold of his arm and stopped him mid stride. "What was the reason?"

"Reason?"

"Why use the webmail account?"

"Is it not obvious? I was afraid someone would uncover our research. There is a great deal at stake here, both money and reputation. Since Ellen and I were partners then, so are we. I do not mind sharing with you. Fifty-fifty." He patted Alex on the shoulder and grinned. Then he looked more serious. "There have been suspicious people—men who I do not trust. They ask a lot of questions and I think my email was hacked into."

It made sense. Marek's experiences sounded similar to his own, but Alex was still unclear about the answer. "So what is the webmail account?"

Marek shook his head. "My friend, you must understand. After Ellen's death and the burglary at Lord Carnarvon's exhibition, I knew there was a problem. Was it not fair for me to be more worried? When you got in touch afterwards... to be honest, I was a little concerned you were perhaps not who you said you were, or perhaps were now working for someone else, so I deleted the webmail account."

Alex began to protest his innocence, but Marek asked him to wait before he disappeared inside a building. He emerged a few minutes later with an armed policeman in tow.

For a second, Alex panicked: Marek with an armed man! But then Marek grinned and waved for Ahmed to pick them up. "We need a police escort," he explained.

They waited together until their driver pulled up. Marek said, "So, I was saying I was unsure about you, no? Last night you told me everything about the Map-Stone and so now I am happy." He patted Alex's arm. "Come on. Let's take a look at the palace."

They climbed into the Nissan. The policeman had them wind down the window so that he could stand on the step and hold on to the car through the door. They followed the route taken the day before, around the town and then south along the modern cemetery. Ahmed stopped beside the Great Aten Temple.

Rebecca asked a question about the number of altars, probably looking for forty.

"Offering tables," Marek answered. "Nine hundred—"

His ringing phone interrupted him and he answered excitedly.

"I can't hear you," he said after a few moments. "The signal here is poor. Could you try a text?" He gave up and shrugged at the others. "That was my friend in Cairo. Maybe he has translated the hieroglyphs." He laughed. "But I think we are close here."

Alex shook his head. "I don't see it."

Marek beckoned, and the policeman intervened as they approached a network of stone walls, making them skirt around the side.

"The water came up to here—the Royal Quay." Marek raised his eyebrows knowingly. "The royal barge would have been moored here. We have a typical double meaning of the boat hieroglyph, I think. The royal boat and referring to the palace of the sun."

"So?" Alex said, looking around. "What are you showing us? What have you worked out?"

Marek turned and pointed west. "Through the courtyard ran a straight path to the river's edge. You'll see there are a few trees spotted around? Well, they're more regularly spaced than appears now. I checked last night. There's a clear pattern and the excavation team who have modelled this believe there were… forty."

Alex said nothing. The forty was part of the numerical code, not the location. He was now sure of it.

"Forty trees would be the forty pillars," Marek said enthusiastically. "The royal barge would be to the right beside the Great Palace of the Aten… or god's sun boat."

Rebecca asked, "And the geese?"

"To the south we have a stone quay where the main working city began. So the end of the courtyard would have been the start of a more natural setting. It is thought there would have been a garden and a reed bed. As you probably know, geese played an important part in ancient Egyptian life, and undoubtedly, this is where the royal geese would have lived. Also, of course, close by we have the records office where Meryra, the scribe, would have worked. This section would have had great significance." Marek turned back to the pylons. They were standing at the second. "And here is Nefertiti's gateway. Alex, what do you think? Am I right?"

It was possible, but didn't seem specific enough. There was no sense of an origin to the map and the geese were somehow linked to a throne... although he still wasn't willing to share that with Marek.

Alex walked forward to a square area at the back of the temple and looked around. The policeman waved him away from the walls.

Alex said, "Nefertiti's gateway...?"

Marek wasn't paying attention. He'd glanced at his phone. "Sorry, Alex. What did you say?"

"What was this area?"

Marek seemed to shake some thoughts from his head but continued to look thoughtful. "Er... the sanctuary. In fact, it was a small version of the one in the Great Temple." He looked back at his phone.

Alex said, "What's up?"

"I am mistaken," Marek said, but instead of being disappointed, his eyes flashed with excitement. "I get it! My expert friend has decoded the name we worked out last night. He's convinced the order was wrong. It is not the name of a royal boat." He held out his phone so that Alex could see what was written.

"In transliteration," Marek said, "the sounds are *Hw-t-wr-t.*"

Alex frowned. "Okay, what does it mean?"

"The Palace of the Great Barque."

Rebecca said what Alex was thinking: "Isn't that effectively the same thing as you said last night?"

"Similar, but more specific."

"What about the other hieroglyphs: the throne and the flag?"

"The flag will be what we thought—the determination of a location. The throne... well, as I said before, I think it means a temple..." He was grinning at their expectant expressions. "One minute," he said.

Marek needed a cigarette and made them wait as he led them back to the Nissan. When he finally removed the cigarette from his mouth, he looked at Alex and said, "Still not worked it out?"

When Alex shook his head, Marek said. "It is not so much what it means, because it is a name. A place known as Hut-waret—somewhere of amazing historical importance. The capital city of the Hyksos, when they ruled Lower Egypt around the Thirteenth Dynasty. Believed to have been located at Tell el-Dab'a."

"But that's the wrong period," Alex said, disappointed. "How does this help us?"

Marek laughed. "Well, if it was a couple of years ago, then no, it would not help. But recently, an Austrian archaeological team discovered evidence of New Kingdom settlements at Tell el-Dab'a. That, my friends, is where we need to go."

Joachim hadn't followed the group back to Amarna. After the Englishman had spotted him in Akhenaten's tomb, he knew he had to keep out of sight. He sat in a bar and sipped coffee awaiting instructions.

His phone rang. It was the old man. Gershom.

"Yes?"

Gershom said, "The tomb is not in Amarna. They are looking in the wrong location."

"Where is it?"

"Tell el-Dab'a."

Joachim didn't know the place and the old man explained roughly where it was in the Delta.

He said, "If we know where it is, then we don't need MacLure anymore. If you're still saying we can't get rid of him, then let's just leave him. There's more than one way to stop him being a nuisance."

The old man cleared his throat.

Joachim prompted, "Is that a yes?"

"It's a no. We can't be sure we know everything. Getting to the location isn't enough. Mr MacLure might still be of use to us."

"Tell el-Dab'a then. I should leave straight away."

"One other thing. We have a problem with the site," Gershom said. "There's a village and an excavation team working the area. We need a diversion."

"You have an idea?"

Gershom explained his plan.

Joachim was dubious. "It is a good idea, but can you arrange for that?"

The old man may have been offended, but he grunted, suggesting humour. "Leave that to me, Joachim. By the time you get there it should be in place." There was a pause then he added, "And if it's not, then you will need to improvise."

Chapter 50

Ahmed estimated the drive would take three and a half hours, and Alex dozed most of the way in the back with Rebecca, until a jolt of brakes woke him. They were outside Cairo and Marek explained an accident had blocked the first bridge over the Nile. In laborious single file, the traffic made its way beside the river and crossed at the next bridge, then doubled back to pick up the ring road.

Alex managed to piggyback off a variable Wi-Fi signal and killed some time by browsing the Internet for information on Hut-waret.

Two ancient Egyptian places were referred to in the Bible: Pithom and Pi-Ramesses. Alex discovered that Pithom was believed to be the place the Greeks later called Avaris.

An archaeology team from Vienna University had been working the Tell el-Dab'a area for almost fifty years but had made their big breakthrough in 2009 when they discovered eight-metre-thick fortified walls under cultivated land that had once been almost surrounded by a Nile tributary. The structure matched expectations for Avaris, and the discovery of a warrior's mud-brick tomb seemed to be confirmation of the Hyksos period.

The phone signal became more intermittent, but Alex managed to read that a number of palaces and temples had been identified. The discovery of horse burials again appeared to point to pre-New Kingdom occupation. The team had also discovered Eighteenth Dynasty groundworks, although the Austrian team concluded this was restoration by Pharaoh Horemheb.

An email arrived. He saw the name Mutnodjemet—the member of the EgyptConfidential forum—but the connection failed completely before he could open the email.

Once off the ring road and on a motorway, they made good progress. When Ahmed pulled into a service area, Marek announced he desperately needed a cigarette, so they stopped and both he and Ahmed hungrily sucked in the nicotine.

Alex and Rebecca stretched their legs. He located a shop selling mobile devices and purchased a dongle with prepaid Internet browsing.

"How much further?" he asked Marek when he returned to the car.

"We are already in the Delta, about forty miles north of Cairo. Not long now—about half an hour perhaps."

It took considerably longer. Ahmed clearly didn't know the way, and the warren of roads that criss-crossed the green canals seemed to confuse him.

Alex used the time to decode more of Yanhamu's story. He found another short section referring to being a soldier in the army. But also, something that made his heart race.

Meryra would construct hidden tombs for them with coded maps, so their vital spirits could reunite on Earth and in the afterlife.

"Yes!" Alex exclaimed, before he bit his tongue.

"Aberdeen won," he said when Marek looked questioningly at him. "Big match last night."

He closed his laptop, heart still racing. This simple passage confirmed everything they believed. Meryra had created the maps to find Akhenaten's and Nefertiti's final resting places.

Outside, the countryside was green farmland. A far cry from the harsh desert of the rest of Egypt. They were following a major canal. Then Ahmed drove through a small town and Marek announced they were now on the right track. And track it became, because they bumped along a dirt road through fields.

Ahmed pointed ahead at a small hill. "That must be Tell el-Dab'a."

Rebecca said, "Tell means hill, right?"

Marek swivelled in his seat. "Yes, yes, a very important and strategic point here in the Delta."

"But," Rebecca responded, "Amarna is called Tell el-Amarna—that town wasn't on a hill."

"You are right!" Marek laughed. "It is one of the great mysteries... no, actually I asked Ahmed yesterday and he said it is a mistake that dates back to British rule. Some British bureaucrat mistakenly added the Tell part to the name."

Alex asked, "Do modern Egyptians despise the British for that period?"

Marek spoke to Ahmed in Arabic, and they both laughed. Looking to the rear seats, Marek relayed the conversation that Egyptians had thousands of years of foreign rulers, including the Hyksos, the Hittites, the Persians, the French, the Romans, and the Greeks. In fact, the most prosperous times were under the foreigners, as opposed to King Farouk, who had had only his self-interest at heart.

Alex asked, "What made you laugh?"

"Ahmed used a phrase," Marek explained. "It translates something like 'It is better to trust the foreigner you know, than the brother you know you cannot trust.'"

"Here," Ahmed announced, and stopped the Nissan.

They had passed through a cluster of houses and had pulled up outside a building that looked something like a low-lying block of flats.

Alex noticed a large number of blue signs as they climbed out. They had the word *Danger*, with Arabic beneath. "What do they say?" he asked Marek.

"There has been a gas leak." Marek headed for the building's entrance. "I will ask at the hotel."

Rebecca raised an eyebrow. "Hotel?"

Minutes later, Marek returned, a wide grin splitting his face. "It is all right, the problem is over. It seems the village was cleared but the hotel owner refused to go and the leak was fixed last night. He is very angry with the local government—his main business is linked to the archaeological dig and he doesn't know when the team will return. But in case we need to stay, I have negotiated a very good price."

A surly-looking man came out of the entrance and headed for them.

"One of the local excavation workers. He stayed behind when the others left," Marek explained. "He is called Tariq and"—Marek rubbed his fingers together indicating baksheesh—"he's kindly volunteered to show us the site."

Marek instructed Ahmed to wait at the hotel and he took the driver's seat. Tariq climbed in beside him and spoke in Arabic.

Marek said, "I will have to translate because he claims to speak little English." He dropped his voice. "The truth is, I suspect he can't be bothered." He started the engine and pulled away from the hotel and skirted the hill.

Tariq spoke and Marek explained they were heading to a massive archaeological site covering over a square mile—and that was before you counted the Pi-Ramesses site to the north.

They travelled along farm tracks and crossed a canal before stopping at their first location. Tariq distributed maps showing how different the ancient landscape had been—the area had once been mostly surrounded by water, with several islands, unlike the dry land they now stood on.

"This palace was bordered by water to the east and north," Marek translated.

Tariq talked as they walked.

Alex cut in. "It's not Eighteenth Dynasty. New Kingdom. That's the period we're interested in."

"The old citadel probably dates to the Twelfth Dynasty," Marek translated.

Alex pointed to some columns. "What about theses? Are they from a later period?"

Marek smiled. "Yes, this is what we're looking for!"

Tariq led them deeper into the ruins while Marek translated. "These columns supported platforms. They're Eighteenth Dynasty—a smaller palace built on stilts about seven meters high, possibly for flood protection."

Alex paced out the main palace area—about ninety-two strides wide. When he suggested the monumental doorway with pylons might suggest a temple, Marek explained there was no evidence of a temple.

Disappointed with the first site, they continued. Tariq was well-versed, or at least believable in his assertions about periods. Very little was distinctly New Kingdom, although from scattered stone ruins, it was hard to tell.

Alex was overwhelmed by the number of sites. There were multiple settlements and five palaces, more than 400 tombs and large cemeteries. Six temples had been formally identified.

At one point, Alex heard the name of a pharaoh: Amenemhat I. He questioned Tariq and the guide briefly switched to English explaining that an untouched fragment of a stele was located there. "But the temple is built over an even older structure."

Marek showed no interest. "What about here?" he asked, pointing to the map.

The excavation site, on the hill closest to their hotel, had revealed large wall sections.

"New Kingdom," Marek confirmed. "Temples?"

Tariq reverted to Arabic and Marek translated again. "Possibly with a palace."

Alex paced it out and looked around. "Four separate sites," he said. "Could be four temples."

The next site had temples and other structures and Alex paced out the largest at twenty by thirty yards. Beyond this main temple was another temple, a defence tower, a small house, and cemeteries nearby.

At the next stop Tariq didn't bother getting out. He said the site had once been underwater and had limited excavation. "There may have been one palace here, or two connected ones. Magnetometry shows two large courtyards with rooms. There's a fortified wall with a tower."

"So nothing to see?" Rebecca asked.

"And not New Kingdom," Marek said. "There's one more site and that one might be the right period."

As the light faded, their final stop revealed a vast excavation area with a lattice of walls. Marek translated Tariq's uncertainty: "They're not sure if this is a large residence or a series of regular houses arranged in rows."

"Twelve in a row," Rebecca noted. "How many rows were there?"

"They don't know," Marek replied. "There's also an interesting structure in the northeast corner—possibly a tower."

"No temple or tomb?" Alex checked.

"No."

He shook his head, disappointed. "So, no obvious New Kingdom tomb anywhere in the area."

"No," Marek agreed. "Back to the hotel. Perhaps tomorrow... or perhaps there is nothing left to find. After all—"

"I'd like detailed maps of the four potential New Kingdom sites," Alex interrupted.

After a brief exchange with Tariq, Marek said the hotel owner had charts that might help, though he added with a shrug, "It'll undoubtedly cost us more. What are you looking for?"

Alex considered. He'd hoped for inspiration, but it hadn't come. He'd planned to ditch Marek because of his doubts about him, but maybe Alex did need the other Egyptologist's help.

"A clue like the geese... or lines that match what's on the Map-Stone. But... my theory is there's mathematics involved."

"Math?" Marek frowned.

"Think of the secret code in the Amarna Letters. In my experience, everything comes down to the understanding of mathematics."

Chapter 51

In his hotel room, Alex studied the detailed diagrams provided by the owner. Any numbers written on the maps were modern and irrelevant. But something nagged at him. Numbers were relevant, it was just a matter of locating them.

He'd expected a temple to be orientated east–west like Akhenaten's, but not one of the temples was like that. The group of four nearest the hotel interested him the most. He studied the layout. There was something that he couldn't put his finger on.

He took a break from staring at the outlines and thought about the symbols written on Meryra's Map-Stone.

He decided to browse the Internet for inspiration, although it took him fifteen minutes to work out how to sign on using the prepaid dongle because it was in Arabic. When he finally gained access, he logged onto Ellen's secure site about the Map-Stone.

He studied the images over and over. His attention kept returning to the thrones. Alex knew the symbol was often associated with Isis. Three thrones. Was it a separate clue within the code?

The throne and the geese. The throne in the place description... possibly pointing to a temple. And the throne on its own.

Wait a minute. He zoomed in. There was a mark in front of the solitary throne. Was it deliberate or just an indentation? If deliberate, it might have been a sun... Ra or Aten and the Isis throne? No, Aten was drawn with rays and the size... too small to be a sun.

He looked through all of Ellen's drawings. None had the mark, but he was sure it was there. This wasn't an indentation or a natural discolouration of the stone. This was deliberate. A message...

He drew it a few times, helping him think.

The concept of numbers flashed into his brain. Three, four and five.

Alex sat back as though poleaxed. That was it!

The throne wasn't just on the Map-Stone, it also represented the three-four-five triangle. Special numbers. A special triangle—*the golden triangle*.

He studied the map of the excavations. Certain he'd found it, he traced out a simple version of one of the temples: Temple IV.

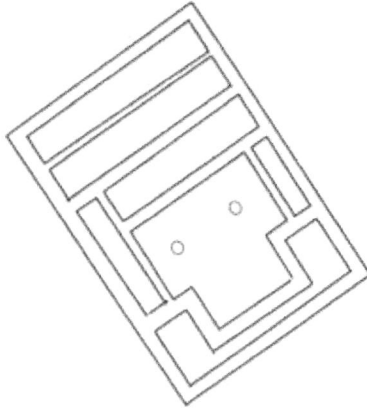

Drawing only the foundations, he saw it immediately: the Isis throne was clearly part of the structure. The plan showed that the bottom righthand corner was subtly based on her throne. The dot on the Map-Stone appeared to correspond to the object Marek had assumed was a building sign. From the foundation diagram, it looked like one of two pillars.

Excited, he texted Rebecca:

It's the temple on the hill closest to the hotel!

As he put down his phone, he remembered to check the email from Mutnodjemet. Clicking on it, he saw there was no message, just a link. He followed that and a new window opened with a private posted message. As he started to read, cold gripped his heart.

Didn't you know? Marek was found dead in his flat in Cairo. Suicide, the report said, with foul play ruled out. Strange, I can't find the link now. Could someone have removed it?

Chapter 52

Marek wasn't who he claimed to be.

The room phone rang, jarring Alex from his thoughts. He picked it up, his heart pounding.

"Alex, it's Rebecca. Are you coming down for dinner?"

He could hear background chatter. Could Marek—whoever he was—overhear?

"Are you alone?" Alex asked cautiously.

"No, Marek and Ahmed are here. We've been waiting for you."

"Don't react to what I say."

"What?"

That reaction might tip off the imposter. Alex's mind raced. How could he convey this? "Look, sorry. Tell them I've got Montezuma's revenge. I'm not feeling well. Tell Marek I'll be fine after a good night's sleep. Okay?"

"Alex...?"

He repeated the instructions and hung up.

At 3am, he packed his things and called Rebecca's room.

"Alex, what's going on?"

"Get dressed. I'm coming to your room."

She said something, but he didn't listen. He put the phone down, opened his bedroom door as quietly as possible, and stepped into the dimly lit corridor. He wedged a pen between the door and jamb to keep it from slamming shut, then took a step. The floor creaked. He stopped, listened. Nothing. He moved again, slow and hesitant. Three more steps and he was outside Marek's door. He paused, took deep breaths, and stepped past. From somewhere in the hotel, a low rumble of snoring reached his ears. He hoped it was Marek.

Alex glided over the rugs, turning a corner, and took five more steps to Rebecca's room. In the still of the night, his gentle knock sounded loud.

No response.

He was about to knock again but thought better of it. He texted her: **Open your door. I'm outside. Be quiet!**

The wait seemed interminable, but just as he was about to knock again, he heard movement. The door opened a crack, and he pushed in, taking the handle from her and closing it with a wince as it clunked shut. Rebecca was in her pyjamas.

"Rebecca!" he whispered urgently.

She backed up to the bed, sat, and patted it.

"Get dressed now!" Alex whispered again. "We need to get away. I was right about Marek."

"Alex…"

He waved at her to keep quiet.

"Alex…" She patted the bed again. "I think you should calm down. I'm worried about you."

"No, no! Look—" He pulled out his laptop and showed her the email from Mutnodjemet and clicked on the link. "I was right not to trust him. All those signs that he didn't know everything. That really isn't Marek."

She shook her head, trying to process. "But the message doesn't give details. How do you know this isn't just a windup? Or maybe it's a conspiracy nut. Maybe they're paranoid…"

He grabbed her shoulders, looking into her eyes. "I'm convinced. There've been too many inconsistencies. And today there was a partial stele. He didn't ask to see it. That's Marek's specialisation, for God's sake! He should have been interested, should have wanted to see it, even though it's not why we're here."

Rebecca stood. "All right, we'll get out of here." She dressed quickly, and Alex helped cram her things into her case.

"We should go to the police. Agreed?" he asked as she closed it.

She nodded.

"No chance of a taxi," he said, "so we'll have to take the Nissan. I guess we'll need to hot-wire it."

"It's been a while, but I should manage."

He was astounded.

She grinned. "The wrong crowd and a misspent youth, remember?"

They crept out into the corridor, jamming it with a pen to keep the door from slamming. They walked lightly in the opposite direction of Marek's room, down a flight of stairs, and into a lounge area. Most of the lights were out, and no one was around—no night porter, no receptionist. They needed to cross the foyer to reach the front door.

Alex wondered if a small hotel like this locked the front door at night. When he reached for the handle, it turned, and the door opened easily. Outside, the air was cool. They stood, scanning for movement. In the moonlight, everything seemed tranquil. Nothing stirred. The Nissan was parked only fifteen metres away. With exchanged nods, Alex and Rebecca started towards it.

A man stepped out from beside the vehicle, handgun aimed at Alex's chest. The light caught his face. It was the man from the BMW and the tomb, the one who had grabbed Pete from the train.

A noise behind them. Alex spun to see Marek approaching. Marek smiled, gun pointed at Rebecca's head. "Drop the bags," he commanded, his voice shockingly loud in the still night.

Rebecca let go of her case and dropped her handbag. Alex's bag hit the floor.

"On your knees. Hands behind your backs."

They knelt.

The blow to the back of Alex's head was immediate. His world went black.

Chapter 53

As Alex came round, he had flashes of images and for a few minutes he was confused. Then he became aware of being uncomfortable, the air was warm and it was hard to breathe. Cigarette smoke. His hands and feet were tied.

Opening his eyes, the first thing he saw was the back of a seat. He was squashed on the floor in the back of a big vehicle, possibly a four-by-four. Awkwardly and gradually, he manoeuvred into a kneeling position and then fell sideways onto the seat and sat up.

"Good morning," Marek said, friendly, as though nothing had happened. He sat in the passenger's seat and breathed out smoke into the already dense atmosphere.

Alex coughed. "Where's Rebecca?"

Marek gave a slight chuckle and indicated with his thumb. "She's in the hotel. My friend is keeping her company."

Alex said, "You bastard. If you hurt her, I'll—"

"Then you had better hope we can follow your map. My friend has a very bad temper and he always gets his way."

Alex stared out of the window towards the hotel and then back at the man he knew as Marek.

"Who are you... really?" Alex asked.

"My name's Wael."

"You seem to know a great deal."

"I am a real Egyptologist."

"Did you kill Marek?"

"No."

"Who did?"

At that moment, the side door jerked open and the BMW man, Joachim, took hold of Alex's collar and pulled him out. "Enough chat." When the three of them were standing beside a Land Rover, Joachim gripped Alex's shoulder.

"The girl has told me it's temple four—the one on this hill—that we're interested in."

"You bastard," Alex hissed, fighting against the bindings. "If you've hurt her—"

The man slapped him. "Don't worry about what I've *done*, worry about what I *will* do. If you don't help us, then I shall just have to have some fun, won't I?"

Wael said, "Who is keeping an eye on her?"

"Ahmed," Joachim said dismissively. He took a piece of paper from a pocket and showed a diagram to Wael and then Alex.

Wael said, "Why this temple, Alex?"

"The dimensions."

Wael shrugged. "And that means?"

"The short end is twenty-two and a half metres long. The side is thirty metres and if I draw a diagonal line across the temple, the triangle I have is thirty-seven and a half metres," Alex said, proudly unable to restrain himself. "It's in the ratio three, four and five."

"So it's the magical ratio of numbers we are looking for." Wael grinned for a moment then frowned. "This helps us how?"

"Why should I tell you?"

The other man growled, "Because of the girl."

Wael pulled the other man aside. Alex couldn't understand what they said, but it was urgent and angry.

He figured the men despised one another. Could he use that to his advantage somehow?

They stopped talking and Wael turned to Alex and spoke calmly. "It is for your professional pride, Alex. My people only want the treasure that is here. If you want, you can have all the glory. Perhaps we may allow you to keep something valuable."

Alex thought, but there seemed no option but to cooperate.

He said, "All right. Let's go up to the temple, but I have two conditions. Firstly, you cut these bindings—after all, I won't be able to walk with my legs tied and I need my hands to draw."

Joachim cut the bindings with a knife and returned it to a sheath on his belt. All the time he kept his cold eyes on Alex, like a snake trying to mesmerise a trapped rodent.

"All right," Wael said. "See, we are reasonable. What is your second condition?"

Alex said, "You let Rebecca go."

"You're in no position to bargain," Joachim scoffed, but then he signalled towards the hotel. Returning his attention to Alex, he said, "I will let her join us. Perhaps it will add to the incentive."

Rebecca appeared at the entrance, her hands tied in front of her. Ahmed had hold of her arm, but when he let go, she ran to Alex. He put his arms around her. "Are you all right?"

She nodded and he told her everything was going to be all right.

"Let's go," Joachim said, and pointed up the hill.

They walked up the sand and gravel path to the summit. Wael led the way. Ahmed and Joachim walked behind them.

"Marek's real name is Wael. Claims he's an Egyptologist," Alex said to Rebecca. Then, calling to Wael, "The mummy research in Cairo was fake—to convince us you were genuine, right?"

"Yes."

"But when we asked for you at the museum..." Alex nodded at the sudden realisation. "The security guard... you paid him off."

"Of course." Wael stopped and pointed to the ground where paths converged. Most of the area was bald, but there were a few stones to depict the ruins.

Alex was dismayed. "You know this is impossible! How can I possibly make sense of this? Where are the forty columns? Where are the geese?"

Joachim placed his arm across Rebecca's chest, pulling her close and placing his gun against her temple. "I think you know how to read the map. You are a smart guy. I suggest you think hard and work it out."

Alex took the paper from Wael and studied it. Immediately north of the temple was believed to have been an offering area, beyond that another temple. The walls of the second, smaller temple were less regular and his thoughts were that this was from a much earlier period. This location was the focal point of the area. There should only have been one temple. He walked to the south-eastern corner and looked around and then studied the diagram. The previous night he had realised this was not just a series of walls with the magical triangular ratio, the walls weren't symmetrical—they were deliberately different lengths.

He asked, "How long was an Egyptian standard measure?"

"A cubit was the standard measure. It is the length of a forearm to the fingertip," Wael said. "Not very standard."

Alex knelt and measured the smallest gap with his arm, then the next biggest. Then he walked around and estimated the rest and laughed.

Wael joined him. "What is it, my friend?"

Alex returned to the south-eastern corner of the ruined temple. "What do four hoops—heel bones—mean?"

"Forty." Wael shrugged as if it were obvious. "And then the pillar. We agreed we are looking for the forty pillars."

Alex shook his head. "No. We made a mistake. They aren't hoops, they're ropes—coiled ropes. And normally they would mean one hundred."

"So we're looking for four hundred pillars?" Weal asked.

"Normally, yes, but here the coil relates to the triangle not the pillar. Ellen either didn't recognise it or knew it wasn't a number but a..." Alex drew a spiral in the dirt. Under different circumstances he would have grinned.

Joachim snapped, "What?"

"More double meaning. The spiral doesn't just represent one hundred, it also shows—"

"The Fibonacci sequence?" Wael asked.

"Precisely! And what does the Fibonacci sequence do?" Alex paused a beat before answering his own question. "It gives us *sectio aurea*—the golden section. In the Fibonacci sequence the ratio of two consecutive numbers tends towards phi. 1.61803399. So it's similar to pi."

Joachim huffed but Wael held up a hand to stop him interrupting.

Wael said, "Go on, Alex."

"The proportions of the Parthenon are famously based on this ratio. This temple's proportions aren't perfect, perhaps something is missing from the diagram, perhaps we need the full 3D effect, but this is very clever. The proportions here are both the three-four-five ratio and close to the Fibonacci sequence."

Joachim said, "I don't care what it means. Just get on with it!"

Wael glared at his companion and immediately said, "And that helps us how, Alex?"

"Well, I think of Fibonacci as squares rather than a spiral. The squares have sides 1, 1, 2, 3, 5, 8, 13 and so on. The same is true for golden rectangles. You know A0 folds in half to form A1, which folds to form A2 and so on." In the dirt he drew a rectangle and then one on top of the first like an upside-down L.

He said, "The second rectangle here has its length that is twice the width of the first rectangle." Adjacent to the second, he drew a third rectangle. "This is like the A2, if my first rectangle was A4 and then I draw another—A1— that connects us back to the first."

The final series looked like this:

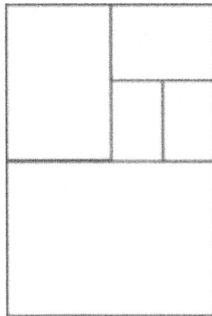

Wael said, "All right, I get the point."

"Well, now draw a diagonal line across one of these and you get a triangle."

"Naturally."

Alex drew a line bisecting the first rectangle. "And the amazing thing is the triangle is approximately three, four, five in dimensions. It's a golden triangle equivalent and the progression is like a Fibonacci sequence—maybe even more special!"

Alex continued to convert his sequence of four rectangles into triangles. "See, a Fibonacci-type spiral appears."

Joachim shook his head, unimpressed.

Wael prompted, "So this means…?"

"Four hoops didn't mean forty. They weren't heel bones. They were deliberately rotated to mean four stages of the sequence. The pillar relates to a circle on the temple layout. It indicates the Isis throne." He added the throne to the diagram and then walked to the bottom right-hand corner of the temple. He knew he hadn't disclosed the throne and dot to Wael/Marek but the Egyptologist didn't question him.

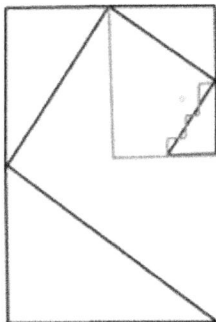

"We needed the location of the temple. But we also needed the start of the map. This is the origin. It's where the first triangle is, the start of the sequence." He indicated a line from the middle of the base to the top end of where the throne would fit. "That would be the hypotenuse. It aligns with the north, yes?"

He didn't wait for a response, but walked the length of the first triangle, counting his paces. When he stopped he indicated a triangle following the line of the temple wall. "The second triangle starts here, goes to the top right corner and finishes top left. The third triangle brings us back." He pointed left, along the line of the base. "It ends at a point the width of the temple on the far side."

Then he started walking again, counting his paces to the top wall of the temple and returned to the bottom corner. "The fourth triangle comes right round and will end over there, the length of the temple away." Pointing south-east, he set off walking in line with the side wall, counting the paces.

When Alex had counted the same number of paces as the length of the temple, he stopped. "The first triangle had sides of three and four. The fourth triangle is eight and twelve. Twelve again. And the eight in the code confirms this is right." He looked back to make sure his line was straight, adjusted his position slightly, then pointed to the ground. "This is where the map leads. Whatever it is, is buried here... possibly a tomb..." He looked at Wael, shrugged and half smiled. "I'm afraid there's no access, the dig hasn't covered this area."

In the corner of his eye he saw Joachim advance. Alex turned just in time to see the man lash out, pistol-whipping him into oblivion.

Chapter 54

The mini digger roared to life on the hill, belching diesel fumes as it worked. A second Land Rover was parked beside the first, both vehicles stationed outside the hotel like silent sentinels. A man Alex hadn't seen before operated the machine, excavating the area known as Temple IV with reckless speed, caring little for preservation as he unearthed the ancient walls.

Rebecca cradled Alex's head in her lap, their hands tied, though their legs were free. Ahmed stood nearby, a gun lazily aimed in their direction. Wael hovered close, his eyes flicking nervously between the excavation and Alex. Joachim directed the dig, his eyes focused on the task at hand.

Alex watched the chaotic excavation and then locked eyes with Wael. "Call yourself an archaeologist? Do you approve of this?"

Wael's silence was telling. Concern etched in his features.

Rebecca offered Alex a drink from a water bottle, helping him sit up. The digger had cleared an area, revealing steps descending to a stone door. Joachim signalled the digger to back off and ventured into the excavated site, approaching the steps.

Wael joined Joachim at the stone door, his excitement palpable. "Geese, one in each corner—the four geese!" he shouted back. "And the Isis throne again."

The Isis throne at the origin and an Isis throne at the end.

This was it. The tomb they were looking for.

Joachim shoved Wael aside, feeling around the stone doorway before stepping back. The two men conferred animatedly, Wael retreating as Joachim signalled the digger operator. The scoop positioned itself before the stone door. Like claps thunder the ground began to reverberate as the digger thrust forward.

"Don't damage it!" Alex yelled, but his words were lost in the thumps and crashes.

Alex turned to Wael and shouted, "If you're expecting treasure, I think you're mistaken."

Wael turned his eyes from the digger to Alex..

"Just to be clear, the gold hiero on the Map-Stone doesn't mean gold!" Alex shouted. The sound abated and Alex quickly added: "There's no gold in the tomb. The hiero refers to the geometric progression identifying the temple: the golden triangles. You were right, it was *pure* gold."

Wael's expression turned scornful. "Perhaps, but our interest is not really treasure, gold or otherwise."

The digger started again and jarred against the stone door. It tilted. Another strike and a gap wide enough for a man to crawl through appeared. As the digger backed away, Wael darted forward, shining a torch into the dark space. After a brief hesitation, he disappeared inside, reemerging moments later.

"You were right. It looks like a maze in here," Wael called out before disappearing again.

Alex nodded to Rebecca, remembering how she had recognised the lines on the ceremonial block as resembling a maze.

Joachim ordered Ahmed to keep his gun trained on them and then entered the tomb.

Rebecca whispered something Alex couldn't catch. Her eyes followed the digger operator as he climbed out on the far side. Alex looked up at Ahmed just as Rebecca swept his legs away. In one swift motion, she was on her feet, standing on Ahmed's gun hand.

She must have untied her hands, for she now held the gun. She pointed it at the stunned digger operator, instructing him to untie Alex. With the gun as her leverage, she made Ahmed and the digger operator walk down the hill towards the cars, prodding them along.

Alex followed, glancing back repeatedly, but the others didn't emerge from the tomb.

At the cars, Rebecca grabbed the keys and told Alex to tie the prisoners' hands. They locked them in the back of the Land Rover and threw the keys away. Rebecca then jumped into the driver's seat of the second Land Rover, Alex beside her.

After fumbling with the ignition, Rebecca slammed the gears into reverse, speeding out of the town. Faces watched them from the safety of their homes, either used to the antics of crazy archaeologists or recognising trouble.

Rebecca navigated the main road, turning right and then onto a dual carriageway. "I don't know where I'm going!" she laughed, almost maniacal relief in her voice.

Alex's heart pounded in his chest like a trapped bird. He took deep breaths, sinking into his seat.

At a service stop, Rebecca parked around the back, and they cleaned up in the bathrooms. They reunited in the restaurant and ordered coffee. Initially deciding against food, the enticing smell soon had them ordering large portions, savouring every bite as if it were their last meal.

Lost in their own thoughts, they ate in silence. When they were done, Alex stared out the window. "We've got to go back," he said.

"No, we need to inform the authorities."

"We've dealt with the so-called authorities before. We're foreigners without passports, and we're linked to trouble. They'll just lock us up—arrest first, question later. I don't want to see the inside of a cell again."

"So, we go back?"

"Hold on." He disappeared for a few minutes, returning with a book. He opened it to a map of the region.

"We wait till dark and find another way around. We make sure they're not there and then take a look." He pointed to an area just south of Port Said. "We're about here. There are a thousand roads through this delta. We can go around here." He traced a line zigzagging west and then south. "We can come around to the north and stop at the buildings to the west of the site."

"So, we'll check it out from a distance and won't go near if they're still there?"

"Exactly."

Rebecca agreed and they drove to Port Said. By the time they arrived, she had persuaded Alex to get a hotel and wait a day before returning. Driving back only to find the men still there would be infuriating.

Without passports, they found a small hotel where they weren't asked for identification. They checked into separate rooms, each sinking into a relaxing bath. Later, they walked to the beach, watching the sunset from a bar. After a couple of beers, Alex began to unwind.

"I still can't get over it," he said.

"What?"

"The golden ratio, phi, is so similar to pi. It can't be a coincidence that the Bible refers to the area where the temple is as Pi-Ramesses. Phi is attributed to the Greeks, but they must have got it from the Egyptians. And the pyramids, generally thought to be based on pi, but actually follow the golden ratio."

Rebecca didn't share his enthusiasm. "Don't you find it amazing?" he asked.

She forced a smile. "About the mathematics? Not really. Sorry, Alex. I'm more interested in whose tomb it is. Who do you think?"

"It must be Nefertiti's. I think Meryra either built the tomb or helped with the design and created the Map-Stone. I don't understand why the block was in Amarna though."

"Are you certain Lord Carnarvon didn't take it from King Tut's... sorry, Tutankhamun's tomb? Wouldn't that make more sense since you think Meryra took other things there, including documents?"

"Two reasons. It wasn't Carnarvon's style to lie about where he obtained something. He was too honest about finding papyri in Tutankhamun's tomb. Secondly, there's the timeline. From the Amarna Letters, Marek—the real one—was sure the trip to the Valley of the Kings was earlier. We think the Map-Stone was taken to Amarna with other records after the queen had died."

"What about Akhenaten? Where's he?"

"If only I knew!" Alex ordered more drinks, a twinkle in his eye as he looked at Rebecca. "You know, some people believe Moses was actually Akhenaten."

"That can't be true. You said yourself Akhenaten died."

Alex raised his hands. "I agree. But there are many who think the Exodus happened around this time. Remember, Akhenaten's—and by extension Nefertiti's—followers were considered outlaws."

"Yes, I recall you winding me up by saying *Ibiru* meant outlaw and sounds like Hebrew."

"You know, one thing that's always bothered me about the Bible is the story of Adam and Eve. They're the first people, right? Eve is made from Adam's rib, but they can't have been the only ones. When Cain kills Abel, he's branded so others would know. Later, Cain marries and has a son."

"Called Henoch," Rebecca said quietly.

Alex nodded. "If there weren't other people, then Cain must have married a sister—which he didn't."

Rebecca sipped a tequila sunrise. "I don't know if it's the alcohol or that I'm just suddenly very chilled out, but I'm not going to argue with you." Her laugh encouraged him to continue.

"I'll tell you something that might surprise you. There's a theory that Akhenaten and Nefertiti were the Adam and Eve of the Bible. Their city, Akhetaten, was a new beautiful paradise—Eden. Akhenaten upset God and they were expelled from the city."

"And you believe that?"

"Not really. It's a fun thought, though. The city must have been incredible, like nothing the people would have experienced before. Obviously, you can't see it nowadays, but there would have been irrigation channels with gardens and trees everywhere. The streets would have been paved, some with beautiful paintings—there's one in the Cairo Museum. Parts would have been open to the sky for the worship of the sun, but scholars believe there were giant awnings strung between buildings so people could walk in the shade. The temples would have been beautifully painted with blues, yellows, whites, and greens, bringing the buildings to life. Even the statues would have been painted with lifelike colours. It must have been an incredible time—a time of art, music, and peace."

"Until it all came to an end."

"But wonderful while it lasted."

"If it was allowed, I'd give you a kiss." She squeezed his arm affectionately. "For an atheist, you've just painted a very religious experience."

Chapter 55

Gershom stood on the hill, surveying the expanse of Tell el-Dab'a. "So this is the temple," he murmured, a shadow of curiosity in his voice.

Wael gestured to the area encompassing what they had believed were two temples, now understood to be one. Like A1 paper folded to form two A2 sheets. "The temple of Osiris," he confirmed. "It all fits. It makes more sense for it to be here in the Delta, the heart of the religion, rather than in Amarna."

"And the map led you to the entrance of the tomb?" Gershom's eyes traced the crude excavation to the open stone entrance.

"It did," Wael replied.

"Where is Joachim?"

"He's inside, laying explosives." Wael's voice betrayed his disgust.

"What troubles you?" Gershom asked, eyes narrowing.

"I am an archaeologist first and foremost. This destruction goes against everything I stand for."

"First and foremost, you are a member of the sacred brotherhood," Gershom reminded him sharply. "I understand your concerns, but this is necessary. We must eliminate the evidence."

Wael's eyes pleaded with the old man. "But there *is* no evidence!"

"What do you mean?" Gershom's voice hardened.

"Come, let me show you." Wael led the way down into the crater, waiting for Gershom to catch up. They ducked under a stone lintel, entering a dim corridor. Wael flicked on a torch, guiding them through the twisting maze.

The old man's walking stick echoed against the stone, a rhythmic click-clack that mirrored his hesitant pace. After several turns, Gershom asked, "The map was clear about navigating this maze?"

"Yes, yes, we had no problems until..." Wael's voice trailed off as they rounded another corner, revealing the glow of Joachim's torch.

Joachim stood in a room, attaching explosives to the walls. There was nothing else save for the hieroglyphs adorning its surfaces.

"The burial chamber?" Gershom inquired; his tone sceptical.

Joachim paused, his frustration evident. "Empty. It seems the tomb was robbed long ago."

"And there's nothing more?" Gershom pressed.

"There's an identical room on the opposite side, but this is the true burial chamber. The inscriptions indicate it belonged to a significant woman—undoubtedly the right tomb, from the Eighteenth Dynasty—but there's nothing here worth destroying."

Gershom pondered for a moment, tapping his stick as if making a decision. "We leave. Remove the explosives, Joachim. Wael is correct. There is nothing here we should be afraid of."

Joachim hesitated as though considering an argument, then began disconnecting the explosives. Gershom patted Wael's arm and led him out of the chamber. Together, they retraced their steps to the surface.

Outside, Wael breathed a sigh of relief. "Thank you."

"You have served the Brotherhood well," Gershom said. He pointed to a Land Rover parked outside the hotel. The driver raised a hand in acknowledgment. "Return to Cairo and resume your life."

"And you?"

"I will pray." Gershom watched Wael descend the hill before turning back to the temple. He found a secluded spot and stood still, lost in thought. Slowly, he pulled a book from his pocket, lifted his head to the sky, and began to chant the ancient sacred words, passed down through generations for over three thousand years.

When he finished, the sun was like liquid gold on the horizon. For ten more minutes, Gershom stood in silence, watching it disappear, feeling the same awe the ancient Egyptians must have felt as they imagined the sun being swallowed by the goddess Nut, only to be reborn the next day. This was the Aten, the sun disc on the horizon. Gershom nodded to himself; how much simpler it would have been if they had embraced Akhenaten's worship of the sun god.

As Gershom turned to leave, he saw Joachim watching, his eyes cold and devoid of appreciation for the moment. Joachim could never lead the Brotherhood. But then, neither could Wael.

"Everything is in place," Joachim said.

"Did you ever think Wael would find the tomb?" Gershom asked.

"It was possible. Perhaps he could have located the temple, but I doubt he would have understood the golden triangles and the sequence." Joachim's voice was dismissive.

In the fading light, they walked down the hill, Joachim matching the old man's pace.

"But the chamber we found isn't the final tomb," Joachim continued. "The maze is unsolvable without the map. And MacLure knows he didn't tell us everything. Are you sure he'll come back?"

"He'll be back, either tonight or tomorrow," Gershom said, glancing back at the temple. "And the explosives?"

Joachim smiled tightly. "As I said, the explosives are in place."

Chapter 56

The moon, just three days shy of full, cast an eerie glow over the ancient hill. Rebecca had parked in the shadow of some farm buildings, precisely where Alex had indicated, and they followed the path to the foot of the mound. Dressed in black—newly acquired from a day of shopping for appropriate clothes in Port Said—they each carried a powerful torch. Alex wore a tool belt, stocked with a claw hammer and screwdriver. He didn't have Rebecca's martial art skills and found comfort in knowing the tools could double as weapons if needed.

He checked his watch: just after 1am. They stood hidden beside a wall, eyes fixed on the spectral hill. Nothing stirred. After thirty minutes, they decided to move.

A dog barked sharply from the direction of the main cluster of buildings. Someone shouted. Alex and Rebecca stopped, crouching low, listening intently. Another dog barked, this time farther away. Silence followed.

"We're exposed here," Rebecca whispered urgently. "We need to get inside."

Alex nodded, and they swiftly moved to where the digger had excavated a crater, exposing the tomb's entrance.

In the moonlight, Alex saw a metal grill, like a section of a security fence, covering the doorway. A red and white sign warned of danger.

Taking a side each, they carefully lifted the grill and moved it aside. Alex led the way, climbing past the stone door. He switched on his torch, and Rebecca's beam soon joined his. The passage was just wide enough for one person to pass through with their head bent. Its walls, floor, and ceiling were unadorned stone blocks. They walked forward five paces, small stones and sandy earth grating under their feet.

At a T-junction, Alex recalled the Map-Stone and turned left. Rebecca followed a step behind.

Alex pulled up sharply, staring at a blinking red light on the wall. "What the...?"

Rebecca leaned in close to peer at the object wedged between the blocks. The red light was a digital display.

"Jesus! It's a timer. This place is rigged to blow," Alex said, his voice tight with alarm.

"According to the timer, we have just under two hours," Rebecca noted, her eyes wide.

Alex checked his watch again. "Let's hope that's enough," he muttered, sweeping his torch ahead. Two hours seemed like a long time, but his breathing quickened, and he began to hurry. Three steps later, he turned right and then immediately left. At the next junction, another timer blinked on a package affixed to the wall, mirroring the first. Alex pressed on, turning right, then right again.

This is much bigger than I expected," Rebecca whispered, a note of unease in her voice.

Alex turned to look at her. "You okay?"

In the torchlight, her face looked ghostly pale. "I don't like confined spaces."

"Not long," he reassured her, taking four more paces before stopping at what appeared to be a dead end.

Rebecca shone her torch at the wall. "Wrong way?"

Alex stepped forward, sideways, and disappeared. His torch lit a sliver of the wall where he'd vanished. "Optical illusion," he called back.

Rebecca followed, squeezing through. They weaved through a few more tight turns before arriving at a chamber.

"No more explosives since the false wall. Looks like the other guys didn't get this far. Probably found the mirror image of this chamber," Alex noted, scanning the blank walls with his torch.

"Nothing here," Rebecca observed, sounding deflated.

"Another illusion," Alex suggested. He moved to the far end and shone his torch back. The overlapping stones revealed a gap in the floor.

He sat, manoeuvred into the hole, and shone the torch down and right. Steps descended into a well of blackness.

"Oh God," Rebecca breathed.

"If it's too confined for you, wait here," Alex offered.

"I'm coming," she said firmly.

They dropped almost six feet and began to weave through this new level, the sides barely shoulder-width apart, forcing them to crouch.

"Alex."

"Okay?" He turned, shining his torch toward her. She held a piece of limestone in her hand, marking the wall.

She smiled wanly. "I'm marking our route. It's helping me stay focused and not worry about being trapped down here. But we've just come back on ourselves."

"I can't do it," he admitted. "I thought I could make sense of the lines on the Map-Stone, but I can't."

"I can get us to the steps. Shall we go back?"

He reluctantly agreed, and after a couple of turns, they were back at the start of the level.

Rebecca sat on the steps, and he squatted in front of her, deep in thought. After a few minutes, he raised his torch to check Rebecca's face. She looked at him, half patient, half expectant. And then he saw it. Over her left shoulder was a symbol on the wall. He jumped up, examining the indentation closely. A scarab. He shone the torch on the other walls, noticing each path was marked with a different symbol. One made him let out a splutter.

"Of course!"

Chapter 57

"It's the knot of Isis," Alex exclaimed, his voice echoing through the ancient passage. "One of the four amulets for protection in the afterlife. It was placed in the hand of the deceased. It was on the Map-Stone. It was faded and looked like a spoon, but it was the kot of isis. Isis is the key of life. You see, Rebecca? *Isis is the key.* Ellen would have loved that her message had another meaning!"

He squeezed past Rebecca, his torch beam dancing along the walls as he checked each corner.

"This way—we follow the Isis markings."

At the next junction, he pointed the light at another Isis knot on the wall, then turned to search the next alternatives. He was moving quicker now, a sense of urgency driving him. After three more switchbacks, he turned to Rebecca, excitement gleaming in his eyes. "Almost there. The next turn should take us to the burial corridor. If I've got my bearings right, it'll lead us back under the temple."

They reached a junction where they needed to crawl to enter the corridor. The air was cool and tasted of dry dust and earth. The walls were inscribed with hieroglyphs.

"It's Neferneferuaten—Nefertiti," Alex said, his voice barely containing his excitement. The hieroglyphs ran along the gently sloping corridor, appearing to tell a story.

"Can you read it?" Rebecca asked.

"No," Alex admitted, running his hand along the wall. "But here we have the death of a child and then another. This section seems to be about Akhenaten's death and the Aten turning his back on the people." He moved down, climbing around wooden ceiling supports.

He switched to the other wall. "This is more positive. Here, Nefertiti seems to have taken on the form of Isis and is with her husband Osiris. Here's a reference to the Palace of the Great Barque. And four geese!" He played the torch back and forth. "I don't understand. Maybe it's a double meaning again. I didn't expect any more geese."

"Wael said that the geese could symbolise the rise of a new pharaoh," Rebecca reminded him.

"He did." Alex pondered for a second. "Would Nefertiti celebrate Ay or Horemheb taking power? It doesn't seem likely."

"How are we doing for time?" Rebecca asked, a note of urgency in her voice.

He checked his watch. "Ninety-three minutes."

"Can we keep going? The sooner we're out of here, the better."

"But this could be the find of the century! We need to record it before it's too late." Alex took out his phone and, using the torch, snapped photographs of the mural. When he had finished, Rebecca was waiting for him at the end of the passage—the antechamber, Alex surmised. There had once been a stone door, but the debris was scattered around a partial slab where it had originally sealed the chamber.

The floor dropped down, allowing them to stand again, though they had to bend their heads. Wooden supports held up the ceiling, but further back, they had collapsed. Earth and other debris covered the ground. Alex cast the torch beam around, noting nothing he would class as treasure, but among the broken pottery, some pieces remained intact, and there were five wooden caskets of various sizes—three smashed, two intact. Beyond the room was an opening: the entrance to the burial chamber. From appearances, it had been broken into from above. Most of the room was blocked with dirt and rubble.

"Tomb robbers," Alex said. "Probably in antiquity. Either they deliberately dug through from the temple or the roof collapsed first. Nefertiti's sarcophagus may be under there, but I somehow doubt it." He swung the light back into the antechamber. Beautifully painted murals covered every inch, telling the same story as before, plus traditional images of resurrection and the afterlife. There was also a scene of the Opening of the Mouth ceremony. Normally, this would have been performed by the high priest, but this was a significant departure; here, the priest seemed to be Osiris himself. Alex took more photographs before turning his attention to the caskets.

The first was about two feet long and deep, and about a foot wide. He lifted the heavy lid. Inside were dozens of clay shabtis and a funerary block.

"This looks like the twin of the Map-Stone," Alex said in awe.

He lifted the lid of the second complete chest. This was the size of a bed linen box and contained a stack of clay tablets and neatly rolled papyri. He pulled one out, barely able to breathe with excitement. Slowly, he unrolled it, afraid its brittle material would crumble. It didn't.

He stared at the image drawn on the paper, unable to comprehend what he was looking at: three columns of coloured circles. Against each was written a single word in hieratic script. He snapped a photo, then pulled out another and photographed that one. It was confusing. This wasn't what he'd expected at all. There was no *Book of the Dead*, but rather evidence of something else entirely. Again and again, he noted Osiris featuring. Suddenly, the religious significance of what he was looking at dawned on him.

He pulled out another and gagged at what he saw.

"Rebecca!" he blurted. "My God, this is incredible!"

He'd been so engrossed in the papyri, he hadn't wondered what Rebecca was doing. Now he heard her footsteps. Where was she going? He looked around and then his blood froze. The footfall was approaching. Rebecca had backed into a corner and was just standing there.

A light came towards them down the passage.

Rebecca's voice was quiet. "I'm so sorry, Alex."

Joachim stepped into the chamber and pointed his gun at Alex.

Chapter 58

Joachim glanced at Rebecca, his eyes gleaming with a mixture of triumph and anticipation. "Is this all there is?"

Rebecca nodded, her voice steady. "It looks that way."

"But it's enough, and we've found it," Joachim declared. "This is a great day for the Brotherhood of Levi. This is what we have existed for."

Alex squatted, pressed back against the wall, his eyes locked on the gun aimed at his chest. Joachim said something more, but Alex wasn't listening. His mind was racing, trying to process the betrayal. He stared at Rebecca in disbelief.

"You're working with them?" his voice was a mixture of anger and hurt.

Rebecca's eyes briefly met his before she stepped between the two men, her demeanour calm but resolute.

"Let him go," she commanded, not a hint of a question in her voice.

Joachim's smile widened.

She continued: "There have been enough deaths over this. I played my role on the understanding that he would be allowed to live. My uncle guaranteed it."

Alex stood and moved closer to Rebecca, reducing the opportunity for Joachim to shoot him. Rebecca sensed his presence and edged to the right. Alex moved with her, maintaining the shield. This manoeuvre allowed Joachim to see the open chest. With his gun still trained on Alex, he sidestepped, removed a bag from his shoulder, and dipped into the papyri-filled chest. Pulling out a scroll, he partially unrolled it using one hand and the edge of the box.

"Shine your torch," he snapped at Rebecca. She complied, aiming it close by. Joachim glanced briefly at the document before dropping it and inspecting another.

Rebecca seized the moment. "Is that more explosive in there?" she asked, pointing at the bag, her voice calm.

"Don't worry, there's plenty of time for us to get out safely," Joachim said, instinctively glancing at the bag.

That was when Rebecca kicked out. A shower of debris and a chunk of stone flew from her foot towards Joachim. He dropped into a squat and fired the gun, but the shot went wide.

Rebecca was already pulling Alex towards the doorway. As she moved, she kicked out at an upright support.

Joachim shouted and fired again. This time, Rebecca grunted in pain. She lunged at the upright, and immediately, the ceiling began to cave in.

Alex grabbed her arm and pulled her into the corridor as dust and debris blasted around them. The ceiling began to crack and a stanchion creaked and snapped. Earth and stone fell. Alex guided her up the passage as it crumbled behind them.

The torchlight easily picked out Rebecca's white chalk marks, and they hurried through the lower level. Each time they turned he fear the worst: they'd find the way blocked, the tunnel collapsed.

Then they were at the place they'd dropped down, and climbed to the first level of the maze. The ground groaned beneath them and Alex wondered if the whole thing would fail, trapping them, sealing the whole tomb.

There was no air. The maze walls closed in and then, finally, they saw the broken entrance. Staggering up the final steps, they collapsed on the ground outside.

Alex lay panting, looking up at the stars. Beside him, Rebecca stood, staring towards the temple. A man leaning heavily on a walking stick stood not ten paces away.

Alex forced himself up. In the pale moonlight, it took a moment to recognise the old man.

Of course.

"Uncle Seth!" Alex said bitterly.

"Where's Joachim?" Gershom said, his voice as thick as liquid tar.

Rebecca replied that the other man had been crushed by the collapse of the burial chamber. Alex looked at her, noticing her arm was slick with blood. Shot by Joachim.

"Rebecca, you're hurt!" Alex tore a sleeve off his shirt and tied a tourniquet above the wound. She put her other arm over his shoulder for support, and his arm went around her. Suddenly, nothing else seemed to matter. Together, they walked out of the crater.

Two paces short of the old man, they stopped.

Gershom asked, "Was the evidence there?"

"Yes. And Joachim laid the explosive," Rebecca replied, looking long and hard at the old man. "He tried to kill us. You promised—"

"What did he see?" Gershom interrupted, nodding at Alex.

"Nothing," she said. "The chamber collapsed."

A long silence. The old man breathed out. "Then I say there will be no more deaths."

"Thank you."

"But nothing incriminating can be allowed to leave this place. It's our sacred duty."

Alex's mind continued to spin with the enormity of it all. Then he started talking before he could stop himself. "You can't destroy this… This is a miraculous archaeological find… You mustn't—"

Gershom fixed Alex with a glare. "Stop! Stop now before I change my mind about you."

Alex stood, struck dumb. He looked at Rebecca for support but she shook her head.

"You need to promise that you'll never talk about what happened."

Alex said nothing.

Rebecca's eyes were wide with concern. "Alex, promise me!"

He rubbed his head then nodded slowly.

She stepped closer and hugged him and whispered in his ear. "I'm so sorry. I had to do it. Had to… But something changed. I really… care about you. Please remember that." She broke the embrace and held something out.

He looked down and saw the keys to the Land Rover.

"Take them."

Gershom checked his watch. "We need to get going before the explosion. And you, young lady, need a doctor."

Alex walked slowly towards the farm buildings and got into the car like an automaton. He started the engine and drove, unblinking eyes fixed, tunnel vision ahead.

He covered the first few miles in a daze, unable to recall the route he'd taken. It felt like a bad dream. He put the window down. Leaning out, he let the rushing air blast his face, waking him up. In the distance, behind, he thought he heard a dull explosion, but it came and went so quickly he was left wondering.

Alex found his way out of the region and turned onto a dual carriageway. Pressing the accelerator hard, he joined the motorway and headed for Cairo. He tried to focus on the road, but thoughts continued to crowd his mind. Everything that had happened. Everything he'd seen. He no longer had the evidence, but Rebecca had helped him. Did she know the truth? Of course she knew.

He might not have the evidence, but he knew too.

He knew their secret.

Chapter 59

Fifteen months later

Abubakar Habib sucked his teeth. "Show me again the area of your planned excavation."

Alex took a deep breath. This had already been approved by the Ministry of Antiquities, but he had quickly learned how things worked in Egypt. There was no point in arguing. It would only aggravate matters. Habib, this minor local official, either wanted power and respect, or money—or perhaps all of them.

Alex called to his assistant. "Mahmood, please make the inspector a cup of your best coffee."

A young Nubian man waved from the next room and there were soon sounds of a pot on the small gas cooker they all shared.

Alex pulled out the approved documents and looked at the diagram of the four hundred square metre patch in the northern hills of Amarna. Despite there being some nobles' tombs, this location had yielded nothing in the past.

Inspector Habib marked the areas of other excavations and also the area where peasants' graves had been found in the plain. "These are not your areas."

"I agree."

Habib pointed at the area Alex was interested in. "There is nothing here." He sucked on his teeth for a moment as though thinking. "Which team did you say you are with?"

Again, Alex pulled out the relevant papers. He spoke with pride, having had the dig approved by Professor Steele at Macquarie University. "The permit is for one year."

Mahmood, the Nubian assistant, scurried in with a small steaming cup of Egyptian coffee. He nodded encouragement to Alex, who returned his smile.

Habib tasted the coffee without comment and set it down. "You will not enter any tomb you find. Is that understood?"

"Absolutely! No entry without you being present."

"If you find anything at all, it must be recorded. I will make visits. If I find any item not recorded, your permit will be revoked. Any items and that is it. No more digging."

"Understood."

"You and your team are staying on the site?"

"We are staying in caravans. We will not leave Tell el-Amarna without notifying you."

"Good. When you and your team come and go, you will tell me first. I must know when you leave. If someone comes or goes and you don't tell me, then that is it also. No more digging."

The inspector went over the details of the permit once again before he finished his coffee. Alex was surprised there was no suggestion of money to be paid, but he knew this was just the beginning.

When he was alone again, he sat back in his chair and closed his eyes. It felt much longer than fifteen months. So much had happened. He had checked into a hotel at Cairo airport and flown back to England the following day. He had returned to his flat in Maida Vale without any media attention. There had been a couple of students murdered, one of which had caught the public's attention because of the mystery surrounding the girl's final movements. And so the headlines and paparazzi had moved away from Alex and the Highclere burglary. He was old news.

He felt a mixture of elation and disappointment. He had made an incredible discovery and yet he knew it wouldn't be believed. Rebecca had lied to her uncle. She knew Alex had taken photographs. But they didn't prove it was Nefertiti's tomb at Tell el-Dab'a.

He cursed himself for not photographing the ceremonial funerary stone—a second Map-Stone that no doubt led to Akhenaten's true resting place. A hidden tomb in Amarna, he thought.

The destruction of part of the hill at the ancient site in Tell el-Dab'a was reported in the local press as a gas explosion. Another gas explosion. Ellen's death and now the destruction of an ancient site. Alex realised that claiming to have discovered the tomb would create unwanted media attention. He could imagine the headlines and the hounding. No, it wasn't worth it.

Alex had searched online for information about the Brotherhood of Levi. There was limited information on the Jewish group, and a conspiracy theory suggested they had senior roles in all Western governments, controlling and censoring, and actively ensured information about them was destroyed. Alex noted that Levi in the Bible was a son of Jacob whose three sons had responded when Moses felt betrayed by his people.

In Exodus, while Moses was on Mount Sinai, the Israelites turned to Aaron, a high priest who created a golden calf for the people to worship. In retribution, the sons of Levi killed three thousand of the followers in punishment for turning to other gods. It seemed reasonable that a modern group would have the same aims.

The golden calf was undoubtedly a bull which was an incarnation of Ra—the sun god. It made sense. While Moses was away, the Israelites had returned to worshipping the sun. Maybe this also confirmed that they had come from Akhenaten's city and the worship of the sun by the name of the Aten. Alex was convinced that Aten and Ra were one and the same.

During the first few days, Alex sketched what he had seen in the tomb.

He also began to write potential academic papers that avoided reference to the missing papyri and Judaism, but focused on what might have become of Akhenaten and his queen.

In the second week, he was amazed to receive an email from Rebecca saying that her wound was healing well and she had finished the article about him.

The article had changed his life. Its publication in a Sunday paper coincided with him finding the item missing from the exhibition. Now that all the pressure was off, he was able to think clearly, able to revisit Highclere Castle and look at the exhibition through Ellen's eyes. What would he have done if he had feared the Map-Stone would be stolen? She wasn't strong so she wouldn't have carried it far. Also, she knew she couldn't take it past a camera.

Alex had found it under the four canopic jars in Tutankhamun's mock burial chamber.

He'd been working on the translation of the hidden messages within the Amarna Letters. When he was happy with the story—mainly the progression of a peasant boy called Yanhamu to becoming a soldier and then scribe, he published it. But he gave credit to Ellen Champion and

Marek Borevsek for their ground-breaking work, giving himself a minor role in the publication.

The paper didn't draw conclusions. Alex did that in his own work. A month later, he published a paper on the theory that Akhenaten's tomb had been moved and coincided with where the Amarna Letters had originally lain.

On the back of his thesis, he switched his doctorate from pre-dynastic Egypt to the New Kingdom, specifically the investigation into what had happened to Akhenaten. Professor Steele at Macquarie was supportive and had gained approval for the dig at Amarna. Officially, Alex wasn't leading the group, but that didn't matter. He was here.

Lord Carnarvon had found the ceremonial stone in Amarna. If it had come from Akhenaten's burial chamber, then the tomb had already been disturbed. Perhaps the Amarna Letters had also originated in the hidden tomb of the heretic pharaoh.

After the initial exchange of emails with Rebecca, he heard nothing more. Now and again he would read an article by her and he guessed she was travelling the world. Her association with Alex and Egyptology gave her credibility that seemed to extend to other ancient civilisations—but always from the human angle. Her latest piece had been on a temple hidden in the jungles of Cambodia. Alex didn't doubt for a moment that she was physically there.

He went into the kitchen and made himself a cup of Earl Grey tea, black. He returned to his desk and relaxed, the scent of the tea wafting away the stressful meeting with the local antiquities official. Was this how Carter and Carnarvon used to feel about them? He suspected it was worse in the mid-1920s because of the political tensions between Britain and Egypt. The changing rules of discovery and reward must have been infuriating to the two men who spent so long and so much trying to find the boy king's tomb. Their expedition had started because Carter had found evidence suggesting Tutankhamun's tomb was in the Valley of the Kings. The many similarities made Alex smile.

He opened a drawer and looked at the papers he had compiled since returning from Nefertiti's tomb.

He picked up the most intriguing. It was a series of colourful circles with names in them. He knew it had been a vital discovery, but a little online investigation filled gaps in his understanding. The diagram was known as the Tree of Life, part of the Jewish Kabbalah. The very name was a clue since both the ancient Egyptians and the Jews had a Tree of Life. The ancient Egyptian tree was from the story of Osiris, whose coffin was saved from the river by catching in the tree's roots. Effectively, the tree was the doorway to the afterlife.

Alex learned that, in Judaism, the Tree of Life was used to explain many things from religion to psychology. The relevance to Sigmund Freud was not lost on him. The circles represented characteristics and also archangels. It was the latter that Alex found most interesting, because the papyrus had names written beside them. For Alex it was conclusive evidence that Judaism was based on the ancient Egyptian religion.

He understood the sensitivity of what he'd seen, but it didn't make total sense. Was it really enough to kill over?

Mahmood came in and Alex quickly hid his notes.

"Mr Alex, we are ready to start the dig."

Alex pointed to the map. "We're starting here," he said.

The Nubian shook his head, frowning. "But nothing points to finding a tomb—"

"You know," Alex said, "I'll be happy if we only find little clay tablets."

Chapter 60

Alex stood outside his tent, squinting across the excavation site against the harsh Egyptian sun. The hills of Amarna stretched before him, holding secrets he was determined to uncover. His mind went over his discovery. A week ago, they had uncovered more clay tablets, and Alex had found an encoded message. The author was undoubtedly Yanhamu. They were fragments, but they made sense of questions Alex had been asking of the ancient Egyptian. He'd put them in order, guessing the sequence of events.

My men were waiting at the bend before the necropolis gates. Two officers transferred Meryra's mummy and treasures from my cart to their carriage.

Akhetaten's body was missing, but these necropolis guards didn't know that.
We took the coffin containing Meryra and told the guards not to touch the trunk.

The trunk! Alex punched the air. The thrill of discovery. Something that archaeologists lived for. Yanhamu had completed Meryra's task and placed the chest of papyri in Tutankhamun's tomb. He had a good sense that these documents were similar to the ones he'd seen in Nefertiti's tomb.

The passage also confirmed that Yanhamu had taken Meryra's body to the Valley of the Kings. He shouldn't have been buried there, but it sounded like Yanhamu had pretended that the coffin had contained the despised, heretic pharaoh. He'd been interred in a simply, unadorned tomb and Alex believed this was the one known as KV55.

Another decoded tablet, wasn't about Meryra's mission, but was more personal.

In seeking vengeance, I had found instead friendship, trust, and truth. Revenge had lost its allure, for my sister's wish was for me to possess a pure heart. Scorpion, after all, was doomed to be devoured by the soul-eater. Life in this world, like the ripples on the pool, was fleeting, while the afterlife was the eternal Great River, flowing from the dawn of time to its end.

Had Yanhamu achieved retribution for the death of his sister? Whether he had or not, he had found peace with her murder.

The extract made him think of Ellen. She'd be proud of what he'd achieved and new PhD subject. In a sense, he was not just doing this for himself, but also her.

In Ellen's final message to him, she'd used an ancient Egyptian phrase about meeting again in the Field of Reeds. Seeing his friend again, discussing Egyptology. A reassuring thought. He nodded to himself. Religion, whether based on an invisible god or the sun, gave hope.

Staring across the ruins at Amarna, he wondered what had become of the young peasant boy, Yanhamu, who had become the scribe. What happened next? The answers may be out there on clay tablets, buried in earthenware jars.

Pharaoh Akhenaten's tomb was probably out there too. No doubt with a maze and secret passages. Maybe one day the second Map-Stone would be unearthed. Or maybe it had been destroyed in the destruction of Nefertiti's tomb in Tell el-Dab'a.

A voice broke through his reverie. Mahmood approached holding out the satellite phone shared by the group.

"Mr Alex, there is an important phone call."

Chapter 61

"Hello?"

"Alex? It's me."

His heart skipped a beat, but he maintained a neutral tone. "Rebecca or do I call you Talyia? Or another name perhaps—a genuine one?"

"Rebecca, if you prefer." As her voice filled his ear, Alex's mind raced. Why was she calling now, after months of silence? What new revelation or danger might she bring?

"Well done on getting the position and licence to dig," she said, her tone carrying a hint of something Alex couldn't quite place.

"Rebecca, I—" he began, but she cut him off.

"Things have changed, Alex. I've changed."

He wasn't listening. He needed to know. "Rebecca… can you tell me that the Brotherhood had nothing to do with Ellen's death?"

"That was the gang, her landlord got involved. And I won't deny that the Brotherhood disposed of them while trying to find Ellen's research."

"And the genuine Marek Borevsek?"

She hesitated then confirmed his death had been at their hands—although another accident.

"And, I still don't know who shot at me by the river in Putney," he prompted. "That was the Brotherhood, wasn't it?"

"The plan had been to scare you... to run with me."

"It worked," he said cynically.

"But, they shot that East End thug... that wasn't planned. So, it was needed after all."

"Nevertheless, I don't like the people you're associated with, Rebecca."

"Listen to me, Alex. I'm telling you things are different now. My uncle has died. Uncle Seth, Gershom, was the high priest of the Brotherhood of Levi and he's gone.

"Okay," he said uncertainly. Then listened intently as Rebecca revealed that she had inherited the mantle of High Priest.

"But," she said, "I don't want it. I've broken all ties with the secretive organisation. It still exists, of course it does, but I'm not involved and they no longer need to find and destroy the secrets in Nefertit's tomb."

"Are you saying things will now change about disclosing the links between Egyptian religion and Judaism?" Alex asked, his mind whirling with possibilities.

Rebecca's response was unexpected. "No, I am not! Anyway, that wasn't the great secret. I thought you'd worked it out."

Alex's brow furrowed. What had he missed? They'd previously spoken about Sigmund Freud and his book, *Moses and Monotheism*. In it, he argued that Moses was influenced by the sun god, Aten, worshipped under Pharaoh Akhenaten.

Alex said, "What I saw in the tomb supported Freud's belief. The secret was that Judaism is based on the ancient Egyptian worship of the sun.

"No," she said.

"No?"

"That was the great misdirection."

"Misdirection? By Freud? But the evidence... are you saying that it was about Nefertiti... that she thought she was Isis?" He shook his head. *Why would that—?*

"The god was Osiris, Alex. Not the sun," she said.

His mind stopped spinning, focused. There were lots of images of Osiris in Nefertiti's tomb.

"The worship of Osiris?"

For a beat there was silence. Then Rebecca confirmed it. "Moses was the high priest of Osiris. Moses was just part of his priest's name. Osar-Moses."

Rebecca explained.

As the sun began to set over the ancient city, Alex absorbed the revelations she shared. The true story of the Exodus, the fate of Nefertiti, the connection between Egyptian gods and Jewish archangels—it all began to fall into place.

The Brotherhood of Levi wanted to keep it all a secret, especially because the god of Moses was Osiris, god of the afterlife. Also considered the god of the dead.

Ironically, Osiris was widely worshiped until the rise of Christianity under the Romans.

But one question still nagged at him. He thought about the trunk. "What about the missing papyri? There really were papyri in Tutankhamun's tomb, weren't there?"

"Yes," Rebecca replied, her voice heavy with the weight of hidden history.

The desert wind whipped around Alex as he stood outside his tent, still clutching the satellite phone. His conversation with Rebecca had taken an unexpected turn, delving into the dark secrets surrounding the discovery of Tutankhamun's tomb.

"So the papyri were too sensitive," Alex mused aloud. "Lord Carnarvon did take them?"

"Yes," Rebecca confirmed.

313

A chill ran down Alex's spine as he voiced his next question. "And he was murdered?"

Rebecca's response confirmed his worst suspicions. Lord Carnarvon, it seemed, had paid the ultimate price for refusing to surrender the ancient documents to the Brotherhood of Levi.

As they discussed Howard Carter's role in the cover-up, Alex wondered how many lives had been destroyed to keep the secrets. How much of history as they knew it was a carefully constructed lie?

A moment of silence fell between them. Alex checked the phone, fearing the connection had been lost. "Rebecca?"

"Still here," she replied. "I was thinking... If you don't mind my candour?"

"Go on," he said uncertainly.

"Well, your paper on Akhenaten's tomb and the Map-Stone was interesting but... remember I watched that documentary on Queen Hatshepsut, how her lover had built a secret passage connecting their tombs?"

Meryra would construct hidden tombs for them with maps, so their vital spirits could reunite on Earth and in the afterlife.

Meryra had created a virtual bridge between the heretic pharaoh and his queen. An eternal connection. "Yes," he said.

"The story of Akhenaten and Nefertiti is as much a love story as an academic thesis."

"But academic—"

"Shush," she said. "You can never tell the truth about Osar-Moses and everything that followed, but you can tell the world about the fascinating real lives and loves of people 3000 years ago." She paused. "What I'm suggesting is that you need a writer. Someone could take your facts and turn them into something the general public would devour... just like they did about Tutankhamun."

"The mummy's curse?" he said sceptically.

"No! The public love stories of ancient Egypt. You yourself said there are still many mysteries to be solved."

Alex said nothing.

"Take the translations of the Amarna Letters," she said. "The secret messages. Think Wilber Smith. Yanhamu's story could be reconstructed and—"

"Into fiction?"

"I think it's called faction. Fiction based on fact. But if you prefer it could be more documentary than novel. But there's no reason—"

"It's very early days," he said cautiously, warming to the idea—if she was leading at what he hoped. "I've found more clay tablets. More of Yanhamu's journal. I believe he completed Meryra's mission and delivered the mysterious trunk with Meryra's secrets."

"The contents of which—"

"—will never be disclosed," he said, his enthusiasm unabated. "Understood. But I also believe it suggests the body found in KV55 is that of Meryra. Taken there by Yanhamu in place of Akhenaten."

"What about revenge? Did Yanhamu make Scorpion pay for killing his sister?"

"I don't know, there's still some of the story missing, but I'm getting there."

"Fantastic!" she said enthusiastically. "It sounds like you've made significant discoveries."

"Yes."

"So could you?" Rebecca pressed.

"Could I...? Have a writer, you mean? I guess so... although... Do you have a recommendation?"

"Me, dummy," Rebecca laughed, and Alex could picture her crooked smile.

His pulse raced. "In that case, definitely yes, I could do with a writer. When can you get here?"

"I'm in Cairo," she revealed. "I'll be at your dig site by tomorrow morning."

As the call ended, Alex stared out at the darkening landscape of Amarna. Tomorrow, Rebecca would be here. Together, they would continue to unravel the threads of history, piecing together the story of Yanhamu and perhaps the discovery of Akhenaten's tomb.

But even as excitement coursed through him, a nagging doubt remained. The Brotherhood of Levi might be without a leader, but were their secrets truly safe? And what other dangers might lurk in the shifting sands of Egypt, waiting to be unearthed?

With a deep breath, Alex turned back to his tent. Tomorrow would bring new challenges, new discoveries, and perhaps, a new chapter in his own story.

THE END

Book 2:
The Mark of Eternity

From encrypted messages to Egyptian tombs,
the truth is buried deeper than the dead

When a mutilated body is discovered, FBI Special
Agent Charlie Reed, fears the return of a brutal serial
killer. Called the Surgeon by the media, his tell-tale
technique has everyone wondering why. Then, just as
abruptly as the killings begin, they stop—leaving more
questions than answers.

Agent Reed follows a trail of symbols across continents
to Egypt where the Surgeon has resurfaced—and he's
no longer killing at random. He has a shocking
objective.

Egyptologist Alex MacLure receives a cryptic message
from a young AI student believing he's uncovered a
conspiracy tied to the pyramids and a forgotten
symbol of power. But before MacLure can investigate,
the student vanishes—and MacLure is arrested for a
murder he didn't commit.

Forced into an uneasy alliance, MacLure and Reed
unravel an ancient code that points to a terrifying
truth: the Surgeon has a mission and is dangerously
close to succeeding. It becomes a race against the
clock. And the hour is now…

Read the first chapter now...

THE EGYPTIAN STONES

THE **MARK OF**
ETERNITY

AN ANCIENT CODE

A DEADLY KILLER

A RACE AGAINST THE SANDS OF TIME

MURRAY BAILEY

EXTRACT FROM THE MARK OF ETERNITY

Atlanta, Georgia

When he first saw flesh in the dog's jaws, Eddie didn't think much of it. His two hounds were often finding bones. Only this time it was different. The dogs had been running out by the church. And when he took the human hand from Deion's jaws, Eddie worried he'd be in trouble.

JJ was nowhere to be seen and didn't come when called, which concerned Eddie too. But first he decided to find where Deion had been digging and just replace the hand. No one would ever know.

Then he spotted his second dog, far too intent on his bone to respond to calls. But this one wasn't a bone, it was an arm. And that wasn't all. Eddie watched a lot of TV but he'd also seen the posters. This arm was distinctive with a Maori sleeve tattoo.

Eddie didn't think he was in trouble anymore. He knew he'd found the latest missing boy.

Special Agent Charlie Rebb watched FOX News. She finished blending the super-greens smoothie and used it to wash down a couple of Advil. What was worse, the green gloop or the thumping headache?

Her phone rang. It was her partner, Peter Zhang.

"You watching this?" he said.

"Morning, Peter."

"Yeah, morning. Have you got the news on?"

"If you mean, am I watching the media circus at the church, then yeah. It's crazy."

"Five bodies they've pulled out of there."

"Hold on," she said. The pastor of the church was being interviewed. The display gave his name as Reverend Piccard. Behind him was a cluster of doleful members of his congregation.

"We are all deeply shocked," Piccard said. "The community is in shock. But at the same time, we must have faith in the risen Lord. The Son of God must be delivered over to the hands of the sinners, be crucified, and on the third day be raised again." Piccard reached out and the people behind closed in and held hands.

Peter said something but she cut him off. "Wait, I want to hear this."

The reporter said, "Reverend, Mark Simmons had been missing from Georgia State University for forty days. There's been a state-wide hunt for him. And now we discover he's been under this church—under your church. Forty days under your church." She paused, adding weight to the statement. "Tell us how you found out about the body. How you learned about the other bodies?"

In Charlie's ear, Zhang said, "We don't know Simmons was under there for forty days! He could have been someplace else and been moved."

"Shush!" Charlie put the phone down on the counter so her partner couldn't interrupt.

Reverend Piccard repeated the story that everyone knew by now: a local man had found "the poor boy" while out walking his dogs. He said, "The man called the police and I got a call from them at home yesterday at around 10am. Of course, I came straight here and we have been praying ever since. This is a wake-up call." Reverend Piccard looked into the camera, speaking to the TV audience. "The human race is out of control and corrupt. Evil is abound. Greed and self-gratification have replaced God and godliness. We are being punished for turning our backs on the Lord. Only by accepting Christ can we hope for salvation."

2

"Has he said the words 'fire and brimstone' yet?" Charlie heard her partner scoff.

The reporter had managed to get a word in: "—and this morning the police issued a statement about there being multiple bodies under your church."

The reverend swallowed and nodded. A woman beside him closed in as though for comfort or protection.

The reporter said, "What can you tell us about those other bodies?"

Piccard looked like he was on the verge of tears. "Those poor boys... I've been told there are four more that the crime scene people have found. Five poor boys. We should all take a moment today and pray for their souls..." He paused. "I am sure we will learn in due course who they were, but for now I say, Father, into your hands I commit their souls. Christ our saviour rose on the third day. He will rise again. He will lead us from damnation and the serpent of evil will be driven out once and for all."

"This is crap," she heard Zhang shout. "Listen, I'll be there in fifteen to pick you up." He disconnected.

Twenty minutes later she was in his car and heading for the church in Dunwoody, north of the city.

He caught her rubbing her forehead.

"Headache, Chicago?"

She didn't respond. He knew the nickname wound her up and he kept using it. Just because she'd previously lived in the suburbs of Chicago. It'd been where her husband's job had taken him—before it all went wrong. Before she discovered what a two-timing little douchebag he was.

Zhang said, "That headache. Marcie says it's because you drink too much coffee."

Special Agent Zhang was a few years younger than Charlie. Maybe just the wrong side of thirty, although sometimes he could seem much older. He'd been married to Marcie for five years, and she always had an opinion.

Or maybe it was just his way of expressing his own opinion. Charlie hadn't figured out which it was yet.

What she had figured was that Peter was struggling. Marcie didn't work and had health problems. At least that was what she claimed. Hypochondriac was what she appeared, and yet Peter would never say it. Her treatments for mystery illnesses were eating away at Zhang's savings. But worst of all were the sleepless nights.

Peter used to talk about her symptoms and insomnia. But not lately. It was like he'd resigned himself to the situation. It was never getting better.

As a good partner, Charlie knew she should be more understanding. But it was hard. Zhang was a difficult guy. Aggressive and sarcastic, he wasn't the person you let cry on your shoulder.

"Too much coffee," he repeated.

"Actually, it's because I need a goddamn coffee," she said. "I'm trying a health kick and there's more kick than health at the moment."

"Wow! So no coffee?"

"That's what I'm saying. Not for two days now. If this headache doesn't quit in another then I'm back on the caffeine."

They went through the centre of Dunwoody and took Mount Vernon Road before turning left.

He said, "Headache ain't so good for you know what."

Charlie thought, *I guess you should know.*

"And speaking of which," he said, "how is the new guy, Pablo?"

"Paolo."

"Close enough," he said. "About time I met him, isn't it?"

"No."

"Oh come on, Chicago!"

She pressed her thumbs to her temples. "Quit calling me that."

He chuckled. "Just winding you up. Getting under your skin. It's what partners do. Psych 101, that's all it is. Just be grateful you're not from some hick state like Kansas. Then I could have some real fun."

She turned to him, feeling a wave of despair. "For f—"

"We're here," he interrupted.

The church stood proudly on a slight rise, with sunlight glinting off white shutters and a steeple. A giant white cross dominated the cut grass frontage. As they turned into the driveway, Charlie read the gate sign: "Church of the Risen Christ—New Beginnings". Beneath that was Reverend Piccard's name. Charlie noted that it was on a removable strip. Maybe they didn't expect him to stay here long. Maybe after this he wouldn't anyway.

"I've not heard of this church before," she said.

"Fairly new," Zhang grunted. "They seem to be springing up all over the state."

"Doesn't look new," she said as they badged a uniformed cop and were waved through.

Behind and to the right were the media crews. They were penned off and well controlled. Ahead of them was the church parking lot. There were two police cars, an unmarked, an ambulance and a coroner's van.

Zhang stopped in the entrance.

"There are parking spaces," she said, but she knew why he did it, why he stopped here. It was like a statement: we're in charge because we can park where we goddamn like. She knew he played the same games with her. She was the senior and yet he liked to act like he was in control. It was the little things, like the nickname to wind her up. She'd come across it all the time from men in her career. But she suspected there was more to it from her partner. Maybe it was his way of compensating for problems at home.

They got out and both put on their FBI jackets. Zhang put on sunglasses, retro ones that he always wore for the image. She spotted the officer-in-charge, but for a moment Zhang was going nowhere. He surveyed the scene and then pointed at the church.

"You said it doesn't look new," he said. "You're right. I think they take over older churches. You know, ones that aren't doing so well. CRC seems to be doing all right."

Her brain took a moment to realize what CRC meant. Church of the Risen Christ.

She said, "You seem to know an awful lot."

"The internet." He smiled pointedly. "While you were watching TV, I was doing research."

They walked around the side towards the detective-in-charge. Charlie showed her ID and introduced them both.

The detective sighed like he'd been waiting for them to arrive and was a little pissed that he was losing the case.

"Detective Nick Garcia," he said. "Atlanta Homicide." He nodded towards the rear, where the uniformed officers were standing behind a media screen. "Just pulled out another one."

They quickly confirmed that all of the bodies were of young men. So far, only Mark Simmons had been ID'd, on account of his distinctive tattoo.

Number six was lying on the grass naked and on his front. The body was smeared with black mud.

"Caucasian male, probably early twenties," the detective said. "Obviously no identification. My gut says it's another missing guy."

Zhang beckoned the investigating coroner over. He introduced them both before saying, "Preliminary cause of death?"

"Of course, hard to say, but for the moment this one's strangulation. Ligature marks on the neck and wrists. A few lacerations on the body but they appear post-mortem. Looks like more than one animal got under there recently.

Probably wild animals broke in before the two dogs found the hole." He nodded towards the church. The base had boards running around it, and at the rear they were broken.

"Would you flip him over?"

The coroner signalled to the uniforms, and they carefully lifted number six and turned him onto his back. The whole procedure was smooth and respectful.

From the torso it was hard to tell the guy was white, there was so much muck. Charlie guessed they'd pulled him out by his feet, face down.

The ligature marks were less obvious on this side. His eyes were closed, and his face looked peaceful, like he was just resting.

Zhang asked, "Had a look at the others?"

"Still only preliminary. This is the only one with obvious ligature marks. I'd say it's the second most recent."

"Mark Simmons being the most recent?" Charlie asked.

"Yes. He was also the only incomplete body. I don't think the two dogs tore off the hand or the arm. I can't be certain. The damage is all post-mortem, but probably a different animal or animals."

"Let's take a look at the site," Zhang said.

The detective and investigating coroner joined them as they knelt by the broken panels and looked under the church. Spotlights lit the otherwise enclosed area that was about twenty yards by six. It wasn't much more than an uneven crawl space—which explained why the body had been dragged out—maybe as much as three feet high in some places and almost nothing in others. Two investigators were at work, probing the space for more bodies.

Detective Garcia said, "None of the bodies were more than a few inches under the soil."

"So far," Charlie said.

Garcia grunted agreement.

She said, "There will be more."

Zhang said, "You can count on it."

He touched her arm and indicated they should move away. When they were out of earshot he said, "Did you notice?"

"Yes," she said quietly. Not because she didn't want the homicide guy to overhear, but because her stomach was knotted. It had been three years since they'd found anything else. Found any more bodies.

He said, "Looks like the Surgeon is back."

END OF EXTRACT

Scorpion and the Tomb

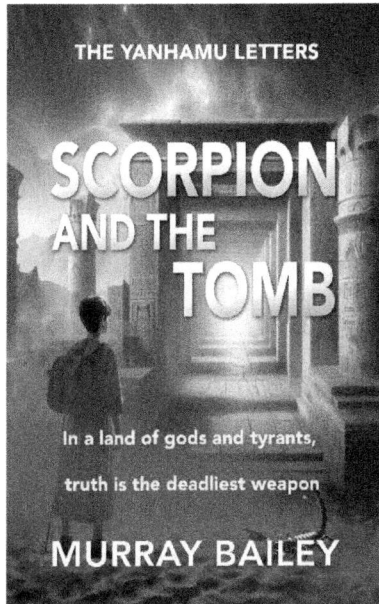

A gripping tale of destiny, vengeance, and love set against the backdrop of ancient Egypt during the reign of Pharaoh Ay. Yanhamu, once a peasant then magistrate's assistant goes in search of his sister's killer.

But as soldier in Pharaoh's army, he is drawn into the intrigue of politics when a cryptic mission leads him to the heart of the empire.

murraybaileybooks.com

IF YOU ENJOYED THIS BOOK

Feedback helps me understand what works, what doesn't and what readers want more of. It also brings a book to life.

Online reviews are also very important in encouraging others to try my books. I don't have the financial clout of a big publisher. I can't take out newspaper ads or run poster campaigns.

But what I do have is an enthusiastic and committed bunch of readers.

Honest reviews are a powerful tool. I'd be very grateful if you could spend a couple of minutes leaving a review, however short, on sites like Amazon and Goodreads.

If you would like to contact me, I'm always happy to receive direct feedback so please feel free to use the email address below.

Thank you
Murray

murray@murraybaileybooks.com